TAKE MY BREATH AWAY

An Alternate Selection of the Literary Guild®/
Doubleday Book Club®

PRAISE FOR *A DEEP AND DREAMLESS SLEEP:*

"Looking for a complex psychological thriller that deliv-

"A spectacular and magnificent psychological suspense
thriller . . . like a du Maurier classic."
—*Affaire de Coeur*

"The plot is as twisty as anything Hitchcock ever filmed
. . . Daphne du Maurier with a very nineties spin."
—*The Purloined Letter*

St. Martin's Paperbacks titles by Meg O'Brien

I'LL LOVE YOU TILL I DIE
A DEEP AND DREAMLESS SLEEP
TAKE MY BREATH AWAY

TAKE MY BREATH AWAY

MEG O'BRIEN

St. Martin's Paperbacks

TAKE MY BREATH AWAY

ISBN: 0-312-96158-8

Printed in the United States of America

St. Martin's Paperbacks edition/May 1997

10 9 8 7 6 5 4 3 2 1

*This book is dedicated with much love to Peggy,
Tiffany, Josh, Courtney, and
Jonathan*

*The children ... in whose wisdom, faith, and love
the future lies*

Acknowledgments

A special thank you to new friends and old: To Mary and Phil Walker, Chris Morgan, Angelita Rae, Patsy Blue, Lu Wilcox, Bess Thompson, Lorraine Campbell, Kathy Kessell, Jamie Hollomon, Gwen Glover, Susan Skeale, Marc Zweier, Lea Pinkus, Denise Nelson, Sammy Roberts, Ken and Nora van Doren, Linda Haddeman, Violet Rose Manteufel, and Janet Hagberg.

A very special thank you, as always, to Barbara Stone and Cathy Landrum, for their friendship and generous research assistance . . . and last but certainly not least to my editor, Jennifer Enderlin, for her invaluable editorial wisdom.

The following tale includes stories of true people, true events. Much of what occurs in these pages, however, is a product of the author's imagination.

But then . . . what is imagination?
And how can we know?

TAKE MY BREATH AWAY

CHAPTER 1

I don't know when I first began to see that he was watching me. Perhaps it was in Hecock's, the open-air bar and restaurant in Lahaina. I was sitting at a window watching as much as I could of the Old Lahaina Luau. I was within spitting distance of the people dining, and there were local men and women in grass skirts, with torches, winding through the tables down to the beach. Someone was chanting in Hawaiian on the stage, but since the stage was up against Hecock's wall, I couldn't actually see much, only the occasional hula dancers who'd come out to the edge of it. Now and then I'd look around at the other diners and think they must be locals, as they didn't seem awed by this wonderful sight, as I certainly was. Beyond the beach the waves lapped softly, the air was balmy and clean. I was drinking a Blue Hawaiian, my own body swaying slightly to the strains of Hawaiian music, and nothing could have been better. My dream—to have a month in Maui to both relax and write—had come true.

Except for the man who kept meeting my eyes. He wasn't smiling, not obviously coming on to me. Simply staring. He was broad-shouldered and had dark curly hair, a look about him of the islands, yet not, I thought, purebred Hawaiian.

Although that, of course, is a misnomer. The "pure-breds" were said to have come from the Marquesas Islands in 500 A.D. Many years later the Tahitians arrived, and then good old Captain Cook with his hearty crew of libidinous whalers. They got so out of hand that when the missionaries forbade the willing young Hawaiian women to board the boats for nights of party, party, the sailors stormed the town and waged war. The missionaries built a fort to protect themselves, and some gave their lives—all in defense of a tiny island that would one day be home to seafood restaurants, bikini shops, a Hard Rock Cafe, and even a Planet Hollywood.

So what does this say? I don't know, except, maybe, that sex will out.

When I saw this man look my way the first time I smiled slightly, then glanced away, as one will do. The second, third, and fourth times it felt a bit awkward. It might have been different if he'd smiled back. But that stare made me uneasy. I kept wondering: Do I know him from somewhere?

After awhile I left Hecock's and walked around Lahaina, stopping at the activities booth in The Market Place to ask about a sunset cruise. The woman there, who wore a flowered sarong and had long blond hair pulled up in a sun-bleached ponytail, told me I could get a huge discount on activities by simply attending a time-share presentation. I'd done that on a trip to the Caribbean and knew there wasn't anything simple about it. It was far easier to come up with the full fare than put up with the high-pressure tactics that arose the minute the finance manager made his appearance.

The activities woman, Betty, was friendly, though. She asked if I was visiting Maui alone, and when I said I was, she made a sad little grimace. "Maui is no place to be alone. There are too many romantic things to do. Gazing at stars from Haleakala, making love on the beach . . ."

"Well, I'm here to work," I said, smiling, "so maybe it's just as well I'm not distracted that way. Besides, in the month I've been here, I've met a lot of nice people."

She nodded. "Just be careful. There are a few sharks around Maui, and they aren't all the deep-sea kind."

I smiled, but her green eyes narrowed. "There are plenty of handsome young men looking for well-to-do females traveling alone. They're in every tourist town."

Laughing, I said, "Well, I'm certainly not well-to-do, so I guess I'm safe."

She leaned forward, palms on the counter, and said confidentially, "Listen, if you're on a budget, you can save so much just by doing a time-share. You don't have to commit to anything. Just show up, let them feed you pastry and coffee, and listen to their spiel. It won't take more than an hour or so, and when it's over you say "no thank you," get your discounts for whatever you want to do—luau, dinner cruise, helicopter ride—and leave."

"I can't believe you're telling me this," I said. "You mean I should go there intending not to buy? Isn't that ripping them off?"

"It's not a rip-off, it's a game. You play your part, they play theirs."

"I don't know . . . it sounds like this role is too much work for me."

We chatted a few minutes longer and I repeated my thanks but no thanks on the time-share, walked down to the harbor and booked a cruise at the *Kaulana* dock for the following night. The price was a little higher, here, but not much. Then I drove my rusty blue "Maui cruiser," a rented '86 Chevy Sprint, back to Kihei. Along the way I stopped at a lookout point, as I often did, to catch a glimpse of the stars. There were thousands visible, the kind of tented sky poets write about: huge, bright, glimmering points of light stretching from one horizon to the other. And there, to the south, the Southern Cross. It never fails to thrill me that I can see that from here. I imagine the old sea captains charting their way with it, out on that great wide sea with no land in sight, nothing to guide them but the heavens.

Parked beside me this night were trucks with camper shells and a few passenger cars. No sign of life in any of them. Either the occupants were sleeping here for the night or down at the beach. Anywhere on the mainland I'd have been more cautious than to stop along an isolated road like this at night alone. But I'd learned that in Maui, there are few crimes of bodily injury. The big problem here is the theft of items from cars or hotel and condo units. Even on the Visitor Channel they tell you to lock everything up tight, and for that matter, to take all valuables with you and not leave them in your car. One must therefore build up suitable muscles and aerobic strength before coming to Maui, as one is likely to end up hiking down trailheads and through shopping malls burdened with fifty-pound totes that are filled to the brim with cameras, jewelry, money, and the like.

For most writers, of course, that's hardly a problem, as we tend to have little money and our jewelry often comes from Target. A camera is my one big pleasure, and burden. I never go anywhere without mine.

On this particular night I'd slung my purse over my shoulder, but left my camera on the back seat of the

Sprint, as I'd intended to stand for only a moment, nearby. But I kept wandering farther out on the bluff, just to get the feel of being alone and not surrounded by other cars. I was scanning the northern sky for Cassiopeia's Chair when an unusually brisk wind came up, giving me a chill. Almost simultaneously I heard a click of metal and the crunch of a shoe against gravel. I looked quickly behind me and saw no one. My gaze darted automatically to the Sprint, but there was only a quarter moon; it was too dark to make much out. I started back that way and, remembering suddenly the man at Hecock's, I didn't feel as safe as I had.

I was relieved, therefore, to reach the Sprint and find no one there. Relieved, as well, to glance inside and see my camera still on the seat in back. I slid behind the wheel, reached into the pocket of my shorts for the key, and started the engine, pulling back out onto the highway. I was surprised to find that my hands were shaking.

The next morning I sat on my lanai at the Hale Pau Hana, working on my latest novel, tentatively titled *At Risk*. It was supposed to be a rather hard-driving story of murder and mayhem in Chicago, but was rapidly turning into romantic suspense, the locale—no surprise—being Maui. In it, a young author, much more lovely and successful than I, marries a handsome older man of royal Hawaiian descent who whisks her away to his absolutely gorgeous pineapple plantation where they live happily ever after. One important perk is that she never has to write books anymore for a living and gets to simply sit and watch the clouds go by.

But back to reality. My apartment at Hale Pau Hana was on the second floor, and looking down I saw three

women in the pool doing aqua-cizes. I liked it that
there were a lot of older people there, with plenty of
wrinkles, lumps, and cellulite, which they seemed to
happily ignore. Though I'm in my thirties and not particularly lumpy, I'm also not a bikini babe, nor do I
have any incentive to be one, as it all seems pretty
silly at this point.

Surrounding the pool was a grassy area with palm,
papaya, and banana trees, and beyond that, perhaps a
hundred feet off, the beach and the surf. At night I
liked to sit on the beach and think, as it was always
empty, with only the pounding of the waves for company.

This was the first year my income had allowed me
to have this kind of vacation, and of course I wasn't
used to it yet, the gearing down. So even though *Hale
Pau Hana* means *House of No Work*, I'd brought my
notebook computer and spent at least a couple of hours
on my lanai every morning, till the battery ran down,
working. I'd decided after a week that there couldn't
be a better place to work, not on heaven or earth. With
all those people around, I didn't feel lonely. On the
other hand, they could see I was working, so I didn't
have to sit around and chat about their golf scores all
day. There were, at last count, 7,399 golf courses on
Maui. (An exaggeration, but not much.)

Sometime around two o'clock I went inside and
took a shower to get ready for the sunset cruise. While
I combed out my thick brown hair I talked to the
gecko on the ceiling above my head, as a friend of
mine, who happens to be a psychic advisor, once advised. "You don't really belong here, little gecko," I
wheedled. "Wouldn't you rather be out on the nice
sunny grass eating bugs?"

Geckos are supposed to be good luck, but personally, I think that's something a Chamber of Commerce

publicity person made up so we won't be horrified at having lizards in the house. "You'll learn to love them," they say, but I hadn't, yet, and since there was seemingly no way to get rid of them, my friend advised the reasoning approach.

This particular gecko didn't buy my plea. So I finished up with him hovering, and hoped his little legs wouldn't tire, sending him plopping down on my head.

Five minutes after my shower I was dripping with sweat again. I pulled on a tank top and shorts, then it was into the Sprint, and this time up South Kihei Road to Long's Drugs, to drop off film for developing. I told the clerk I wanted the twenty-four-hour service, digging into my purse and bringing out one of the two rolls I'd used up the day before. Then I took my camera from its carrying case on my shoulder and opened it up for the other roll.

The camera was empty.

I have what might almost be called a fetish for photos. Especially sunsets. I'll use entire rolls just hoping to catch one perfect shot of a sunset, which is just what I'd done the evening before. I'd been down in front of the Old Lahaina Cafe, on the beach, before I'd gone to Hecock's. From there I'd caught a glimpse of the *America II*, which was docked at Maui for a few days, and I'd gotten some great shots of it with the sun behind its white sails, making them glow with pink and red against the horizon. At times people had walked in front of my lens, so I'd taken another shot, and another. But I knew there were some great ones in the bunch, and I'd been excited about seeing them. I would absolutely not have been careless with that film, if only because of that rare opportunity with the *America II*. If I'd removed it from the camera earlier, I'd have remembered.

So I stood there at the film counter in Long's that

morning feeling like someone who'd pulled into her driveway only to find her house had gone. Just to be sure, I dumped the contents of my purse out on the counter. The film wasn't there.

My first reaction was a sense of loss. The next was irritation. And finally, a tremor of fear.

The man at Hecock's. He took it last night. At the lookout.

I can't explain why I thought that. It was some instinctual thing, and I didn't know whether to trust it or laugh it off as silly and paranoid. *The noise I heard was him—taking the film from my camera.*

Easy does it, a saner voice said. So what if he did? This may have nothing to do with you. There were other people in those photos. You might have caught something that could be incriminating, if it fell into the wrong hands. A cheating husband?

Of course. That was it. The man in Hecock's was married, and he was here on Maui with another woman. I'd unwittingly snapped a photo of them together. Earlier, say, on the beach.

But what did he think I'd do with it? Sell it to the *Enquirer*, for heaven's sake? Was he someone well-known—though not to me?

The explanation somehow didn't satisfy me. Leaving Long's a few minutes later I found myself looking around the parking lot, even checking the doorway of the T-Shirt Factory for anyone lurking there. It was empty. In the lot itself I saw plenty of tourists, and some surfer types in cars that were even more beat-up than mine. No one seemed particularly interested in me.

Getting into the Sprint I checked the backseat for villains, the way my grandmother, who raised me, had tried her best to teach me to do. "Always look in back," she'd say, "before you get in the car. A kidnapper could be hiding there." That she told me this when I was five, or ten, made a bit of sense. Continuing to warn me of it when I was twenty, however, seemed a reach. My wonderful Irish grandmother dedicated many hours to implanting her own fears, suspicions, and superstitions in my mind while I was growing up, thinking only to prepare me for the kind of tough life she'd always had. I find it nearly impossible, therefore, to live the sort of carefree, no-worry way that some do—even on Maui, where the official Maui motto is Hang-Loose.

On the other hand, I supposed I shouldn't complain. That same suspicious mind served me well as a suspense writer. I was always looking around metaphorical and mystical corners, delving into people's minds, searching for unworthy motives and clues.

It is not at all surprising, therefore, that my next thought was: *He'll turn up again.* After all, I still had a second roll of film. And if indeed the man from Hecock's had taken the first, he probably knew about it. And wanted it.

The other thing almost everyone around here knows is that Long's in Kihei will absolutely not hand over developed photos to anyone other than the person whose name is on the package. One must have ID if one doesn't have a receipt.

So to get that other roll of photos, the man from Hecock's would have to go through me.

CHAPTER 2

I'd done a cruise before, but not the cocktail kind. I'd done the dinner thing, packed with tourists elbow to elbow at cafeteria-style tables. There was a canopy overhead, or whatever they call it on boats, so you couldn't really see the sky. There was also a singer at one end with a guitar. As the sun was going down they brought on the hula dancer, and not to be impolite, everyone watched her instead of the sun. It was awful.

This boat, the *Kaulana*, was like a smallish ferry, a catamaran, wide-open on the upper deck and with bench-type seating along the sides. I helped myself to a free mai-tai on the way up, and found a spot facing west, near the prow. Sipping my drink, I slouched down in my seat, propped my feet on the rail, and relished the breeze as we left the dock and motored out into the calm Pacific Ocean. There was live music on board, a two-man group with guitar and keyboard. Loudspeakers carried their music to the upper deck, and it was far too loud for my taste, but otherwise lent itself nicely to the party atmosphere. The *Kaulana* wasn't crowded, mostly honeymoon types and some older couples who may have been in Hawaii to celebrate their anniversaries. The sun was warm on my face, the catamaran riding the waves up and down, up and down, the gentle movement soothing and relaxing. This was what I'd come for . . . not the hors d'oeuvres, not even the drinks, though the mai-tai tasted great, but the feel of the water beneath me, lifting and swaying—carrying me out to places unknown, uncharted territory where anything can happen. A dashing, romantic pirate, for instance, might appear and whisk me off to his ship, where he'd ravish me and declare undying love, just like on the covers of the romance novels. Or there might be a giant sea turtle rising out of the deep to gobble us up . . . or perhaps we'd sail off to faraway ports and end on an undiscovered isle where we'd be killed off one by one, as in Christie's *Ten Little Indians* . . .

See, that's the trouble. Even the romantic fantasies end in mayhem for me.

For the moment, however, all was peaceful on the *Kaulana*. Captain Kim, as I'd heard him called, was guiding the catamaran from the wheelhouse up here, and he had loaned his binoculars to a couple who must have just arrived on the island, as they wore leis. At one point I looked back to see the place where the mountains of Maui parted, between the supposedly "desirable destination" of the west end, with its Ritz-Carlton, Hyatt, Marriott, *et al*, and—to the south—the dormant volcano, Haleakala. For the most part in clouds, the ten-thousand-foot volcano broods above the lava fields and desertlike beach areas of Makena, Wailea, and Kihei. The west-end mountains are softer, greener. In between is the Iao Needle, that majestic green phallic symbol nestled between the other higher mountains in the Iao Valley. The view was so awesome I got up with my drink and walked around the wheelhouse toward the other side to watch the chang-

ing colors on the mountains as the sun dipped lower
and lower into the west.

Rounding the wheelhouse, I stopped to glance down
to the lower deck, which was longer than this one.
Below were the musicians, both in ponytails and
Aloha shirts, blasting away. I paused for a moment to
watch them. Something made the back of my neck
prickle, and I thought at first it was the brisk sea air.
But then I felt compelled to look back around the upper deck. And there he was, leaning lazily against the
back of the wheelhouse, hands in the pockets of his
denim shorts, staring at me.

I hadn't deliberately been thinking of the man from
Hecock's, though the puzzle of the missing film had
been ever-present in the background of my mind, nat-
tering away: *Was it he who took it? And if so, why?*

Our eyes met. Mine flickered away, then fastened
on his. Other passengers were by now mingling and
talking casually to each other, so it seemed almost
natural when he took the few steps toward me and
said, "Hello. Do I know you from somewhere?"

I shook my head. "I don't think so."

He smiled. "No, of course not. I'm sure I'd remember you if we'd met." He stuck out his hand. "I'm
Dan. Dan Kala."

I took the hand. "Kate," I said.

"Kate . . . ?" He let it hang, clearly asking for a
surname, which I ignored.

He smiled again, but less assuredly. "Are you enjoying the cruise, Kate?"

"Yes. Are you?"

"I am now."

Under other circumstances I'd have felt relieved to
know where we stood. *He's flirting with me*, I'd have
told myself. *And that's what it was all about at Hecock's too*. Well, things could be worse. I could have

gone the whole month without anyone even giving me a tumble, spending most of my time on my lanai with a computer, making up romance and mayhem in my head.

But my grandmother also taught me, along with all those fears, to know trouble when I saw it and to meet it head-on. So instead, I planted my hands firmly on my hips and said, "Listen, Dan Kala, I'll tell you what. Why don't we cut to the chase? I'd like my film back. Let me have it and I won't tell anyone you took it, or what's on it. Okay?"

CHAPTER 3

A look crossed his eyes that could have been either confusion or a pretense at confusion. "I'm sorry. Film? What film?"

"A roll of film is missing from my camera. Are you saying you didn't take it at the lookout last night? You didn't follow me there?"

He shook his head, still apparently bewildered. "Absolutely not. I was in my hotel room last night. In Ka'anapali."

"Not for dinner, you weren't. Try Hecock's."

He smiled then. "That's where I've seen you before! You were staring at me. I remember now."

I flushed. "I was not staring at you, it was the other way around."

He laughed. "Hardly. But have it your way."

"It's not 'my way.' It's the way it was. You were staring at me all evening, and a short while later a roll of film was stolen from my camera."

"Well, I'm sorry about your film, but—"

"The only thing is, you blew it. There's another roll, one you weren't able to find. And now here we are on the same boat, at the same time. I don't much believe in coincidence—do you?"

"Actually, no . . ." he said thoughtfully. "But I do believe in synchronicity."

"Synchronicity. As in?"

A slight pause while he seemed to be searching for the right words. "As in my finding you here. To be honest, when I saw you there at the rail a few minutes ago, I did remember you from last night. I was too embarrassed to admit it."

"Embarrassed?"

"Well, I wanted to come over and introduce myself in Hecock's, ask you if you'd like to join me for a drink. I chickened out. And ever since then I've been thinking, *Maybe I'll see her again. We'll pass on the street, or she'll be shopping and I'll round the end of an aisle and there she'll be . . .*" He shrugged and grinned. "And now—*voilà*—here you are."

Now I was the one to hesitate. He was right about synchronicity; it was something I'd experienced many times myself, especially of late. That strange, inexplicable business of thinking of someone and there they are. Or needing something and suddenly it appears.

Was that all this actually was, then? If it hadn't been for the missing film, I probably never would have questioned running into this man again. After all, Lahaina's a small town; one runs into the same people all the time. And there was certainly no logical reason to think this man had taken my film. If I hadn't had such a suspicious mind—if I'd done anything other than write suspense for a living, or if I hadn't been plagued by my grandmother's fears—I never would have jumped to such a conclusion in the first place.

The man from Hecock's began to move away. "Look, I'm sorry I bothered you. It's been . . . well, interesting, talking to you. I hope you enjoy the rest of the cruise."

"Wait."

He paused and turned back.

For some reason I didn't fully understand, I decided to throw caution to the wind. "I'm sorry too," I said. "I've been on edge."

He came back to stand at my side against the rail. "It seems as if you've been having a bad experience of Maui."

"Not really. I love it here. It's just that on my way home last night I stopped at a lookout to watch the stars, and I thought I heard someone at my car. This morning, a roll of film was missing from my camera. Since you'd been staring at me . . . or at least, it seemed you were staring at me . . . I thought it might have been you at the lookout." I smiled and shrugged. "I'm a writer. My imagination sometimes runs wild. I thought you were following me."

His brow furrowed. "Well, I can tell you as a certainty that I wasn't at your car. And I didn't take your film. But your conclusion doesn't seem all that wild to me, given that you honestly thought you were being stared at—possibly even followed—by a stranger. Just what lookout are we talking about here?"

"I'm not sure it has a name. It's just off the highway, about halfway down the road toward Kihei."

"And you stopped there at night, alone? Is that safe?"

"It has been. So far."

"Still . . ."

I was beginning to feel a fool. "Let's forget it, okay?"

But Dan Kala looked thoughtful. "Maybe it was the menehune."

I lifted a brow. "Menehune? You mean the little people? The spirits?"

"They're said to take things sometimes. It's a possibility . . . don't you think?"

He didn't smile, and I felt a chill.

"I somehow don't like the idea of invisible little mischief-makers poking through my things," I said.

"Still, they seldom keep the things they take. You'll probably find your film again, right where it was supposed to be."

"Even though it wasn't there this morning?" I smiled. "Like with a key, or a lipstick, you mean. I'll empty out my purse or drawer and swear what I'm looking for isn't there. Then, later, it is." I turned to him. "The problem with the menehune theory is, what about when this happens in New York, or San Francisco, or in some cornfield in Iowa?"

He smiled. "Well, now, if you want to know what I personally believe, I think the menehune were the ancient Hawaiians' explanation for certain mysterious disappearances that occur everywhere, all the time. Just as the Irish believed in leprechauns."

"While the true explanation is . . ."

"That these things slip into another dimension, a rip or tear in time, and then sometimes—not always— they slip back."

"On their own accord, you mean?"

"Or with the help of the little people, who are said to live everywhere throughout the world." He grinned. "Who knows?"

I was intrigued by now. This was the sort of discussion I enjoyed. I often wrote in my books about such things, as they fit hand-in-glove with the old stories and legends I'd studied in college.

"On the other hand," Dan Kala said, "your film may have been swiped by any one of the ordinary car thieves that abound in Maui."

"Right. Because a roll of Kodak is so valuable

in exchange for drugs these days.'' I looked at him askance.

''You're probably right,'' he admitted. ''It does seem odd.''

I took a sip of my mai-tai, ready to let the subject go for now. But I seemed to have caught my shipmate's curiosity.

''What were you taking photos of?'' he asked.

''Oh . . . the sunset, the boats . . . people on the beach.''

''Sounds innocent enough. Unless, of course, your lens happened to catch a well-known married man with a traveling companion other than his wife. A politician, say? He might have thought you were paparazzi.''

I gave a small start. Warning flags went up. ''You know, it's downright amazing you thought of that. It's just what I'd been thinking.''

''Really? Well . . . did you?''

''Catch someone with his mistress instead of his wife? I'm not sure. How would I know?''

I was hoping to get him to say something that would tell me he knew precisely whom I'd taken a photo of. Then I'd know, one way or another, about him. But Dan Kala laughed and shrugged.

''Speaking theoretically, there's only one way I can think of,'' he said. ''Most married people don't talk to each other in restaurants. Couples who talk to each other in restaurants are usually either single, or very good friends. And if the man happened to be wearing a wedding ring . . .''

''And extremely attentive to his dinner date?''

''A dead giveaway.''

''Except that he wouldn't wear a ring, would he?'' I pondered.

''Perhaps not. Some do, however, if only to flaunt

the fact they've a wife as well as a mistress."

I glanced involuntarily at his ring finger. It was bare—signifying, perhaps, nothing.

"You know," I said, "you sound like quite an expert at these things. Are you a detective? Or do you speak from experience?"

"You mean, am I married? No. Never have been. You?"

"No."

"Ever come close?"

I hesitated. "Once." Turning away, I stared across the water at the mountains behind Lahaina.

"Sorry. Guess I hit a sore spot."

"No. It's just that it's an old story, and not a very pleasant one. Why don't we talk about you? What are you doing in Maui? Do you live here?"

"In San Francisco. I'm on business here for a client."

"Really? I live there too. What do you do?"

"Consulting. Which, come to think of it, is a bit like being a detective."

"In what way?"

He met my curious gaze head-on. "You really want to know this?"

"Sure."

"All right, then. Why don't we go down and get you another drink first? It looks like yours is just about dry."

On the deck below, we loaded up a couple of plates with celery, carrot sticks, crackers, and dip. People were dancing, now, in the area just in front of the band. We found seats away from there, near the prow. The sun was sinking low toward the island of Lanai, which was capped by the usual clouds. On either side the sky stretched from horizon to horizon in brilliant ribbons of pink. A dinner cruise boat went by, and people on the top deck waved. We waved back.

My new shipmate piled cheese onto a cracker and popped it into his mouth. When he'd finished chewing he washed the rest down with a deep swallow of his drink, which was plain guava juice. I'd been studying his profile in a subtle way, pretending to look first fore, then aft, and on one of my excursions fore I noted a crook in the nose, as if it had been broken at some time. Certainly not football or boxing, I thought, as he had a tall, lean body that tended toward lankiness rather than pugnacity. The dark hair was close-cropped but longish in the back, halfway down to the collar of his white shirt. Damp curls in front came forward but did not quite fall over the forehead. The hand holding his glass was slender, though the knuckles were coarse, as if accustomed to manual labor of some sort.

"Tell me about you," Dan Kala said, turning slightly to me. "Your first trip to Hawaii?"

"Yes."

"Any particular reason you chose Maui?"

"Well, my mother was a native Hawaiian. She was born here on Maui, though she moved with her parents, I'm told, to Honolulu when she was seven. She died when I was three."

"What about your father?"

"He was in the navy. Apparently he settled in Honolulu after Vietnam. He met my mother, they fell in love, and he married her. Just before I was born, he brought her home to California."

"Is he still alive?"

"I don't know. He ran off when my mother died, leaving me with my grandmother—my father's mother. We never heard from him again."

Dan Kala frowned. "I'm sorry."

"Don't be. It turned out all right. My grandmother

was a good person. She was much older, and it was tough for her to raise me alone, but she managed. We were very close.''

''You talk as if she's gone.''

''She is.''

''So you haven't anyone left in your family? You're alone?''

Alone. Odd, I'd never precisely thought of it that way. My head was so peopled most of the time by fictitious characters, all of whom populated my life at various times, it was difficult to ever feel truly lonely.

Except when a book was done. That, I've often thought, is why writers fall into depressions that often last for weeks, when they've finished a book. All those wonderful, vital, fascinating people—gone, just like that. Gone with one stroke of a pen and two words: THE END.

''I guess I am pretty much alone,'' I said. ''At least as far as family's concerned.''

''So is this a kind of homecoming for you? To explore your roots?''

''Actually, I'm not sure I'd know where to begin. I was told my mother's parents were both Hawaiian. Beyond that, my grandmother McKenna didn't know. She thought there would be plenty of time to learn those things, so she never got around to asking my mother about them.''

''I'm surprised . . .'' he began, then hesitated.

''Surprised? At what?''

''The, uh . . . the color of your eyes. They're the bluest I've ever seen. Almost turquoise . . .'' He paused again. ''Unless those are tinted contacts.''

I smiled at him. ''No. They're real. But why would that surprise you?''

''It's just that you look . . . No, never mind.''

''Tell me.''

He shook his head and smiled. "It isn't important. So you're actually just here on vacation?"

I was beginning to feel a bit strained by all the questions—as well as an undercurrent I didn't fully understand.

"Partly," I answered to be polite. "I'm working a bit."

"Does your book take place on Maui?"

I started to answer, then stopped, looking at him. "How did you know I was writing a book?"

He had been about to take another sip of juice. His hand paused midway to his mouth. "You said you were a writer, didn't you? Upstairs? Earlier?"

"But I could be writing for magazines."

He smiled. "You mentioned something about a wild imagination. I assumed you must be writing fiction."

I wasn't completely satisfied.

"Just what is this consulting work you do?" I asked. "You said it was much like detecting."

The smile widened to a grin. "So . . . she still doesn't trust me. Okay, I'll tell you. I have clients from around the world who need certain information about an area before they invest their money there. I find these things out for them . . . or, at least I do as much as I can. It's a bit of an esoteric science."

"In what way?"

He drank the last of his juice and put the empty plastic cup beside him on the seat, to keep it from blowing away. As the sun fell lower into the west, the breeze became stronger. It wasn't by any means cool, but stiff. The *Kaulana* had turned, and we were on our way back to land, now, as were the other cruise boats.

"My clients," Dan Kala said, propping his feet on the rail alongside mine, "want to know which areas around the world are relatively safe, or will be, when the kinds of earth changes they're expecting take place.''

''Earth changes. Such as . . . ?''

''Earthquakes, floods, volcanic eruptions. There's already been an enormous and highly unusual increase in these, in the past couple of years. One has only to read the daily paper to know this. My clients, however, are hooked into information you don't hear about through the ordinary media. And they expect things to get much worse.''

''Such as California breaking off and falling into the sea, you mean? Hasn't that been predicted for a long time now? Sorry to tell you this, but we're still waiting.''

I was only half scoffing; I knew better than to laugh too loud in the face of Mother Nature.

''Actually, my clients believe there will be several waves of geological changes, each one wiping out more and more of the western half of the United States. If they're right, we should all be moving to Indiana. Or better—another planet.''

I looked at him. ''Do you believe this too?''

He shrugged. ''When I first got into this work, I didn't. But the more I learn about it . . . Let's just say I'm fast becoming a believer.''

''And just who are these clients of yours?''

He smiled. ''I can't tell you their names, of course. Part of what they pay me for is confidentiality. But they're people whose names or faces you might know. Government leaders. CEOs of major corporations. Highly renowned scientists.''

''You're kidding.''

Laughing, he said, ''You thought they'd be like that guy who ran into the police station—I think it was on *Barney Miller*—and swore the telephone company was trying to take over his mind?''

"Something like that."

"As I remember, he wore tinfoil on his head to protect himself from magnetic waves, or something," Dan said. He sobered, folding his arms on the railing and staring out over the sea. "And to think we laughed."

I was silent a few moments. Finally I said, "To be honest, I think about these things sometimes. I studied astronomy at Berkeley, and my teacher was half in this world, half from some other mysterious place, it seemed. He'd come to class with what sounded like far-out ideas ... electromagnetic frequencies controlling us from other planets, our government keeping information from us about ancient monuments on Mars, that sort of thing. We all kind of figured he'd had some good dope that weekend. But then I'd sit and think about it later, and some things would make sense. If you separate the wheat from the chaff ..."

"And with all the earth changes going on right now, the increase in volcanic eruptions, the extremes in weather, the oceans rising, there's been a renewed interest in these things. A lot of people think we're on very short time now."

"I don't know about that," I said. "I do think we need to address the issues that are facing us at the moment. For instance, I read that Maui is losing beaches at the rate of two or three feet a year, because of the ocean warming and rising."

"True. But it may be a moot point. There's a guy over on Kilauea, the active volcano on the Big Island, who lives a quarter mile from the rim. He works part-time with geologists up there, and he claims he's not worried. He thinks Hawaii, at least at the higher levels, will be the safest place when things start to come down. As for coastline, it could be twenty-five percent gone."

"And what exactly does 'come down' mean? The end of the world?"

"Not necessarily. A speeding up of natural disasters, certainly. In the last year there have been somewhere around twelve million earthquakes recorded. Some quite low on the Richter scale, of course, but this is more than at any time in recent history. My clients are particularly concerned right now about beachfront property and the threat of tsunamis from earthquakes from Japan to the Indian Ocean."

"And what do you do to reassure them?"

"Actually, reassurance isn't the point. I gather information, and they decide what it means. I might have my own ideas about that, but it's not my job to decipher information—only to pass it along."

"And where do you get this information?"

"From everywhere around the globe. I ferret out people whose life work it is to research the newer discoveries in science, and who are willing to talk about what's going on. My clients believe that the older, mainstream scientists know there are monumental changes coming, but are afraid to come out of their boxes and say what they really think, for fear of sounding like alarmists. The great fear is in losing credibility—and, of course, funding."

"Are these people you ferret out, as you say, 'End of the World' doomsayers?"

"Doomsayers . . ." He smiled. "So far as I can see from talking to hundreds of them over the years, that might be a matter of semantics. A Christian might say the Rapture's coming, and God is punishing the world for our many transgressions. Of course, in the strictly born-again Christian belief, only they will be saved— no Catholics, Jews, or Buddhists need apply. At the same time, many scholars agree that the end of the world is upon us. They simply call it something else."

"I have a friend," I said, "who writes science fiction, and we talk sometimes about these things. She honestly believes there's an intergalactic war taking place, and beings from other planets are already fighting over Earth. She thinks some of us will be picked up by friendly spacecraft and saved, but that billions of others will die."

He smiled. "Not so different from the Rapture story, is it? Substitute the word 'angels' for 'space beings' and you've got basically the same story."

"It's always bothered me that in all the stories, it's only the chosen who will be saved—and that the people who believe that particular story always believe they're the chosen."

"I agree there could be some psychological trickery involved: appeal to people and make them want to follow you by telling them they're special. The *chosen*. The only thing is—and this is something I don't share with many people—but the more I delve into these things, the more I begin to believe the stories could be right. Not that the chosen are Christians only, but that they're people who understand what's going on well enough to have what it takes to survive whatever happens. The 'virgins with the lamps, keeping watch,' so to speak. That could very well be what the Bible was trying to tell us."

I felt the *Kaulana* turn in the water and realized suddenly that the sky had darkened. Only a few last streaks of pink remained over the western sky. Lanai was still topped by clouds, and just to the right of her, Molokai could be seen. I thought how fragile all these tiny islands were, here in the middle of this vast body of water, surrounded by the Ring of Fire. For the first time in Hawaii, I had a sense of the great impermanence of it all.

"I remember from my research that Hawaii was

born as a volcano," I said. "And there's another, submerging but said to be rising, just off the coast here, to the south."

"There are volcanoes all over the world that are rising," Dan said. "At Mammoth Lakes in California, for instance, the volcanic and earthquake activity has been intensifying every day. And parts of the Arctic are breaking off, becoming ice floes that threaten to raise the level of the sea to flood proportions."

"Enough!" I said, laughing. "I come out here for a pleasant little cruise and run into doom and gloom."

He smiled. "Sorry. I didn't think of it that way. I guess I don't see it as doom and gloom, but more as a natural cycle. There have been many such cycles throughout history."

"But how could you take it so lightly, if millions of people might die?"

"I don't take it lightly. Pragmatically, perhaps."

"I'll bet you've got your kitchen stocked high with cans of food and jugs of water, though."

He didn't smile. "It's a pantry. But yes, I do."

Leaving the *Kaulana,* we walked together toward Front Street.

"Where is your car?" he asked.

"Over there, on the other side of the banyan tree."

"I'll walk you."

We didn't speak for a few minutes. As the silence grew, so did my tension. I just wasn't sure what I was tense about.

"It's crowded in town tonight," I noted, just to say something.

"Yes." He stopped walking abruptly. "You know, I'm at the Hyatt in Ka'anapali. Why don't you come and have dinner with me? There's a great restaurant overlooking the water, and we can talk some more.

Then we can walk along the shore afterward. If you'd
like that, that is.''

If he hadn't added the part about an innocent walk
along the shore, I might have hesitated more. I still
wasn't entirely sure of him. But there were things
about him I liked. If nothing else, he could be a new
friend.

The little demon of tension in my gut, however,
laughed at the word *friend*. I might not want to admit
it, but my body was already thinking about Dan Kala
as much more than a pal.

"Well . . ." I said. "All right. But I'll take my own
car."

"Sure," he agreed. "Do you know where the Hyatt
is? Or do you want to follow me?"

"I know where it is." I smiled. "I'll meet you in
the lobby."

"Great."

CHAPTER 4

The restaurant was high above the walk that meandered along the shore past the big hotels. Beyond the walk was a grassy area with a couple of striped tents, and past that the sand and sea. Out over the water, tiny lights bobbed.

Here in the open restaurant we were surrounded by fragrant flowers and gentle, warm night air. A pianist played soft classical music, and a bartender at a center bar with hanging sea-green glasses moved quietly to mix our drinks. The young, over-eager waiter, who seemed to consider his job a sacred trust, brought our wine and ran down the specials menu. This took nearly five minutes, as his recitation included *ohs* and *ahs* and rave reviews for the new chef, "A find, a true gem, direct from Paree." Our waiter's name was Thomas.

We ordered. I, the "Mahvelous, truly mahvelous, mahimahi, fresh from the sea, exquisitely prepared," and Dan a less enthused-about prime rib.

"Is there anything else I can get for you?" Thomas asked when he'd brought our plates. They were steaming, fragrant works of art, decorated with orchids and sugar-glazed hunks of mango, papaya, and pineapple.

"Tartar sauce, please," I said.

Thomas stiffened. He lifted a brow. One does not, I understood immediately, foul the famous chef's *pièce de résistance* with a condiment so lowly as tartar sauce.

But it was what I wanted, and I would not back down. "For the fish," I said firmly.

"Of course." Poor Thomas. He bowed ever so slightly and did not meet my eyes.

When he'd gone to fetch the dreaded tartar sauce, I glanced across the table at Dan Kala, who was laughing quietly.

"I think you've made an impression. Of sorts," he said.

"I've been putting tartar sauce on fish since I was a kid," I said. "I can't eat it any other way."

"Then you shouldn't," he affirmed. And when the waiter reappeared with a small white dish holding a minute, pale white blob, Dan looked at it, smacked his lips, and said, "I think I'll have a side of that myself."

"Of course." The waiter sighed.

I am not a promiscuous person. I know all the ways to have safe sex, and I have sex—ordinarily and infrequently—only with men I have deemed are safe. That limits the opportunities somewhat, but experience has taught me to be cautious.

I sat looking at Dan Kala across from me, thinking: I am no longer the innocent ingenue I was at twenty. I don't have to play the game anymore, that business of pretending I'm not going to sleep with a man when I know damn well I am. That's nice.

On the other hand, I've made mistakes over the years by jumping to conclusions too quickly—one such conclusion being: *He's here at last. The man for me.* I once went to a man's apartment and sipped bad wine while he serenaded me for two hours with a Spanish guitar and an off-key voice. I smiled, drank, and nodded, making all the appropriate, encouraging comments like, "Mmmm, yes, lovely," only to have him go on and on till I thought my head would split, if not my bladder. I finally said I'd have to leave, and he shrugged, walked me to the door, handed me his business card, and asked me to let him know if I'd like to invest in a demo tape. That's all I was to him—a possible investor.

He'd have slept with me, though, if I'd stayed.

On the other hand, there have been a few very brief, bright liaisons over the years. Some have been complete with good, satisfying sex, while others have offered proficiency with all the passion and soul of a Hoover. At times, that's all I require. As for that one man in all the world I can "click" with, without whom there would be no earth, wind, or sky, that's a trifle more elusive. Since Gerard . . .

"Something wrong?" my dinner mate asked.

"No. Why?"

"You were frowning. The Amaretto? Is it all right?"

"Wonderful. And I love this setting. It's very romantic." *Forget Gerard.*

He looked at me thoughtfully. "I would think you'd have a lot of romance in your life."

"Would you, now? And why do I feel the pinch of a lure in my mouth?"

He smiled. "You're right, I'm fishing. But I think you've also had some sadness. Do you want to tell me about it?"

"On a first date? Please. This isn't the Seinfeld show."

He laughed. "You're right. Let me tell you a story

of romance, then. I have a portrait on my wall at home
of a Maui princess. Nahi'ena'ena.''

"Nahi . . ." My tongue stumbled around the pro-
nunciation.

"Nah-hee-ay-na-ay-na," he said. "Hawaiian is easier if you think of it as being pronounced much the
same as Latin. Have you ever studied Latin?"

"Are you kidding? In a Catholic high school? Four
years of it."

"Then you know, for instance, that *a* is pronounced
'ah,' *i* like a long *e,* and *e* like a long *a.*"

"And the Hawaiian syllables?"

"You can break them down and sound each one
out. We even tell *haoles* when to separate vowels that
are alike. Not that they pay much attention."

"And how is that?"

"Take Ka'anapali, for instance." He pulled a pen
from his shirt pocket and wrote on a napkin,
Ka'anapali. "It's sometimes spelled Kaanapali these
days, and pronounced, especially by tourists, 'Can-ah-
pah-lee.' In the true Hawaiian language, however,
there's a separation between 'Ka' and 'anapali.'
Ka'anapali. That 'backward apostrophe' is called an
okina. It tells you to pause a split second after 'Kah,'
then finish with 'ahn-ah-pah-lee.' See?"

"Yes, that's right. I did know about the separation.
Most visitors do just say 'Can-apali,' though."

He shuddered. "It squeaks along my bones when I
hear it . . . like an off-key note."

Smiling, I said, "I'll do my best not to squeak your
bones. But you were telling me about a princess.
Nahi'ena'ena, I believe."

He grinned. "You said that perfectly."

I acknowledged the compliment with a slight curtsy
of my head.

"A portrait of Nahi'ena'ena hangs in a guest room of my home. She lived in the early 1800s, and died at the age of twenty. According to tradition, she had married her brother, the king, a year before. It was a plural marriage, a *punalua*—also according to tradition—and she married another man, as well, in the same ceremony. Months later she gave birth to a stillborn child. Who the father was, was anyone's guess. Shortly after that, she died."

He paused to take a sip of his after-dinner Cointreau, and I said, "Wow. Some romantic story. Sure makes me want to hear more."

Shaking his head and smiling, he agreed. "That isn't the romantic part. The next is. According to what version you listen to, it's said the princess inherited the *mana*—or spiritual power—of the great lizard goddess, Kihawahine. Some say she uses this power to slip back to visit her people from time to time. She particularly visits lovers, people who never quite managed to get together in a previous life, or, as some might say, in another dimension. She helps them to find each other again."

"Really?" I was intrigued. "And do you believe this business of people knowing each other in earlier lives? Or other dimensions?"

"I actually believe in multidimensions more than 'earlier' lives, as in reincarnation, that is. I have no actual proof of this, of course, but I tend to go along with the thinking that other, slightly different versions of us exist on various dimensions at the same time. I think we have similar, only slightly different lives there. And that's the reason we're attracted to someone to begin with. Not because we've known them in an earlier life, but we know them *now*. We may already be together in another dimension, in fact, and somehow the feelings slip over to this one . . . and there you are.''

I sat silently for a moment, absorbing that.

"Have you ever seen this princess?"

"As a spirit, you mean? No. Only in my portrait."

"What does she look like?" I asked.

He hesitated, and again I felt that undercurrent of something going on that I didn't understand.

"Oddly enough," he said finally, "she looks almost exactly like you. The same long dark hair, the wide cheekbones, the mouth . . . only the eyes are different. Hers are brown, of course. While yours are blue. Other than that . . ."

I was startled. At the same time, a chill swept up my spine. "How odd."

"I've been thinking much the same thing," he said.

After that, we moved on to other topics for conversation. My dinner partner was the perfect date: attentive, touching my fingertips once as I reached for my wine, then pulling back, allowing me space. Desire was there, however. I was certain of it. I thought, in fact, he'd suggest we go right to his room. And I was ready. The good food and even better wine had worked their wonders, and despite this odd thing about the princess—which left me with questions I couldn't even begin to fathom the answers to—Dan Kala seemed harmless. He had all those things a woman looks for: humor, intelligence, above-average looks, and apparent selflessness. The things that, when you find them in one man, generally prove too good to be true.

Still, we keep trying, we women. Nothing like being struck down by a two-by-four and getting up again, over and over. One would think we'd watched too many Three Stooges films as kids.

Dan Kala, it turned out, had other plans. As we left the restaurant and entered the hotel lobby, he went to a phone, made a brief call—business, he explained—then spoke to someone at the front desk. I waited in one of the plush, dark green lounge chairs, enjoying the heady scent of a ginger arrangement as it mingled with a lingering high from the wine and Amaretto. My body felt odd—a combination of tension and relaxation. Goose bumps chased themselves along my bare legs, though the air that drifted in through the open lobby doors was warm.

My attention strayed from its study of Dan Kala's nice but broken-nosed profile. A magnificent koa wood clock over the front desk told me it was going on eleven. The lobby was busy for that hour. More couples wandered through, crossing to the doors leading out toward the beach. There wasn't a single woman here alone, it seemed—all couples, many of them apparent honeymooners. One can tell from the amount of attention they give each other.

I pictured myself actually being here tonight alone, without Dan Kala or any other man. Not for the first time I felt a tiny pang somewhere in my gut, or perhaps my heart.

I can live alone. I'd done it for years, so I know how. I've never been a woman who must have a member of the opposite sex by my side continually throughout life, who floats from one relationship to another without ceasing. But life would be so much richer with someone to share things with, I've often thought. I've also considered that the time might come when I'd give up on finding that someone and retire to live in a big old house with a fluttery spinster friend and seventeen cats.

I used to know a couple of women like that, on Magnolia Avenue, when I was a kid. They had old

money and lived in one of the town's oldest and most
elegant houses, made of brick with white shutters.
Long, luscious strands of ivy trailed up the front. For
the longest while I thought Mae and Lucille were just
two women living together—like roommates. I'd see
them puttering out in their rose garden together, chat-
ting away as they worked, or sometimes just sitting
side by side, drinking tea under the arbor. Once, when
I was sort of sauntering through people's yards, taking
a shortcut home, I came upon them holding hands.
Mae—she was the younger—was resting her head on
Lucille's shoulder. *When I grow up*, I thought, *I'd like
to live with a girlfriend too.* It would be so much fun
to have a friend like that to be with every day. (The
sentiments of a lonely child.) As I grew older and
discovered the truth of the situation, I felt a bit embarrassed about those thoughts—as if by thinking that
Mae and Lucille had the ideal relationship, I was
somehow sexually "like them."

I still wonder about that sometimes. In particular, I
wonder if women treat women better than men treat
women. Are there lesbian relationships in which one
woman abuses another, beats her to a pulp on Saturday
nights or Superbowl Sunday? Is there less role-
playing, or does one still take out the trash while the
other mops the floor? Questions like this can drive a
writer wild.

Meanwhile, Dan Kala was heading my way, and I
couldn't deny the charge of pure sexual energy that
raced through me. Projecting as I often do, I saw us
together in his room. There would be soft music playing from tapes he had brought with him on his trip,
which of course would be precisely to my taste. We'd
undress each other slowly, lingering over all the important parts. My fingers would leave his lips and follow the strong line of chest to a slight swell of love

handles on either side. I like love handles on a man.
I think many women do, as they give us the feeling a
man is warm, cuddly, safe. That, of course, is often
an illusion. One has only to study the size and shape
of arrested serial killers to know this. But as I've said,
we women tend to fool ourselves. A man doesn't have
to do a thing. We do it all to ourselves, in our minds.

"Sorry to take so long," he said.

"That's okay. I was enjoying the view."

He had two slips of paper in his right hand. "I have
an even better view for you," he said, holding out his
free hand. I took it and he pulled me to my feet.
"Come with me."

I lay on my back, gazing at a million stars above, as
my legs were stroked with scented oil. The open-
ceilinged tent was on the beach in front of the hotel.
It was closed on three sides, open on the fourth to the
sea, which was less than ten feet away. Waves slapped
the sand; the gentle hands stroking my legs moved
higher, higher . . .

"Turn over," the voice of the masseuse, Leani, directed quietly. "I'll do your back now."

I sighed, so relaxed it felt as if my bones were no
longer connected. "I don't know if I can. I may fall
apart."

Leani, who managed the hotel spa—AVAILABLE
TWENTY-FOUR HOURS, the sign said—gave a soft
chuckle. "People always feel that way."

I looked over at Dan Kala, who was on a massage
table next to me, five feet away. A young Asian
woman Leani had introduced as her assistant, Kim,
worked on him. She seemed to speak little English.
Aside from the body parts being kneaded, we were
both discreetely covered with silky cotton sheets. Dan

had one arm exposed, and Kim was fluttering her fingers over it in the style of *lomi-lomi*, the Hawaiian massage. His eyes were closed; on his face was an expression of bliss. I saw this only from the light of a tall white pillar candle in one corner. Muted strains of Hawaiian music and chant emanated from a tape recorder.

"This isn't exactly what I was expecting," I said as Leani held the sheet up, giving me privacy as I turned.

Dan opened an eye. "I thought you'd enjoy the stars. Are you complaining?"

"Hardly. I may never leave this place."

Leani laughed softly. "When people leave here they are staggering. They have to sit down on the grass to catch their breaths."

"Especially us *haoles*, I'll bet. We aren't used to pampering ourselves."

She tucked the sheet around me, making sure my feet were covered and warm. Pulling the top edge down to my waist, she ran her fingertips lightly over my back. "That's how the word *haole* came about," she said. "Did you know that?"

"No. Tell me."

"*Haole* means 'no breath.' Our people called the white settlers *haoles* because they didn't kiss when they met, as we did. They would only shake hands. Therefore, we could not feel their breaths on our cheeks." I could hear her smile. "At least, that's one version of the story. 'No breath,' you see?"

"Yes. I do see. They were afraid to feel."

We were silent for a while. The only sound was that of the gentle stroking, the waves, and now and then the quiet voices of couples strolling along the grass behind us, on the walk. The massage oils were lightly scented with cedar, and frangipani, the plumeria of the traditional lei. With every touch, I relaxed even more.

An hour after she'd begun, Leani and Kim tucked the satiny sheets around us, and Leani said, "There's no one else scheduled here tonight. Rest a few minutes. Take as long as you need. We'll come back and pick up after you've gone."

She nodded to Kim, and the two women left. I glanced over at Dan. His eyes were closed.

"I've never had a massage before," I said slowly, my lips feeling like Silly Putty. "It was . . . wonderful."

He smiled. "I learned long ago that body work is not a luxury, but a necessity. I have a massage three times a week at home."

Turning on his side, he looked at me. The sheet fell from his arm; in the candlelight, his skin glistened from the oils. "It will help you to be centered," he said. "That way, you'll be more prepared for whatever ups and downs come your way."

I wondered, silently, if he knew of any particular ups—or more particularly, downs—that were heading in my direction.

"Massage does that?"

"It helps. It gets to the cells, where the old, forgotten emotions and memories lie waiting."

"To pounce, you mean."

"Something like that."

We lay there quietly a few moments more. Finally, I sat up, again holding the sheet to my breast. My limbs felt heavy, and I imagined my blood had turned to molasses, like the burning sugarcane. I knew Dan was watching, and there was, suddenly, a familiar pulsing ache in the area of my groin. It was so strong, I drew in a sharp breath and froze.

He cleared his throat. "I'll, uh . . . if you like, I'll dress first and wait for you outside."

"Okay."

I heard him rise, pull the sheet around his middle, and slip behind the small curtained cubicle provided for changing. I heard the sheet rustle to the ground, then the clink of a belt buckle as he took his jeans from the hanger. I heard the little hop of one foot, then the other, as he pulled them on. The pulsing ache became a pounding, a rapid pounding in my brain.

When he came out of the cubicle, I met his eyes. He paused, and if ever there was desire in a man's whole demeanor . . .

He smiled, shook his head as if to clear it, and continued on outside the tent. My gaze followed him till I couldn't see him anymore.

My legs were unsteady as I slid from the table. *The massage*, I told myself. *It's at least partly that.* But even though I hadn't felt this way for a long time, I recognized it well enough—this heavy, overpowering lust that makes the hands shake, the mouth feel like dust.

I salute you, Dan Kala, I thought as I slipped into my shorts, nearly falling for lack of balance. *As a technique, this isn't half-bad.*

On the floor were a couple of pennies and a dime that had apparently fallen out of Dan's pocket when he either put on, or took off, his jeans. I reached down out of habit to pick them up and saw a worn business card in the corner. I picked it up as well, and without glancing at it, shoved it and the coins in my pocket, thinking the card, at least, might be important to him.

He was sitting on the grass beside the tent waiting for me. His knees were drawn up to his chest, his arms hooked around them, and he didn't see me at first, as he was staring off toward the sea. I'd have given more than a penny for his thoughts, as his expression now seemed dark and brooding. As I reached him, he spotted me and stood, holding out a hand.

"That was wonderful. Thank you," I said, falling slightly against him. It was just as Leani had predicted; my legs had turned to sponge.

"I'm glad you enjoyed it," he said, righting me. "Are you all right?"

I laughed. "Just a bit off-kilter. But I feel great. What about you?"

"Fine," he said, though he didn't smile. "Kate, I've been thinking . . ."

"Me too," I said softly, putting my arms around his neck. "And the answer is yes."

There, I thought. *That should make things easier. No use beating about the bush.*

But he put his hands on my arms and removed them. "I'm sorry. We . . . I can't do this, Kate."

I flushed, feeling embarrassed. "I don't understand."

Surely I hadn't read him that wrong?

He sighed. Moving back from me, he ran his fingers through his hair distractedly. "I know I led you to think . . . You have every right to be upset. I really am sorry."

I began to get my balance back, emotionally as well as physically. "You know," I said wonderingly, "this is amazing. Let me make sure I've got it straight. You pick me up, you wine me and dine me. You even treat me to a massage till I'm as relaxed as one of those ancient Hawaiian virgins just before they tossed her into the crater. Any other man would be having his way with me right now." My eyes narrowed. "But not you. What the hell is going on?"

"It's not that I wouldn't like to spend the night with you," he said quickly. "You're a beautiful woman, Kate. Another time—"

I laughed. "Oh, please, don't patronize me. Look, it was a wonderful evening. Great food. Great *lomi-lomi*. You don't owe me any more—only an explanation. What the hell are you up to, Dan Kala?"

He touched my shoulder. "Nothing, Kate. Nothing. It's been a long day, that's all. I've got several meetings in the morning . . ."

I shook my head, no longer embarrassed but somewhere between bewildered and angry. The way a man feels, I suppose, when he's put out his cash and expects a payoff at the end of the night, only to be dumped. I hadn't put out any cash, but I'd incautiously led from the heart, which can be far worse.

"I'll walk you to your car," Dan Kala said. He took my arm.

I shrugged off his hand. "I know how to find my car."

"I'm sure you do, but I'd like—"

"Thanks anyway," I said firmly. "Thanks for the dinner, the conversation, the massage. It's a night to remember. Truly."

"Kate—"

I turned away, walking at an easy, moderate pace to the parking lot and my car. I didn't even shed a tear till I'd reached the highway. Then, though they didn't break loose, they stung my eyes. Not tears of sadness, but anger—at myself, for being such a silly, romantic fool.

Pulling into a space at the Hale Pau Hana, I was still not quite over it. Men stick their necks out all the time to ask a woman for sex, but when a woman appears to do that, even in these so-called modern, enlightened days, she somehow seems less than nice.

I took the elevator up to 205-B, stuck my key in the door, and flipped on the lights. At the door to my darkened bedroom I reached inside, flipped on the switch to the ceiling fan, and tossed my purse onto the bed. Wearily, I made my way down the hall to the sliding glass doors leading out to the lanai. Opening them, I inhaled all the scents of sea and garden. Somehow, they seemed less vivid now.

Let a man into your life, I thought, *and see what you get.*

It was after two A.M. But the birds were still singing. If they could stay awake all night, why not I? It wouldn't be the first time I'd written tons of pages on frustrated sexual energy alone. I sat at the dining room table, opened my notebook computer, and pressed the button to turn it on—expecting to see my current book flash onto the screen, since I'd left the computer in the resume mode. Instead, my blood literally ran cold.

Ask him who he really is, someone had typed across the screen.

CHAPTER 5

After the initial shock, the terrible feeling of not being alone crept in. First, the hearing went on alert. Then every muscle turned weak with fright. It all seemed to happen at once.

There's someone here. I swung around. *Where? In the bedroom?*

I got to my feet unsteadily. *A weapon. I need a weapon.*

On the kitchen counter was a large square container of tools—spatula, soup spoon, wire whip. Next to it, a wooden block held knives. I tried to slip over there quietly, casually, as if only crossing to the sink for water. All the while, I kept an eye on the hallway to the bedroom and bath. My hand closed over a butcher knife with a long, sharp blade. I didn't ask if I'd have the courage to use it, but grabbed it up, afraid that any moment someone might appear in that hall and take away my ability to question.

No one did. Still listening, straining my ears for any minute sound, I kicked off my shoes and tiptoed across the living room toward the hall. Holding the knife in front of me, I called out. "Is anyone there?"

No answer. Not that I'd expected one, but perhaps

some small sound, a surprised, muffled scrape of shoe on the rug, a crack of protesting bone as the intruder moved out of a cramped position into an attack stance. Anything to give me a clue as to what I was up against, rather than enter that room cold.

Nothing.

I tried to calm myself enough to think it through. If someone were in there, someone who'd wanted to do me harm, there had been ample opportunity when I first came in. A quick step behind me, a wire looped around the throat . . .

I gave a shudder. These things don't happen, I told myself. Not in real life, not that often . . . only in my head. It's the downside of writing suspense all day long. The pictures form at the keyboard; we put them on disk, then paper, and we think they're gone. But in the darkest hours, when the neighbors are asleep, the wine's worn off, and the company's gone? There they are, winking slyly from behind a creaking closet door.

Taking a deep breath, I stepped forward.

There was no one in the bedroom at all. My purse was on the floor, but it had probably slid from the bed when I tossed it. In several rapid, fear-filled motions I threw open the closet doors, lifted up the bed skirt, went into the bathroom and flung open the shower curtain, just to be sure. Whoever had been here was gone.

Back in the living room, I stepped out onto the lanai and looked from right to left, along the grassy area below. Lights illuminated the palm trees and swimming pools, walks and shrubbery. No one stood there watching.

On the beach, then? Aside from one spotlight focused on a narrow strip of sand, the beach was dark. I couldn't know.

Shaking myself to relieve tension, I thought: *There's no one there. Stop this. Better to focus on who had written that message. And what it meant.*

I sat on the chaise lounge in the living room, wrapped in a throw. Though the temperature was probably still in the eighties, my flesh was cold. I tried to think things through, sort out all the questions and confusions. But my mind jumped wildly from the message on the computer to Dan Kala to the missing film, all of it going round in circles till none of it made sense. Finally, I couldn't think anymore. Drifting into sleep despite myself, I came awake with a jerk moments later, thinking I heard a noise at the front door.

No one knocked. No one rang. *A neighbor walking by*, I thought. *Or the paper boy. That's all it is.*

Sometime in that strange half-awake, half-asleep state, I dreamt of a woman with dark eyes and long, dark hair. She stood a few feet away, partially hidden behind a white, gauzelike veil of fog. She seemed to call to me, though I could hear no words. I felt sad that I couldn't hear her, and I took a step forward and raised my arms as if to touch her. She jerked back, a hand going to her mouth as if from shock that I'd come that close.

I could see her eyes, then, as they locked on mine. I felt drawn in by them, drawn to the questions she asked but that I couldn't hear. I reached again, and this time she didn't step away. Her eyes grew more dark, more frightened. They seemed to cut right into mine.

"Who are you?" I whispered.

And then I thought I knew. I was so certain of it, in fact, I drew back my right arm, flattened my palm, and slapped her hard across the face. "Damn you!" I cried. "Damn you, Margo Reed! Damn you to hell!"

*   *   *

The slap woke me up. Oddly, it felt as if my palm actually stung. I looked at it. It seemed pinker than usual, as if the slap had been real.

The sun was rising by then over Haleakala. Though the volcano was behind me, and I couldn't see either it or the sun, I could tell by the tinge of pink on the koa trees and the sea. My limbs were still cold, though the air was warm. I shifted on the chaise lounge, pulling the cover up to my chin. *Margo Reed. Dear God.*

It wasn't all that odd I'd dreamt of her. She'd phoned and left messages, three of them, in the past month. She'd left them on my machine at home, one as recently as two weeks ago. That meant she didn't know where I was.

For that, I was glad. I hadn't seen or talked to my former best friend in several years. I didn't know what she wanted from me now. I didn't want to know.

My mind wandered back . . . to California, to Berkeley, and college. How is it possible, I wondered, that I was ever that young? That trusting? And then I thought wryly, *How far have I actually come?*

I was on a scholarship at Berkeley, full of passion for learning. I flung myself into it all, from astronomy to English lit, from Greek myths to religions, and it took me forever to decide, finally, on a liberal arts major. My levelheaded, practical friend, Margo, laughed. "There are unemployed bodies of liberal arts majors strewn all over America! For God's sake, Katie, get your head out of the clouds. We're heading into the technical age. Computers are where it's at now."

But as much as I liked the act of writing with a computer, and the ease of editing, I never was intrigued by their more esoteric parts. My one love over the years had been an astronomy program. It was the first thing to pique my interest in coming to Hawaii, building up a longing in me for heavenly bodies that can only be seen from the Southern Hemisphere. This, even more than any thought of searching out my roots, drew me here.

The truth is, I was always, as a student, a dreamer—drawn more to romance than hard news. More to fiction than fact.

Which is why, I suppose, I fell in love with Gerard. He came, he said, from Paris, and indeed he had a beautiful French accent to back that up. His parents were rich, and the only reason (he said) that I'd found him working as a waiter at the campus pub was because he'd had a tiff with his family over his goals. They wanted him to stay in France, take over the family business. He wanted to travel, see the world, become his own man. They'd refused to support him in that, Gerard said, so he'd up and left one day, vowing to become independent, to build a life of his own. The Laniers, he said, owned châteaux in the French countryside. Lush green vineyards, virtually oozing with five-figure wines in the soft summer sun.

As I began to fall in love I was tempted, largely because of my tendency toward romanticism, to forget Gerard's vow to remain independent of all that. Or perhaps I saw it as a temporary rebellion, the sort of antipathy toward one's parents that one outgrows, given time, and, of course, the love of a good woman. I'm a bit embarrassed to recall this, as even in retrospect—and given the forgiveness of time—I was, quite clearly, a fool.

I began creating little pictures in my head of living with Gerard at one of those châteaux, being the mistress of the manor, so to speak. It wasn't so much the money and luxury I craved, though of course I didn't mind the idea of having them. It was more what those ancient châteaux symbolized: a home, security, a place in the world where I'd finally "belong." Though my grandmother did her best, as a child I'd always longed for the kind of huge, happy, stable family I imagined the Lanier family to be.

This illusion (for that's what it turned out to be) clouded my vision. I offer this as my only excuse for falling in love with, and believing in, Gerard Lanier.

Oh, he was charming enough. Even Margo had a bit of a crush on him for a while. But when she saw I was falling for him, hard, she backed off. "No man is worth spoiling a good friendship," she said, giving me a hug. "Besides, you know me . . . I'm after one man one week, another the next."

Sobering, she'd twirled a lock of her shiny black hair around a finger and added, "You know, Katie, I don't think I'm ever going to be in love. I don't think I really like men. You simply can't count on them. Know what I mean?"

I didn't know what she meant, not at the time. It took me till much later to wonder if I'd ever like men again.

The first revelation came when Gerard and I had been seeing each other for six months. We'd managed to arrange long, passionate afternoons and sometimes evenings of making love at his apartment, which was near the campus. It was small and simple, but you could hear the university campion strike hourly, and I'd usually bring small bouquets of flowers from a street-corner vendor to set the scene. Gerard would bring the wine.

"California wine," he'd pointed out in the beginning. "It's the best." And I'd poked him in the chest and teased, "You're just saying that to get back at your family." But he didn't respond by laughing.

We'd cook something for dinner together, Gerard sometimes handling the pasta, and I the salad and bread. Afterward, we'd make love, then lie in bed and talk.

One of the talks we'd had was about marriage. I was ready, and I said we could work it out—the college expenses, the apartment. The old "two can live more cheaply than one," myth. (Wouldn't you think that as a student of myths and legends, I might have known better? The only way two ever live more cheaply than one is if one of them gives up what he or she wants.) But there I was, all starry-eyed and with my nose hot to trot at the gate, just panting after that old (wedding) bell.

Gerard said, "Don't you think we should wait?"

"I don't see why . . . we're in love, and we spend half our time together anyway."

"I think we should wait . . . at least until we're out of school."

"But that's three years from now. Two and a half, anyway."

One night I'd let myself in early, and I was at the black and white granite counter crushing cloves of garlic when Gerard came flying through the door, looking happier than I'd ever seen him.

"I got it!" he cried, dashing over to me and grabbing me, kissing me boisterously. "Katie, I got it!"

I looked up at him, wondering. I remember now that the scent of garlic was strong on my fingers as they touched his face. I remember that scent being strong all night, and that the oil from the cloves stung my eyes later when I lay in bed and wiped at tears that, no matter how much I chided myself, wouldn't go away.

"Got what?" I laughed uncertainly.

"The job in Seattle! For heaven's sake, Kate!"

"The . . ." I shook my head, dazed. "The what?"

"You can't not remember. The one for the vineyard up there."

I dropped my hand. "Gerard . . . what are we talking about?"

His face clouded over. "Don't act stupid, Kate. We've talked about this. I told you I'd met a distributor from Washington, and he'd mentioned my background to a vintner he knew. Remember I flew up there and talked to him last month? Well, he wants me to come up there and work for him! Isn't that great?"

I went cold, then hot. I felt like Alice must have, dropping down that awful hole. "Gerard, I don't remember any of this. You flew to Washington? When?"

He looked at me sadly, shaking his head and smiling. "My poor little Kate. What's wrong with you? Have you been studying too hard?"

My mouth worked, but no words came out. I would never have forgotten something as important as this. I would *never* . . .

It was true I'd been working hard. My classload was heavy, and I'd begun writing in nearly every spare moment. Often, I forgot to turn out lights when I went to bed, or to set the alarm. Half the time I couldn't remember to grocery shop. But to forget that Gerard was thinking of *leaving*?

My legs went weak. I turned away from him, leaning on the cold granite counter.

"I thought you'd be happy for me," he said in a slightly pouty tone. "You said you wanted only what was best for me."

After a moment I faced him again. "Gerard, I don't remember any of this at all. When did we talk? When did you tell me this? For God's sake, I thought . . . I thought we were getting married."

"Katie, of course we'll be married! But we agreed it was far too soon for that. I said I'd get a job first, remember?"

"Yes . . . yes, of course I remember that. But you never talked about leaving Berkeley. Or about leaving school. I had no idea."

"Katie, I told you last month I was flying to Seattle for the interview."

"You didn't! You didn't tell me that at all!"

My mind cast back for details, and the only thing I could remember was a weekend when Gerard said he was too busy to see me. It was exam week, and I was up to my ears in studying as well, so I didn't think too much about it. On the following Monday when we met at his apartment, he never mentioned a thing, that I could recall, about the weekend. The only thing I remembered was having missed him, and being so glad to be with him, to have his arms around me and to be lying with him in that funny little bed that squeaked, with the neighbor downstairs who thumped on the ceiling with his mop handle, shouting for us to be quiet. I remembered how we laughed, and how we deliberately thought up new positions that squeaked the bed even more, just out of high spirits and the kind of devil-may-care that existed when we were together.

If men only knew how seductive it is to be with someone who laughs at the same precise moment over the same precise things . . . They wouldn't have to worry so much about technique, or the importance (to them) of the size of a simple body part.

But that moment of unreality in the little apartment on Telegraph Avenue was not fun. Gerard's face darkened. His voice turned cold. "Obviously, it wasn't important enough for you to listen when I told you about Seattle—let alone remember."

"I listen to you, sweetheart," I said, hating the way

my voice became placating and unsure. "I listen all the time."

He turned away, his back straight and stiff. "I don't think we should talk about this now."

We spent the next hour toying with cold food. Gerard opened a bottle of cabernet and began to drink. I didn't touch it. Reality was already too far distant from me; I couldn't imagine making things worse. As the night went on, he drank more and more. Finally, he fell asleep in the armchair by the window. I went to bed alone.

The next day I tracked Margo down in her dorm next to mine, with the thought that I might cry on her shoulder. To my astonishment, she took up for Gerard. "To be fair, you have been horribly distracted," she said. "There have been a few times when you haven't remembered things I told you."

I was stunned. "What kinds of things?"

"Oh, nothing important. Just times we were supposed to meet, and where. Little things like that. Remember when we were supposed to have coffee at the Blue Duck, and you forgot?"

"I . . . yes, of course I remember that. I was writing and I forgot the time and stood you up. But I remembered later and apologized. Anyway, Margo, that was different. I never in a million years would have forgotten something so major as Gerard leaving school to take a job in Seattle."

She took my hand. "Well, maybe it's like he said? You didn't listen? To be honest, Kate, I've been worried about you myself."

Her eyes, which were a dark, rich brown, peered at me worriedly. "Are you on something?"

"*On* something? Of course not!"

"I just thought maybe Valium. Practically everyone is these days."

"I'm not 'on' anything, Margo."

"Well, maybe you should be." She laughed. "Just kidding. But maybe you should see a doctor. There might be something physically wrong."

"Don't be silly, I'm healthy as a clam."

"That's true, you're never sick. Well, maybe you just need more rest."

I decided she was right about that. I began spending more time in the dorm, less with Gerard at his apartment. I told myself I was being sensible—getting more rest, taking care of my health. But a small, secret part of me knew that there was something horribly wrong now. I no longer felt as close to Gerard. Worse, I no longer trusted him. A wall had cropped up between us.

Eventually, it ended. Gerard and I broke it off. Nothing dramatic—more a natural evolvement of things. He moved to Seattle, and I slowly got over the pain and nearly forgot him. Then, three years ago, I read in a newspaper that he'd married: OWNER OF LANIER VINEYARDS MARRIES DAUGHTER OF SENATOR JOHN REED.

According to the accounts, Gerard had written his own marriage vows to the woman he described as his "first and only love," who turned out—(surprise, surprise)—to be my best friend, Margo Reed.

By then Margo and I had grown apart, too, the way college friends often do. But I'd had a call from her a month after the announcement. "I'm sorry I didn't call sooner, Katie. I've been so afraid you might hear about this before I could tell you. Katie, I . . . I've gotten married."

"I know," I said carefully.

"You know?"

"I read about it in the Seattle paper. I was there signing books."

"Oh, Katie, I'm so sorry! I wanted to write and tell you, but I never could quite figure out how to put it. Please tell me you don't really mind. You said you were over him, and after all, it's been years. I never even saw him again myself until a few months ago, and then it all happened so fast. We decided on the spur of the moment, and flew to Las Vegas—"

"Margo," I interrupted, "I don't mind. I've hardly thought of Gerard in years." Amazingly, I realized this was true.

"Are you sure?"

"Of course I'm sure. I just hope . . ."

"What?"

"I don't mean to spoil anything for you. But, Margo, you remember how he ended up being with me. It was all so strange. And I never fully trusted him after that."

"Kate," Margo said reprovingly, "these things are never just one person's fault. You were going through a difficult time then. You were forgetting things, not operating up to par, but you wouldn't admit it. What could Gerard do?"

"Is that what he told you?" I said with the first trace of anger.

"Katie, let's not argue. Looking back, it just seems like a terrible misunderstanding between the two of you. You were both in the midst of exams, both carrying a heavy load and under so much tension . . ."

"I asked you a question, Margo. Is that what Gerard is saying now? That it was all my fault?"

A slight hesitation. "Oh, sweetie, let's not talk about it. Let's just be us, two friends, talking the way we used to."

I could have let it go. Who knew better than I that a woman in love sees through a veil? There's an ancient legend, in fact, that says women were forced to wear veils at their weddings so they couldn't see the truth of their bridegrooms till after the vows were spoken. After that the veil could be removed. The truth didn't matter anymore.

But this wasn't just about my best friend marrying my old love. This was about my best friend believing lies about me—Gerard's lies. Taking his side against mine. It was about losing her loyalty, and feeling betrayed.

So I hung up on Margo that day. And I never spoke to her again.

Not a grown-up or enlightened way to behave, I suppose. I'm not necessarily proud of it. In fact, I think I always believed, deep down, that she would learn the truth relatively quickly, leave Gerard, and call me up to apologize.

She never did. Over the past three years I've thought about that and wondered. But every December the Christmas cards arrive—the happy-family photos on the front, always a silver bucket holding champagne beside them, the label in gold script clearly "*Lanier*." Just the two of them. No child appeared.

This past year I barely looked at the card, leaving it to gather dust on the top of my fridge with the rest of the junk mail. I felt, finally, that I'd put them both in my past. Until three weeks ago.

When Margo left that message on my machine, asking me to call her, it surprised me. I was curious. But not so much that I couldn't ignore it. When she called again, I ignored that too.

The last message, two weeks ago, was disturbing. *"I'm worried about you, Katie. I keep having the strangest dreams."*

Still, I didn't respond. In the old days, Margo tended to leave me with hooks like that, as a way to get me to call her back. She could have waited till I was less busy and had more time to talk, but she'd push and push. Pretending to be worried about me was her way of manipulating, of gaining control. I didn't see all that at the time, of course. I imagined her concern to be genuine.

Perhaps Gerard was at least half-right. I imagined a lot of things.

I was at the Hale Pau Hana's front desk the minute they opened at eight o'clock. "Someone was in my room last night," I told Mari-Lu, the manager. "How could they have gotten in?"

She looked surprised. Her green eyes widened. "I have no idea. I didn't give anyone your key."

"Who else was on duty last night?"

"Well, let's see . . . at about what time?"

"Actually, from yesterday afternoon at around three, until about two this morning."

Again she shook her head, pushing the red-gold curls, already limp from humidity, back from her cheeks.

"I was the only one here, till I closed up at ten. I came in at noon because Tina had a date with some surfer guy." She looked worried. "I'm sorry, but I definitely didn't give anyone your key."

"Is there some other way they could get in, then? How about the housekeepers? Would they let someone in?"

"I doubt it. They shouldn't, of course. But let me talk to them and see."

"I'd like to talk to them myself," I said, "if you wouldn't mind."

She gave a shrug and smiled. "I wouldn't mind at all. But first, let me see what I can do. Some of them don't like *haoles*, which of course includes me. But I'm the boss. They're more likely to talk openly with me, than with you. Just give me an hour or so, okay?''

I agreed to leave it in her hands. Thanking her, I decided to drive down to Long's for my photos from the day before. Something told me this whole thing, from the beginning, at Hecock's, to the end, was about the roll that had disappeared. With any luck, there might be something in the photos from the second roll that would hold a clue.

I took a number and waited with my ID at the ready, while the photo clerk helped three people ahead of me. As I waited, my uneasiness grew. I couldn't help but feel someone was watching me, and I kept looking around, pretending to check out the merchandise but really looking for anyone who might be looking back. There was no one, that I could see.

Ask him who he really is.

I couldn't get that out of my mind. Who had written it, and why?

And what was Dan Kala's involvement? Certainly he must be involved.

My head began to ache. I reached up to rub the bridge of my nose. Just as I did that, my vision blurred. I blinked several times, thinking my contacts had picked up some foreign object. It didn't help. I looked around, just to move my eyes about, hoping to ease any tension. The blurring was still there, but seemed only along the sides. Was this what a migraine was like?

I'd had zigzag lights in my vision now and then in recent years, but no one could offer an explanation for them. An eye doctor suggested they might be migraines, but without the pain. As they never seemed to get worse, or to be linked with any other physical problems, I learned to ignore them. They always went away within a half hour or so.

This was something different, however. No zigzag

lights. It was more as if I could see things moving along my peripheral vision. Almost as if someone, otherwise unseen, were there.

I felt cold, but sensed it was only from fear, the kind of fear that comes when one is in public and something goes wrong with the body. For a brief, flickering moment, you wonder if you're going to faint. Or die. And you fight to get back to normal, because it would be so embarrassing to either faint or die, right there in public that way.

In the next instant, the blurring stopped. I held myself still for a moment, afraid that if I moved one way or another it would start again. Then I heard the clerk call to me, "Next." I moved forward, holding out with shaky hands both my driver's license and the stub given to me the day before. The clerk took them and crossed to a counter along the wall, where a hundred or more envelopes were stacked alphabetically, in neat rows.

I was still deep in thought about the problem with my vision and the events of the night before. Therefore, I didn't immediately realize how long the clerk was taking to find my photos. She came back to the cash register and picked up the notebook that people sign when they pick up their orders. She ran a finger down a page and looked at me. "Your pictures were already picked up," she said.

"Picked up? But that's impossible."

She nodded. "See here?"

I looked at the page. The scrawled signature was impossible to make out.

"This isn't my signature," I said anxiously. "You gave my photos to the wrong person. How could that happen?"

"I don't know," she said, running a tired hand through her dark hair. "I wasn't here."

"When were they picked up? Have you got the time written down?"

"No. But it must have been this morning."

"*This morning*. So that's why the "tired, got a meeting in the morning" act—the sudden end to what had seemed the perfect setup for a night of fun and games. Dan Kala must have needed his beauty sleep. I remembered, now, telling him that there was a second roll of film, one the "thief" hadn't got. That's how secure I'd felt about Long's system of checking IDs.

Anger burned in my gut.

"The man who came for my photos," I said. "He couldn't have had an ID in my name. Why would anyone here have turned them over to him?"

The clerk was tired of me now. Her gaze flicked to the long line behind me as someone coughed impatiently. "I don't know," she said. "Do you want to talk to the manager?"

"Would she have been here when my photos were picked up? Would she have seen the person who took them?"

"I'm afraid not. She just came in."

Another cough and a shuffling of feet from behind me.

"Next?" the clerk said again, loudly, looking past me as I hesitated.

There was nothing more to be done here. I picked up my purse and left.

Back at the Hale Pau Hana, I stopped at the office on the way to my room.

"I've talked to everyone who was here yesterday," Mari-Lu said. "They swear they didn't let anyone in. Did you, uh . . . did you want to report this to the police?"

It was clear this was the last thing she wanted. It wouldn't help to have that kind of publicity—one more rip-off at a Kihei condo—right there in the Crime Watch column of *The Maui News*.

"I don't think so," I said. I knew a little bit about the island cops. They were nearly all Hawaiian. They swaggered a lot, their thumbs hooked into their belts, and they liked to hassle the *haoles*. By the time they were through with me, they'd have me convinced I'd imagined everything.

Like Gerard.

No. I thought that instead of cops, I might just pay a little visit to the Hyatt in Ka'anapali.

CHAPTER 6

Good hotels, I knew, will not give out the room number of a guest; the only way to reach someone is to have the desk ring them up. I'd decided to call Dan Kala from the Hyatt lobby rather than my condo. That way, he'd have fewer excuses to put me off. *"I'll be out on business by the time you get here,"* wouldn't work. And if he put me off anyway? Well, he'd have to leave his room sometime. I'd sit right here in the lobby and wait for him to come out of the elevators. I am not a writer of suspense novels and the fine art of detection for nothing.

I crossed to a hotel house phone, past the scent-laden ginger arrangement and the soft green chair, with their memories of the night before. By now the only emotion they stirred up was one of deep-seated anger. I'd been a victim—of something—and though the precise nature of that victimization was not entirely clear as yet, I was no less bothered by it.

Lifting the phone, I listened until a delicately accented voice said, "Hyatt Regency. May I help you?"

"Yes. Would you connect me with Dan Kala's room, please?"

"One moment."

There was a small pause. "I'm sorry, could you spell that, please?"

"Yes," I said a trifle irritably. It couldn't be much simpler. "Two words. *D-a-n K-a-l-a.*"

"*Mahalo.* One moment."

A longer silence, during which I felt contrite for taking my anger out on the poor operator.

"Sorry, there's no one registered by that name. Is he expected today?"

"No." My irritation returned. "He's been registered here for several days."

Another brief pause. By the time the operator came back on-line, I knew what she'd have to say. "Sorry to take so long. Mr. Kala was here, but he checked out early this morning."

Damn. I hadn't expected this. Had he left, then, right after he'd said good night to me, professing weariness and a desire to turn in? Had he simply omitted the fact that what he was turning in was his key?

"Did he leave me a message?" I asked, knowing, of course, he had not. (But hit me with that old two-by-four anyway.) "This is Kate McKenna."

"No, no messages. Sorry."

"A forwarding address, then?" I am a glutton for punishment.

Her voice sounded sympathetic. *One more female tourist dumped by a local gigolo*, came through the wire. "I'm sorry, no. No forwarding address."

I thought quickly. "You do have that information, though, don't you? He must have registered with a credit card."

With that, she clammed up and became more formal. I could, after all, be a stalker with a rabbit in a pot. "The hotel doesn't give out private information on its guests."

Too bad, I thought, *the hotel doesn't have a board*

*in the lobby listing guests whom unsuspecting women
should stay away from.*

But this wasn't the ordinary dumping, was it? Dan
Kala had stolen my missing film before departing, and
I intended to find out why, if it took everything I had.

I was in luck. I found Leani, the masseuse from the
night before, in the hotel spa. She was seated at a
white desk with a tasteful arrangement of tropical
flowers beside an open appointment book. Behind her,
against the wall, was a row of low file cabinets, all in
white. Leani looked up and smiled, recognizing me as
I entered.

"How are you feeling? Did you come back for
more, now that you've tasted bliss?"

I sat in the client's chair on the opposite side of the
desk. "I'm feeling great, thanks to you. And actually,
I think I might just do that—come back for more.
Another day, though. I was hoping you could help me
with something."

She smiled. "Of course. What can I do?"

"Dan Kala, the man I was with last night, has
checked out, and I was supposed to call him at his
home in San Francisco tonight. But I've lost his number. I hoped you might have it in your files."

"Well . . ." She looked unsure now. "We do keep
a record of all our paying clients. By that, I mean we'd
have his phone number since he paid, but not yours.
The only thing is, we're not really supposed to give
out that information. It's confidential."

I let my shoulders slump, trying to look like a disappointed lover. "I know. I guess I figured that. It's
just that I didn't know what else to do. He'll be waiting for my call, and he won't know what happened.
I'm sure he'll think I've just decided to write him
off."

Leani smiled. The Hawaiian people have what they call an "Aloha spirit." Generally they are willing to help, to extend themselves for the visitors to their islands, I'd learned. The Aloha spirit is beginning to wear a bit thin as they take on more and more work to make ends meet and find themselves tired and out of sorts, just like us mainlanders. But I was counting on Leani, and she came through.

Studying me, she said, "Well, I don't think Mr. Kala would mind. He sounded like a little kid when he called, wanting to surprise you with a massage. I guess he really cares about you."

I smiled ruefully. "I was beginning to think I'd met Mr. Right. But if I can't reach him . . ." Sighing, I rested my chin in my hand. "I don't suppose I'll ever see him again."

Leani made her decision. "Oh, what can it hurt?"

She turned in her chair to the file cabinets. Pulling out a drawer she took out a Rolodex, put it on the desk, and leafed through. "Here we go."

Taking a business card from a holder on her desk and turning it to its blank side, she began to write. When she was finished, she handed the card to me.

I glanced at it. My thank you, "*Mahalo*," was out of my mouth before I realized there was something wrong. "Are you sure this is right? It has a Hawaii area code—eight-zero-eight. Dan lives in San Francisco."

She took the card. "Here, let me double-check. No, I wrote it down correctly. But you're right. It is a Maui number. See the prefix?"

She handed me back the card, and I looked at it, confused. It did seem to be a Maui prefix. Was Dan Kala still on the island, then? Had he gone so far as to change hotels to avoid me?

"Do you have an address?" I asked.

Leani shook her head. "No . . . and that's odd. We should have one. Oh, I know. Kim took down the information when he called last night. She understands enough of what people say to write down names and numbers, but sometimes she forgets about addresses. I'm sorry."

"Well . . . you know what they say about true love. It doesn't run smooth." I stuck the card in my purse, thanked Leani for her help, and promised to phone for another appointment.

"Good luck," she said, giving me a conspiratorial smile. "I hope you find your man."

I sat in the Hyatt bar with a glass of pineapple juice, looking down over the swimming pool with its waterfalls and lava slides, and thinking about my next move. In the pool, children splashed and swam beneath the waterfall to a second pool on the other side. Adults sat around the edge sipping drinks and reading trash novels, soaking up sun. Life went on as always, down there.

As for me, I felt as if I'd been picked up by a spaceship in the past twenty-four hours and set down on another planet. Nothing had changed, yet everything had changed. I no longer felt the security of my quiet little world of words.

I could just let the whole thing go, of course. Whatever Dan Kala's reasons were for stealing my film, they might have nothing whatsoever to do with me. In fact, I was more than ever ready to believe my lens had simply caught someone cheating on his wife and, for whatever reason, Dan Kala had been dispatched for the cleanup job.

He might even be a P.I. If I were writing this story, in fact, that's what I'd make him—a P.I. Someone handsome and sexy like Thomas Magnum, though I'd come up with a more believable name for him. Who'd ever take a character seriously, with a name like Magnum? Jen, my editor, would surely say he lacked credibility, and of course she'd be right. Before the book went to copyedits I'd have to do a global search and replace, changing all the "Magnums" to "Morgan," or maybe "Jones."

So . . . Let's say Dan Kala had been hired to get that film away from me. But then, what was all that about last night? Why spend so much time with me? Why go to so much trouble?

Another possibility: and this seemed the most likely. He'd been dispatched to keep me busy while someone else took care of the cleanup—someone who'd been in my condo last night looking for the film while Dan Kala and I were playing emotional footsy over dinner and enjoying a long, lovely massage. And when my visitor didn't find what he was looking for in my condo, he took the next most logical step and checked out the surrounding photo labs this morning until he came across the developed photos at Long's. He might even have gone there first, since Long's has the largest and most convenient lab.

But how did he manage to convince the clerk to hand my photos over? And, more importantly, was he the same person who had typed those words into my computer—*"Ask him who he really is"*?

If for no other reason, that message was why I couldn't simply let this go. That one act had taken this out of the simple burglary category and thrust it into the personal.

I felt a chill even thinking about it. The idea that someone had been in my place, touched my things, and even gone so far as to open my computer, turn it on, and write something like that . . .

What else might be going on in the mind of such a person?

Part of me felt that with any luck, I might never know. But the other part, that dark, inexplicable side of me that writes about mysterious happenings because they take me out of my otherwise boring day-to-day life, saw the opportunity: *Live it this time, girl. Don't just write about it.*

I will admit to a certain element of anger in this— an urge to stand nose to nose with Dan Kala and demand the truth, not to mention an apology. Wining and dining a woman for nefarious reasons is one thing. Breaking into her condo is another.

But what to do? The idea of yelling at him over the phone had a somehow less than satisfying feel. I wanted to land on the guy's doorstep, take him by surprise, and show him he hadn't gotten away with it. Whatever "it" was.

I'd need his address. And if this were happening in San Francisco, I could do that. I could call a friend at the police department, ask him to track down Dan Kala's address by the phone number Leani gave me, and he'd do it.

But, here? I didn't have those connections.

I sighed. The phone it would have to be.

I reached into my purse and pulled out what I thought was the card from Leani. Then, glancing down at it, I burst out laughing. The bartender looked up warily, as if wondering if he had a nut case on his hands. I didn't care. I'd found gold.

This wasn't the card from Leani, but another one, one I'd forgotten completely with all that had been going on. It was the crumpled business card I'd found on the floor of the tent last night after Dan Kala had dressed. I'd meant to give it to him outside the tent, thinking it must be one of his clients' cards. But then he'd pulled that "I've got a headache" routine, and it had completely slipped my mind.

The reason I laughed was because it happens that way sometimes for me: The doors all seem closed until I make a decision to act. Then they blow wide-open.

DAN C. KALA, read the letters on the card in plain black script. CONSULTANT. 10 KOA ROAD, HUELO POINT, MAUI. Beneath that was a phone number.

Digging into my purse for the card from Leani, I compared the numbers. They were the same.

"Gotcha," I said softly. The bartender looked up again.

I smiled.

CHAPTER 7

I sat in my rental car in the Hyatt parking lot, poring over the map from the glove box. Huelo Point, I saw, was on the north side of the island, on the infamous, much-feared Road to Hana. I'd driven all the way out to Hana one day, and it didn't seem all that bad. Certainly there were the ballyhooed six hundred curves and fifty bridges along the way, turning what might otherwise have been a half-hour drive into one that took, on average, three hours. But I wasn't in a hurry, and the scenery—the black-sand beaches, waterfalls, rain, and bamboo forests—were worth it.

I remembered, now, seeing a road marker for Huelo along the way. It was just west of the point where most of the worst curves in the road began, which made it reasonably accessible—a half hour or less from Kahului and the airport. I remembered, too, that the tape I'd rented for the Road to Hana described Huelo and the surrounding area as the place where Carol Burnett and other stars had built homes. Whether they still lived there was a bit vague; I figured Carol was long gone, but they'd left that on the tape to impress the tourists.

I was anxious to head out there, get this whole thing

over with. I glanced up at the West Maui mountains, then south toward Haleakala. Clouds hung above both, and those over the rim of the crater of Haleakala were especially dark and formidable. It must be raining torrents in Hana, I thought.

Still, I didn't have to go that far. And I'd driven the north side of the island often enough to know that there's just as likely to be nothing more than a heavy mist, or even sunshine, by the time one gets there. I decided to take a chance.

Pulling out onto the Honoapiilani Highway, I entered Lahaina and tanked up on gas. Inside the station I bought a Classic Coke for energy, and a package of cheese and peanut butter crackers. Heading south, then north, I branched off at the Kuihelani Highway to Kahului. Tiny droplets of warm rain spattered my windshield, and off to the left a spectacular rainbow formed within the gentle green folds of the West Maui Mountains. I failed to feel awe as I usually do; my mind was more on the upcoming confrontation with Dan Kala. As I closed in on Kahului, my heart began to beat faster. *Another half hour, perhaps less. I'll be there.*

What would he say? How would he explain his actions? Would he simply laugh the whole thing off? Or would he reason with me?

I hate being reasoned with.

After about forty-five minutes I reached the airport and the winding Hana Road. As I drove east, the rain began to come down in heavy sheets. The Sprint's wipers weren't up to it, forcing me to drive slowly, leaning forward to peer through whatever clear spot I could find. The ocean was to my left, visible at times and at other times blocked by banana, papaya, kukui nut, and bamboo trees. Often, mailboxes in clusters were the only indication there were homes nearby.

Many side roads had no signs, and Koa Road wasn't on the map. Huelo Point was, however, and it looked to be a small enough area. Dan Kala's house shouldn't be all that hard to find.

At least, that was what I told myself. I proved to be wrong, just as I'd been wrong about so many things.

CHAPTER 8

At the mile marker indicated on the sketchy little map that had come with my tour tape, I found Huelo with little trouble. It was little more than a large grouping of mailboxes to the left, and a public telephone. Confusing matters, however, was that there were two roads out to the point. I sat in the Sprint with rain streaming all about me, and debated. Finally I just picked one. *Take the right*, a tiny voice said. Given the bad condition of the rutted road, I had a nagging feeling that voice was leading me straight into hell.

That feeling worsened the farther along I got. Dense trees and wild shrubs loomed over the narrow road. Many of the side roads had no signs, and were nothing more than trails. At one point, the main road forked. Decision time again.

Fifteen minutes later I had to admit I was lost. Pulling into a driveway, I stopped to rest my knuckles, which had whitened considerably from gripping the wheel to dodge huge rocks in the road, as well as potholes as big as washtubs. Glancing up the drive I saw a typical Hawaiian farmhouse: green, with a wide porch. A dark-complected man dressed in work clothes stood there, looking back at me. Wondering, I supposed, what I was doing there. I hesitated only a moment, then stepped out of the car into mud up to my ankles. Swearing softly, I called out.

"Hello! Can you tell me where Koa Road is?"

The rain whipped the words from my mouth, and the man simply stared. I wiped my wet face with the back of my hand and raised my voice. "Koa Road. Do you know where it is?"

Still no response. Couldn't he hear?

Taking a step forward, I paused, my mainland fears kicking in. *Don't go any closer*, they said. *You don't know who this is, or what you might be getting into. He doesn't look all that friendly.*

Had there been a NO TRESPASSING sign somewhere? I realized I wasn't sure. The only thing I knew was that I was on a lonely path somewhere off the Hana Road, surrounded by banana trees and jungle. If anything happened to me, no one would ever know.

I began to step backward toward the car. The man came down his steps, carrying something in his hand. There was a grassy lawn between us, perhaps one hundred feet long. I couldn't make out what he was holding, and reached nervously for the door handle of the Sprint. Opening it, I slid inside, pulling my muddy feet in after me.

Locking the door quickly, I stepped on the clutch and threw the car into reverse. My muddy foot slipped off the pedal. The car slammed to a halt and died. The man drew closer. His hair was dark, the scalp bald in places, and crusted. He was frowning now, one hand held behind his back. With the other he pounded on my window, motioning for me to lower it.

In my anxiety to restart the car and get out of there, I flooded it. Shoving my foot down on the accelerator, I held it there and tried again. Nothing. The man rapped again, more loudly this time. I shook my head, sweat pouring off me in buckets now. The man's other hand came from behind his back. It held a papaya.

I stared. First at the papaya and then into the man's eyes.

"Were you looking for the papayas?" he said loudly. "I brought them onto the porch because of the rain."

It was then I saw the tiny sign: PAPAYAS, 99 CENTS/POUND. The words were written on a piece of old refrigerator carton, nailed to a stake in the ground just a few feet in front of my car.

I couldn't answer. My teeth were chattering, and my bones were busy falling apart.

Where had all that fear come from? I had to ask myself. Was it only a by-product of writing mysteries for a living? Or something more?

Accepting what the good man had to offer—directions to Koa Road and a papaya as well—I got the car started at last and made a U-turn, driving back a quarter mile. There on the left was the small church he'd mentioned, another green house, and next to it a dirt road that made me question my sanity for ever even beginning such a thing. But I'd gone too far to back out. Nudging the little Sprint gingerly past huge boulders and over ruts filled with several inches of rainwater, I mushed on, determined not to think what would happen if my valiant little car got stuck.

Which reminded me of something my grandmother McKenna used to say. "Kate," she'd say, "don't even think it. If you think it, it'll happen, sure enough."

The thing about my grandmother is that all too often she was right. I remembered this particular admonition, of course, far too late. It came to mind abruptly just as the Sprint nose-dived into a sinkhole three feet deep and failed to come up for air.

*   *   *

Cussing and beating up on the steering wheel didn't
seem to help. Houses were sparse at this point, and
though I looked back to the little shack I'd just passed,
there was no sign of life. Which is to say there was
no cheerful "Aloha" from its porch, no offer to help
or even so much as a sign that anyone had noted my
predicament.

It was still raining, and hard. Suddenly, Dan Kala
wasn't worth the trouble. According to my directions,
however, I wasn't far from Koa Road. There was at
least some hope of a dry roof and a telephone at jour-
ney's end.

I took the cash and credit cards from my purse,
shoved them into my shorts pocket, and left the purse
behind to free up my arms for easier walking. Then I
slithered out of the car, soaked through and still
muddy from my visit to Papayaville. Things couldn't
get much worse. If I'd had any secret, hidden desire
to wow Dan Kala with my beauty as well as surprise
him, I'd certainly blown it all to hell.

"This old man, he played three, he played knicky-
knack on my knee . . ."

My singing voice wasn't great, but it gave me courage to schlep through the mud on my way to 10 Koa
Road. I pictured myself as Ingrid Bergman in *The Inn
of the Sixth Happiness,* with all those little orphan children, trudging over muddy hill and dale to freedom.
Hell, if Ingrid could do it, I could.

By the time I'd reached Koa Road, however, I felt
more like Julie Andrews in *The Sound of Music,* where
she stands in front of the captain's mansion and mut-
ters, "Oh, help."

"Oh, help," I did in fact mutter at the sight of what
awaited me at the Koa Road juncture: a sign pointing

down its seemingly endless length in the direction of number 10.

"Damn you, Dan Kala," became my mantra finally. "Damn you, damn you, damn you to hell." Since I was already apparently in that netherworld, I figured the least he could do was join me.

Eventually I reached number 10. It wasn't till I was almost upon it, however, that I realized how isolated it was. There never was a 2, 4, 6, or 8. As for the other side of the road, it was nothing but a cliff, with the sound of roaring surf hitting rocks far below.

An iron gate stood open at the beginning of the driveway. On either side, posts made of lava rock were barely visible through lush vines. This entire side of the road, in fact, was nothing short of unclaimed jungle. Philodendrons like the one I had at home in a pot on my TV were trees here, several stories high. Flowers I couldn't identify ran wild, weaving in and out of gloriously untamed white orchids. Golden plumeria threw its strong, sweet scent over everything, and through the tips of trees I saw, finally, the roof of a house.

Next to the driveway was an ornate stone bench that looked to be quite old. I sat for a moment, realizing my legs were weak from the strenuous walk through the mud.

Or was it the mud? Now that I was here, I wasn't so sure I wanted to know the truth about Dan Kala. Or the missing photos. Not to mention who had been in my condo and typed those words into my computer: *Ask him who he really is.*

"Some things are best left alone," my grandmother used to say.

Why is it I never listen?

❧

CHAPTER 9

The beauty of Dan Kala's place surprised me. Even for Maui, this was something out of the ordinary. The driveway, lined with shrubbery and flowers, opened up to a clearing that revealed what appeared to be a main one-story house with a separate, two-story house on either side. A small estate.

Before the main house, which was low, white, and rambling, with a red tile roof, was a natural-shaped pool surrounded by decorative rocks. The bottom and sides of the pool had been painted slate blue, lending the water a cool, exotic look. As I drew closer, I could see that beyond the houses were only cliff and sea. The estate was on a point, jutting out into the Pacific. It reminded me of the Big Sur area of California—the view absolutely stunning at every turn.

A garage to the right was open, but held no car. I skirted a path around the pool to the door of the main house, curious that no one had heard me coming and appeared. But then, they—whoever else might live here with Dan Kala—were probably not accustomed to people arriving on foot.

The door had both a knocker and a bell. I ran my hands over my wet hair, rang the bell and waited.

Nothing. I tried the knocker. Still nothing.

He's in one of the other houses, then.

Or not here at all.

Suddenly I was certain that was the case. Hesitating, I put my hand on the knob. It gave. The door opened, surprising me only a little. Hawaiians, unlike us fearful *haole* tourists, seldom lock their doors, I'd learned. At least, not out here in the country.

Great. Just walk right in, use the phone, call a tow truck, and leave? Why not? What would it hurt?

Looking toward the smaller houses on the right and left, I saw no one peering through a window. No "Neighborhood Watch," then. Both houses had plenty of glass, and decks both fore and aft, so it wasn't likely they'd miss someone knocking over here.

I rang the bell, just for good measure, then listened a few moments and heard no approaching footsteps.

Opening the door wide, I stepped onto a red-tiled floor. "Hello? Hello, is anyone here?"

Still no answer. It seemed I was definitely alone.

I stood still a moment, looking around. What I saw took my breath away. Directly ahead was a large, wide living room with glass doors across the entire front. Beyond them an elegant flagstone terrace held several blue-and-white-striped chaise lounges. Past them swept the most dramatic view I'd ever seen: blue-green water, sheer emerald cliffs and—off on the horizon, through what was now a lightly misting rain—a dazzling band of bright golden sun. The cliffs were what held my attention, however. They were visible across a band of water to the left of Huelo Point, and above them stretched a rainbow.

I am a sucker for views . . . and this was by far the most stupendous view I'd seen yet on Maui.

That's the only excuse I can think of for remaining, for ambling out onto that terrace and sitting there on a large smooth rock in the welcoming, sudden appearance of sun. For drinking in the sight, rather than going immediately to Dan Kala's phone, calling a tow truck, and getting out of there.

The view took my breath away.

And so one's life is changed by seemingly small, insignificant things . . . and perhaps for all time.

CHAPTER 10

"What is this I spy, a lizard? Rather large for a gecko, I'd say."

Despite my attempts to stay awake, I'd been drifting off, stretched out on the rock and dreaming, exhausted from the long walk and the weather. Dan Kala's voice seeped through, pulling me back from something about a woman, a woman with her arms stretched out, reaching for me. My eyes popped open like a shot.

He was standing above me, frowning, blocking the sun. "You look dreadful." He scanned my muddy clothes and hair. "Here," he said, handing me a towel.

I sat up quickly, feeling immediately off balance. My cheeks grew hot. "I . . ."

"I saw your car alongside the road. I've called a tow truck to bring it here. Did you walk all the way from there? In all that rain?"

"I . . ."

"Take the towel. Actually, what you should do is shower off." He gestured with a motion of his head to an outside shower beside a hot tub I hadn't seen before, as it was almost completely hidden by a trellis with climbing vines.

I accepted the towel but still couldn't think what to

say. If I'd been angry on my way here, Dan Kala was fast taking the wind out of my sails. Finally, wiping dried mud from my face, I said, "You don't seem surprised to find me here."

"Well, you did leave a calling card."

I looked at him stupidly.

"The car? Same one you drove to the Hyatt last night?"

"Oh. Right." My brain was still befuddled, and I felt like a five-year-old child. To add to it, Dan Kala was clearly irritated at finding me on his doorstep— or rock—and he had the advantage.

I swung my feet to the ground and tried to gather my wits.

"Don't put *me* on the defensive, Dan Kala. You're the one who disappeared without a trace."

A small smile curved the left side of his mouth. "Disappeared? Pardon me, but this is my home. I haven't gone anywhere."

"You told me you were staying at the Hyatt," I said. "You also told me you lived in San Francisco."

"I do, part of the year. As for the Hyatt, I was there for three days, meeting with clients. Wait a minute . . . don't tell me," he said in an amused tone. "This is a stalking?"

"Stalking, hell! I just want my photos back. And I want to know what's going on. Tell me that, and I'll be gone."

"Your photos? Why would I have your photos, or anything of yours? What are you talking about?"

"You know damn well what I'm talking about. The photos that turned up missing this morning from Long's Drugs. And what about last night? Were you keeping me away from my condo so some cohort could rifle through my things? Or had you hoped to pump me for information over our cozy little dinner?"

"Information—" Amusement turned to anger. "Woman, what the hell are you talking about?"

"I only wish I knew. The one thing I do know is my photos have been stolen, someone's been in my condo messing with my computer, and you've got something to do with it."

"Wait a minute. This film. Is that the roll of film you told me about last night? The one that was stolen at that lookout point you mentioned? Why would you think I had anything to do with that?"

He looked perfectly sincere. And so innocent.

Why didn't I believe him, then?

"Just tell me," I said irritably. "Tell me the truth, for once, and I'll be out of here."

He shook his head. "I swear to you, I had nothing to do with your film. I never took it, never touched it. I've never even seen it."

He paused. Then he took my arm by the elbow, lightly, but firmly. "And now—*if* you don't mind—I would like you to wash before you come inside the house again. You tracked a hell of a lot of mud over my floor." He began to steer me toward the shower.

I jerked away. "Take your hands off me. I'm not taking a shower, and I'm not coming into your house again. I've said what I came here to say, and now I'll be going, thanks very much."

He shrugged. "You must like walking, then."

"What do you mean? You said you called a tow truck. I can wait for it out front."

"It'll be a long wait. And probably a wet one. It's supposed to rain again tonight."

"Well, that won't bother me. I won't be here tonight."

He smiled. "The tow truck can't get here till tomorrow."

"But that's ridiculous! I'll call the rental company."

"I already did. It was an unusually bad rain, and they're swamped with calls." Again, he shrugged. "You must know by now how it is in Maui. Things get done . . . but eventually. Guess we're stuck with each other meanwhile."

I cursed myself for not calling the rental company when I first arrived. "I want to talk to them myself." I turned toward the house.

"Oh, no, you don't." He blocked my way with an arm. "Shower *first*."

I was suddenly very tired. Too tired to go on arguing. "You are an overbearing, insufferable . . . creep," I muttered.

"I've been called worse. Here. You dropped your towel."

Once I got over my anger I had to admit the shower felt wonderful. I watched rivulets of mud travel down my arms and breasts from my hair, and then shivered as they ran along my legs to my toes. An aquamarine shower curtain provided privacy, and through a crack at the front I could see nearly matching aquamarine water where sunlight played on the surface of the Pacific. Coming in from the north were more vast storm clouds, however, and I knew they'd play havoc with Maui later. Meanwhile, their dramatic power and beauty somehow gave me strength.

Stepping out of the shower I reached for the towel Dan Kala had brought me. A glance in the direction of the house reassured me of privacy; it wasn't possible to see through the heavy trellis of vines if one stood in a certain spot. At the other side of the shower was a large guest room enclosed by glass from floor to ceiling on three sides. It was simply but elegantly

furnished in a tropical style, with a bed facing directly
out toward the sea. In one corner was a comfortable-
looking chair and a table with a lamp and several
books stacked high. In the opposite corner was another
small table, with a coffeepot, cups, and a vase filled
with delicate blue and white flowers.

This, Dan Kala had told me, was his guest room. It
was where I would spend the night.

"You might prefer this to walking home."

"I'll phone for a cab," I'd argued.

"They won't come out on these dirt roads. Especially not after a storm."

I scrabbled around in my memory for someone to
call for help. A friend? I'd been so busy writing, I
hadn't taken the time to make friends. At least, not
anyone I could impose on that way.

"*You* could drive me," I'd said stubbornly. "That
way you'd be rid of me."

"Why would I want to be rid of you?" he had coun-
tered lazily.

"Because if I stay, I won't stop asking questions."

He'd shrugged. "Ask away. I've nothing to hide."

Meanwhile, he was making dinner. A scent of garlic
drifted through the open doors onto the patio, and my
stomach growled. I'd come a long way on a soda and
peanut butter crackers.

Drying myself off, I wrapped the huge, fluffy pink
towel around me, then tossed my muddy clothes into
the shower and ran water on them till they were clean
enough to wring out and take inside the house. I wondered if Dan Kala had a washer and dryer. It seemed
he must, living all the way out here.

And what were those other two houses, anyway?
Who lived there?

My question was answered as I wandered back into
the house and heard my host on a phone in the kitchen.

"Sorry, but both cottages are booked for the month of December. I'll have the guest house free for a week in January, but otherwise . . . Sure, I'll put you down for that."

He went on in that vein, taking down information with a pen in one hand while stirring some sort of sauce with the other. The phone he held crooked between chin and shoulder. When he'd hung up, I said, "You rent to tourists?"

"More in winter than in the summer," he said, still jotting down information. "Right now I've got the larger cottage rented out by the month to a local artist."

"Really? I didn't see anyone when I came in."

"She's in New York for a couple of weeks."

He looked at me, then, his eyes fastening on the pink towel, where I'd tucked it in around my breasts. It had begun to slip, and I grabbed it just in time. The way Dan Kala was looking at me, however, it might as well have fallen to the ground and left me standing there butt naked.

"You could use some clothes," he said finally, clearing his throat and turning away.

"You're right. I, uh . . . I thought you might have a washer . . . ?"

"Sure. But let me get you something, meanwhile. Watch this sauce, will you? Don't let it burn."

I looked doubtfully at the bubbling red sauce. Never having been much of a cook, I hesitated. Kala shook his head and rolled his eyes. "Just *stir* it, okay? It won't bite. Let me have your clothes."

I traded him clothes for spoon, and stirred. When I thought he was out of sight, I couldn't resist a taste. It was so good I had another. And another.

"I forgot what a voracious appetite you have," my

host said, coming through a door at one side of the kitchen.

I jumped. "You startled me. I thought you went the other way."

"Every room on each side is connected to both living room and kitchen by a long central hall. Makes it handy." He held out a blue cotton work shirt and a pair of soft, well-worn denim shorts. "Try these. They're probably big. Think of them as hand-me-downs and roll-me-ups."

I gave a start and nearly dropped the spoon. "What did you say?"

"You mean, hand-me-downs and roll-me-ups?"

"Yes. Why did you say that?"

"I don't know. It seemed appropriate."

"It just seems odd . . . my grandmother used to say that, when she'd buy me secondhand clothes . . . 'I got you some hand-me-downs and roll-me-ups.' I've never heard anyone else say that before. In fact, I've always thought she made it up."

He took the spoon from me and turned to the stove. "Maybe she did. I don't think I ever used it before."

For some reason I didn't understand, I felt a chill. "It just sort of flitted through your mind?"

His eyes studied my face a moment. "I told you . . . strange things happen in Maui."

The pasta with its rich garlicky sauce was great, but I still had my back up. Dan Kala might be feeding me, but he wasn't getting off that easily—despite the view.

Which, at any rate, wasn't so good at the moment. The storm had reached the north shore, and the sea had become invisible through it. We sat inside at a dining room table with nothing between us and the pounding rain but a wall of glass. In the center of the table was a white pillar candle, which my host had lit.

"Just in case the lights go out," he'd explained. He'd also tossed a few wild orchid blossoms around the base of the candle, however, alerting me to the fact that this night could, if I weren't careful, turn into a repeat of the one before. The one thing besides a view that I'm a sucker for is romantic candlelit dinners.

Which does not always—necessarily—turn me into an unthinking blob.

"Do you own this place," I asked, browsing for information in general, "or just manage it?"

"Own it," he said in a slightly rueful tone. "Though sometimes I wonder why. It's a lot to keep up."

"You must have help."

"I do. Gardeners and maintenance people. They come a couple times a week when the cottages are rented. When I'm out here alone, I take care of much of it myself—with the help of Kimo, my foreman."

"You live in this house alone?"

He smiled knowingly. "I live everywhere alone. Is that what you were asking? I'm not married."

I picked up my glass of wine and shrugged. "I only wondered if you were cheating on a wife last night."

"I wasn't. I've been far too busy for a wife."

His eyes became vague and there was a small silence as he seemed to lose himself in his thoughts. Outside, the wind howled. Rain streamed against the windows, and the candle in the center of the table flickered from a draft. I felt as if we were on a ship in the middle of the ocean, completely cut off from the rest of the world.

"Is the weather this wild all the time here?" I asked finally to break the silence.

He sighed heavily, laid his fork down, and came back. "No, generally there are only brief misting rains. Most of the land on this side of the island is rain forest, you know, so even though the rains are brief, they're continuous. In fact, we often get as much as three hundred and sixty inches a year. But the severity of this storm is unusual for summer. I'd expect it more in winter."

I felt quite tired suddenly. The wine and food had gone to my head, but instead of making me relaxed or nicely high, I'd turned rather groggy.

"I think I need some sleep," I said wearily, setting down my wineglass and sitting back. "I wish you'd just lay all your cards on the table, Dan Kala. I don't feel up to asking and asking."

His eyes swung my way, dark and strangely sad. "I told you the truth, Kate. I don't have your film. And I don't know anything about it. I wish to God I did. I wish we didn't have so much standing between us."

"Between us?" My eyes widened.

He stared at me then, looking confused—truly bewildered. "I don't know why in the world I said that."

I was angry then. "Just tell me, dammit! Tell me what's going on."

He looked into my eyes for several long seconds. Then he shook his head as if to clear it. Standing, he reached for my hand. "I don't know if I can. But come with me," he said.

I followed my host to the guest room in which I'd be spending the night. It was the room I'd seen earlier, next to the outside shower, and the first time I'd been inside, as I'd changed into his shorts and shirt in a bathroom in the main house. At first I wondered what kind of game he might be playing this time, but then I saw why he had brought me here: On the one solid wall of the small room, behind the bed, was a portrait. A portrait of a woman.

I was stunned.

"Princess Nahi'ena'ena," Dan Kala said softly, watching my face. "You see it too, don't you?"

"Yes . . . yes, I do."

The portrait, except that the hair was longer, could have been of me. The eyes were the same, as he'd said over dinner at the Hyatt, except for the color, which was brown. The cheekbones, mouth, and nose were so similar it felt shockingly as if I were looking into a mirror.

And yet . . . this woman had something I didn't have, or hadn't had for a long time. It was clear in the portrait: a ripe, abandoned passion, a relaxed, sultry look about the eyes and mouth, as if she'd only recently made love. In her hair was a flower, and above the colorful red and white *pareo*, or sarong, she wore, her breasts swelled as if at some time during her sitting for this portrait they'd been touched, and with love.

"She's the one I told you about," Dan said. "The one who died tragically, after the birth of her stillborn child."

"Yes. I remember. Nahi'ena'ena." Just saying her name sent a strange vibration through me.

"The painting came with the house. The previous owners said Nahi'ena'ena haunted the place. They wouldn't take her with them."

"Haunted it? How? In what way?"

"They weren't specific."

I searched his eyes. "And what about you? Do you believe in this haunting? Have you seen her spirit . . . her ghost?"

"Never once. I'd begun to think they only said that to pique my curiosity and make me more interested in buying." He looked at me. "Until now."

"Why now?"

"Isn't it obvious?"

"You mean because we look so much alike?"

"Well, the resemblance is a bit odd, don't you think? It's why I was staring at you in Hecock's. It was a shock, seeing someone who looked so much like Nahi'ena'ena. I couldn't take my eyes off you."

"That's the reason you arranged to be on the sunset cruise with me?"

"I . . ." He hesitated. "Yes."

"But there's something else," I guessed. "Some other reason you went to so much trouble to see me again. What is it?"

He shook his head. "Nothing, really. Nothing at all."

Why did I know he was lying? Why did that knowledge cut so swiftly through me—like a knife paring away layers of seeming truth, exposing the lie for what it was? It stood between us, as obvious as the rain on the windows. And I thought once more of the message in my computer: *Ask him who he really is.*

I looked up at the portrait of Nahi'ena'ena and imagined I saw the question flicker in her eyes, as well. Prompting me. *Ask him. Just do it. Do it now.*

For some reason, I wasn't ready to know. Something made me hold back, and I said instead, "Tell me again about the princess. You said she married her brother? The king?"

"Kamehameha III. They were the last of the *ali'i*, or royalty, to follow the old traditions and marry within the family."

"And she was how old when she died?"

"Twenty."

"How sad."

Standing here before Nahi'ena'ena's portrait, I felt I could almost know that sorrow, in my own heart. The story didn't seem as distanced now as it had when Dan Kala told it to me over dinner at the Hyatt.

"It was too much to bear . . ." I said softly.

He looked at me sharply. "What was that?"

"I . . . I don't know, it was just too much," I said vaguely, holding out a hand to Nahi'ena'ena's image. My fingers stopped just short of touching the canvas.

I shuddered, surprised to find tears in my eyes. "Poor baby. Poor child."

I turned to Dan Kala, to find him staring at me.

"What is it?"

"You're crying," he said.

With the tips of my fingers, I wiped the tears away. "It's so odd. I feel so incredibly sad." Yet I wasn't embarrassed by the tears. It was almost as if they weren't mine. As if they belonged to someone else.

I looked at the portrait again, shaking myself mentally. "These . . . these people you bought this house from. They were afraid of Nahi'ena'ena? I wonder why."

"I've no idea. I've always liked her, myself. I took her from an alcove in the main house and brought her out here, thinking she might like to see the sunsets. She seems to have an affinity for those."

"Really." Did Nahi'ena'ena and I have more in common, then, than our looks? "And how precisely do you know about this affinity for sunsets?"

Dan Kala shrugged. "I'm not sure. It seemed somehow she was communicating it to me. I decided to listen."

"You talk about her as if she's alive."

"There are times when to me, she is."

I turned to glance out the windows at the rain. It seemed there was a draft from somewhere, though we'd closed the door behind us. It wasn't a cold draft, but warm and gentle, carrying with it a scent of frangipani. Looking back at Dan Kala I saw that his eyes were fixed on Nahi'ena'ena. In them, I was startled to find, was something I could only describe as love.

"So what exactly do you do, spend your evenings out here visiting with your little ghost?" I said it in a purposely flip tone, to break the tension I'd begun to feel.

He looked at me, the eyes going flat. He didn't smile. "We have an occasional midnight chat."

"I see. And what secrets does Nahiʻenaʻena impart to you during these chats?"

A frown furrowed his brow. "Why don't I answer that after breakfast? This may not seem so hilarious to you by then."

"Oh, really? Are you trying to frighten me?"

"No. I only meant that by then, you may have had a chance to meet Nahiʻenaʻena properly."

Before I could say anything to that, he turned to the door. "Now I think I'll just get you some fresh towels and coffee for morning," he said briskly, becoming in that instant the keeper of the inn. "There's a two-cup coffeemaker on your table, there, did you see it?"

I nodded.

"When you feel like breakfast, there'll be sweet bread and fruit in the kitchen. Feel free to help yourself."

He opened the door.

"Wait. Where will you be?" I asked.

He gave me a pointed look. "In my own room, of course."

I couldn't help flushing, though I knew he'd deliberately misunderstood just to aggravate me. "I didn't mean tonight. In the morning."

"I have things to take care of around the property. I'll be around."

"And my car? When did they say they'd come tomorrow?"

"Sometime in the afternoon."

Good, I thought. *And none too soon.*

"But if I were you, I wouldn't count on it," he added.

"Oh?" I raised a brow. "And why not?"

"Because," he said patiently, as if to remind a small child of the obvious, "you're on Maui time now."

After he'd left, I stood for several moments looking at the portrait of Nahi'ena'ena. Oddly, I felt as if I knew her, and had for a very long time. Remembering the dream I'd had the night before, in fact, I thought she looked much like the woman with long dark hair who'd approached me through a mist and then become Margo.

I searched back in memory, wondering if I'd seen a portrait of Nahi'ena'ena before this—some image that might have stuck in my mind and caused me to conjure her up in a dream. Not an improbability, as I'd visited many art galleries and a museum here on the island. Still, I couldn't recall a specific instance of having seen another portrait of Nahi'ena'ena. And I was certain I'd have remembered her story, if I'd heard it before.

Still, I couldn't shake the insistent feeling that Nahi'ena'ena and the woman in my dream were one and the same—at least until she'd become Margo. But why would I have dreamed of Nahi'ena'ena? And why, having done so, would I have ended up here tonight, sleeping in the same room with her image?

Sheer coincidence, I told myself firmly.

But you don't believe in coincidence.

All right. Synchronicity, then. "What is there about you?" I said softly to my mirror image. "What are either of us doing here?"

"I've been asking that myself," Dan Kala said from behind me.

I hadn't heard him come in. He stood just inside the door, bearing towels and what appeared to be a fruit basket. I wondered how long he'd been standing there.

"You startled me."

"Sorry." He set the towels on the bed and the basket on the table beside the coffeepot. "I usually give one of these to guests when they first arrive. There's a mango, a couple of bananas, some sweet bread, jam, and several packets of Kona coffee."

"Wow. I'm a *guest* now. Sounds somehow permanent."

He shrugged. "The way you were talking to my princess just then, nothing would surprise me."

"*Your* princess?"

"She was the princess of my people at one time."

"True . . . I hadn't thought about it that way. I still want to know about those secrets the two of you share at midnight, though."

"Be patient," he said, not smiling. "Come morning, things may be more clear."

On that somehow ominous note, he left me. I watched him disappear past the hot tub and beyond the trellis of vines. When I was certain he was out of sight I turned off the lights and, leaving the vertical mini-blinds open, slipped into bed between the sheets. I left my shorts and T-shirt on, as they were clean and fresh from the dryer, and I knew I'd be throwing off the bedcovers in the night. Why I felt that someone might be spying from somewhere beyond the dark, undraped windows in the night, I didn't know.

Grandmother McKenna, most likely, I thought. She never could understand how I could sleep with the curtains open. "Who'd want to watch me?" I'd argue.

"George," she'd say with only a hint of a twinkle in her eye.

"George?"

"You know . . . George, up there on that hill. See him? He's sitting there picking his toenails."

There never was a George. One thing about Grandma, she knew when she was being paranoid, and didn't mind poking fun at herself.

I missed her, suddenly, as I'd never missed her before. A swift, sharp pain of loneliness swept through me. "Why did you have to leave so soon?" I whispered. "It's no fun, being alone in this world."

It took me awhile to fall asleep. The scent of frangipani still drifted through the room, though the door was closed. Birds outside in the trees sang all night long, as they do in Hawaii. It was one of the things I loved most about Maui, though at times their joyful outbursts kept me awake. I nodded off finally, but with one eye open. I kept turning from side to side, thinking about Dan Kala's last words: "Come morning, things may be more clear." What did he mean? At last I sat up in bed and turned around to look at Nahi'ena'ena, wondering if there actually had been some small movement on the canvas—something I'd heard or that my peripheral vision had seen—or if I'd imagined it.

In the dark, only the white of Nahi'ena'ena's *pareo* was visible. The red hibiscus flowers scattered upon it were mere shadows now, like splotches of old blood. When I finally let go my sleep was restless, and when I awoke, I was more tired than if I'd never gone to bed at all. As I came awake I heard words, but they had no meaning, nor could I remember them a moment later. They were like the remnants of a dream one knows one had, but that can't be called back, no matter how hard one tries.

❧

CHAPTER 11

I awoke to a sea that sparkled, the reflection of the sun so brilliant on it I had to shade my eyes. As the bed faced outward and there was glass across the front and on each side, I had a vast, stupendous view. I could see the emerald cliffs off to the left, and on the horizon a smidgen of land arose. One of the other islands, I thought, though I didn't know which one. I would have to get my maps out.

I yawned and stretched lazily. *Coffee. There's a spectacular idea.* Sitting up, I reached for my watch, which I'd placed on the small rattan night table next to my car keys. My hand hovered over it, picked it up, and paused.

My keys. They weren't there.

I had one of those sort of blank moments one gets, when one is startled to find that something's not where it was thought to be. Then I told myself not to worry, that I must have knocked the keys to the floor in my sleep.

Bending over, I ran my hand along the floor, even stretching to reach far beneath the bed. They weren't there.

My feeling was one of irritation, rather than worry,

my next thought being that I must not have put them on the table after all. Perhaps I'd meant to, but forgot, leaving them in my shorts pocket.

But then I'd have felt them digging into me every time I turned over in the night.

I reached into the pockets, first one, then the other, just to be sure. No keys. Not even a jingle. Nor had they slipped out and gotten lost in the bedcovers. I stood and shook them out and then got down on my knees and searched thoroughly this time beneath the bed, and around the night table. Still no keys.

Where, then? Had I left them in the house?

No. Now that I was waking up, I was certain I'd taken them out of my pocket and put them on the night table just before turning off the light. I could see myself doing it . . . laying the keys down first, then the watch, its gold band resting lightly over the "State of Maui" key chain I'd picked up for fun at an ABC store in Lahaina.

Slowly but very surely, irritation turned to anger.

Dan Kala. Damn him, he'd been in here while I slept, playing tricks on me. That had to be it.

But why would he do that? What on earth could his motive be?

Putting together everything he'd said since I'd arrived here, it almost seemed as if, for whatever private purpose he might have, he almost wanted to keep me here. But for the life of me, I couldn't think what that purpose might be.

Go back, my reasoning voice said. *Go back to the beginning. Pretend it's a book. Start at the setup— then figure out the plot.*

The beginning: Hecock's? The restaurant where I'd first noticed him watching me?

He'd said last night that he was staring because of my resemblance to Nahiʻenaʻena. Having seen her portrait, I'd been inclined to accept that explanation. So inclined, in fact, that I'd forgotten all about . . .

Ah, yes. The missing film.

At any rate, I'd shoved it into a back corner of my mind, willing to accept that Dan Kala had nothing to do with it. But is that precisely what he wanted? Was my resemblance to Nahi'ena'ena only a red herring, to lead me astray while Dan Kala worked his other, true agenda behind the scenes?

Once my mind begins to work on story lines, turning and twisting every angle, all else falls by the wayside. A half hour later I found that I'd made coffee and showered without hardly realizing it. Dan Kala and his agenda had become a mystery to sharpen my mental teeth on . . . not so much a danger as a curiosity.

Unfortunately, the other thing about my writing self is that often, when I'm caught up in the process, I fail to take care of myself. The mystery, and finding a solution, becomes all—to the detriment of my safety and well-being.

I should have remembered that.

After I'd eaten the mango and downed two cups of rich, sweet-tasting coffee, I went in search of Dan Kala. Following a path around the main house, I came upon the swimming pool again. Now that the sun was out, colors were so bright they nearly hurt my eyes. The pool was surrounded by a green lawn, at one end of which was a hammock. It hung suspended between two palm trees. About the entire lawn area, affording it privacy from the driveway and the other two houses, were flowering shrubs.

A glance at the garage told me that no one was there. A path, however, led through the shrubs, and I followed it past row after row of flowers, most of

which I couldn't identify. A lush, heady fragrance surrounded me as I passed a mass of yellow blooms that
were several feet taller than I. This, I did know—frangipani, the delicate blossoms from which the most
common lei in Hawaii is made. There were more long-
lasting leis made from other flowers: tuberoses, car-
nations, orchids. But the plumeria, or frangipani, are
the most traditional and least expensive.

This, I thought, must have been where the scent in
the guest house came from last night.

Beyond a turn in the path I came upon Dan Kala
talking with a man who looked Hawaiian, and somehow familiar, though I couldn't think where I might
have seen him before. The man's dark green pants
were rolled up, and beneath them his feet were bare,
his legs muddy to the knee. I hung back and watched
a few moments, though I could hear only an occasional word. "Taro . . . crop . . ." The man nodded
solemnly as Dan Kala talked, then finally his face
broke into a smile. I heard the word "*Mahalo*" then,
"Thank you," and knew he'd heard something that
had pleased him. The two shook hands and the man
walked away, whistling to a big, brown dog that appeared from its resting place in the shade of a tree.

Dan Kala turned to the path and, seeing me, his own
smile became a frown.

Amazing, I thought wryly, the effect I have on men.

At least on this one man—determined to have me
as his house guest, yet unhappy about it at the same
time. Fascinating.

"Good morning," he said.

"Good morning."

"Did you sleep well?"

"Fine. Never better," I answered, deciding to play
along for a bit with whatever scenario my host had
decided to play today.

He looked at me quizzically. "No disturbances? No midnight visitations?"

"Visitations? Of what sort?" *Like you coming in and lifting my car keys?*

"Oh, I don't know . . . I thought you might be uncomfortable, spending the night with Nahi'ena'ena. Some people are."

"No, she didn't bother me."

The sun was bright in his eyes, so I couldn't read them when he said, "That's odd. I'd have sworn . . ."

He hesitated so long I was prompted to ask, "What? What would you have sworn?"

He shook his head. "Nothing."

"No, tell me."

"I guess . . . I guess I thought she might make some sort of contact with you. Silly of me, I suppose."

"And what did you think she'd do? Come down off the wall and hover like a vapor cloud over my head? Go 'Boo!'?"

He took a few steps onto the path and moved into a shadow. I saw it, however, the frown. He wasn't pleased. Somehow I felt I'd won a point or two.

Moving into step beside him toward the house, I said, "By the way, I think I must have left my car keys in the main house. Do you mind if I look for them?"

"Not at all. I do remember seeing them—" He paused, stopping on the track. "You can't find them?"

"Nooo . . ." I said, matching his patience-in-the-face-of-a-five-year-old attitude from the day before. "That's why I'd like to *look* for them."

"Sorry. It's just that I remember you taking them out of your pocket before you gave me your clothes to wash. You set them on the kitchen counter. But I also distinctly remember you putting them back in the same pocket when you changed back into your own shorts after dinner.''

"Funny, I remember that too. Still, they weren't in my shorts this morning. They aren't anywhere in the guest room. Isn't that odd? I've looked everywhere.''

He clearly knew I was baiting him now. Still, his head turned in the direction of the house. For a long moment he said nothing. Finally, he smiled. It was so unexpected, it shocked me, though not nearly so much as the chuckle that followed it.

"Nahi'ena'ena," he said. "That's it, of course."

"Nahi'ena'ena? Right."

"No, don't you see? She made contact, after all! She probably doesn't want you to go.''

"Uh-huh. You're telling me I've been issued a personal invitation to stay here at Pua'lani . . . by a ghost."

"Have you a better explanation?" he asked reasonably.

"You bet your ass I do," I said. "Now give them back, Dan Kala. I'm tired of your games. I want my keys, and I want to go home."

CHAPTER 12

"**M**ay I remind you that you're the one who tracked me down here?" my host said twenty minutes later, his mouth full of scrambled eggs.

"Stop changing the subject and give me my keys."

He'd been stalling—first by taking an unusual length of time to wash up, then by saying he couldn't possibly talk till he'd gotten some food in his stomach. I sat across from him at the table on the terrace, my arms folded.

Ignoring my demand about the keys, he said, "I've been up since rather early. Kimo, my foreman—that's the man you saw me talking to—drove over to tell me there's trouble at the taro fields."

"Fascinating. I still want my keys."

"I've got a few acres," he continued, "down the road. The weather's been odd this year, though, and they aren't doing as well as we'd like."

I held out one hand, palm up. "Any time, now."

"Poor Kimo. He was worried I'd think he hadn't done a good job. I told him it wasn't his fault."

I sighed and pulled my hand back, folding my arms again. "Okay, I'll bite. Why would he think it was his fault?"

"No real reason. But Kimo's a good man. He has great *aloha* spirit."

"Meaning, in this case?"

"Meaning good will. I like that in someone who works for me, but sometimes Kimo takes too much on himself. I told him he needn't worry, it was the government's fault, playing around with our weather the way they do."

"Playing around with it? In what way?"

"That," he said, taking a deep swallow of guava juice, "is for another day."

I narrowed my eyes. "Oh, I doubt that. I don't think we'll be having another day."

He set his glass down and looked at me. "You really think I have your keys?"

"I think that and a lot more. The only difference between now and yesterday when I arrived here is that I don't care about the *why* so much anymore."

He smiled. "And why is it I don't quite believe that?"

"Hell, I don't know. Why is it you . . . anything?"

"And what about Nahi'ena'ena?" he pressed. "You're not the least bit curious?"

I gave a small shrug. "About what? So she looks a little like me. She's Hawaiian, I'm part Hawaiian. You go back far enough, we probably both have the same ancestry. That's not so unusual, given all the inbreeding right on up to the last century. There must be a lot of us with similar features."

"You look more than a *little* alike," he said.

"Well, it happens. You're not suggesting I'm on Nahi'ena'ena's family tree, are you?"

"I'm not suggesting anything. Just curious. Aren't you?"

"No."

He studied me silently.

"Look, maybe I just don't want to be bothered. Maybe I'd like to leave both you and Nahi'ena'ena behind—like those previous owners who didn't take her with them. By the way . . . just how long ago was that?"

"A little over three years."

"Well, in all this time you must have come up with some clue as to why they were afraid to take her with them."

"Not really. They may have been overly superstitious. It does get rather gloomy out here at times. Between the winds and the rain . . . and of course, we're not too far from the Big Island here, with its active volcano and earthquake tremors. That tends to unsettle some people."

"You actually feel earthquakes here?" I couldn't hide my surprise. "Somehow I never thought of that. In fact, I hoped I'd left all that shaking behind in California."

"There hasn't been anything strong felt here in years. But yes, we do have our tremors. Personally . . ."

He hesitated.

"What?"

"I don't mean to frighten you. But I think we're overdue."

"For a major earthquake, you mean?"

"That, and perhaps a volcanic eruption. With so many dormant volcanoes coming alive around the globe, and the active ones becoming more active, I wouldn't be at all surprised to see a major eruption here . . . sometime in this next year or two."

"You mean, on the Big Island, right? Not here at Haleakala?"

"Most likely not. Haleakala's been dormant for one

hundred and fifty years. But then . . . one never knows.''

I studied the horizon. Nothing but water all about. And behind us, just across the Hana Road, the slopes of Haleakala. Where would people run to if she erupted? In the old days, lava had not only reached the shoreline but poured far out into the sea.

"Can you ever see the Big Island from here?" I asked, nodding toward the sea.

"From certain points on the island, yes, but only when the weather is clear. If you'd like, I'll take you to my favorite island-spotting point.''

I shrugged. "Thanks anyway. I'm going home.''

He sat back in his chair, folding his arms. "And how will you do that—especially without keys?''

"I'll have the Sprint towed to a locksmith in Kahului. I'll just walk down to meet the tow truck and ride in with it.''

He smiled. "That gives you another day here, then.''

I blinked. "Another day?''

"Sure. Today's Sunday. You won't find a locksmith open in Kahului.''

Irritably, I said, "You really think you hold all the cards, don't you? You—''

"And I remind you again,'' he said calmly, "it was you who drove your car into that sinkhole. I didn't even know you were coming. If I had, I'd have warned you about the roads.''

"Yeah, well, it was you who stole my car keys in some feeble attempt to keep me here, though God knows why. I'd think you'd want me out of here as much as I'd like to be out.''

I shoved back my chair and stood. "In fact . . . I'm leaving. Provided you haven't disconnected the phone so I can't call out, I'll call the rental company to come for me. I don't know why I didn't think of that sooner. And if they can't come, I'll damn well walk to the main road and thumb a ride."

He laughed. "You aren't a prisoner here, Kate. Of course you may use the phone. I had hoped you might want to know more about Nahi'ena'ena, but if not . . . I'll be happy to drive you home."

I looked at him, disbelieving—and strangely deflated. "You're serious?"

"Of course I am." He shrugged and spread his palms. "You're free to go. But then, if you do . . ." His smile was enigmatic. "You'll never know . . . will you?"

"For heaven's sake," I said irritably. "Never know what?"

"Why you came here in the first place."

"I already know that. I came here because . . ."

I fell silent, no longer as sure as I had been a day before.

By morning, things may become clear, Kala had said. But they weren't clear. They were more confused now than ever.

"Ah, ha," he said knowingly. "You want to know about the resemblance, don't you? Why don't you admit it? It's eating you up inside."

He was right, of course. Despite my bluff, I'd wanted to know more about Nahi'ena'ena from the moment I'd laid eyes on her portrait.

"You told me you haven't looked up your mother's relatives on Maui yet," he said. "Why not?"

"No special reason. Except that I don't even know if there are any. It's been a long time."

"Still, they could be here. Why haven't you at least looked into it?"

"I don't have to explain that to you," I said sharply. He smiled. "Of course not. But why so touchy?

What are you afraid of? You're part Hawaiian. Don't you want to know about your roots?''

I frowned. ''Of course I do, eventually. You make it sound like I'm ashamed of being part Hawaiian.''

''Are you?''

''No, I most certainly am not. I . . . it just doesn't seem very real to me. I never knew my mother. Or, for that matter, my father.''

''All the more reason, I would think, to want to search your roots.''

I folded my arms again and glared. ''Look—why are you pushing this so much? What do you care?''

''I don't, really,'' he said, turning cool suddenly. Giving a casual shrug, he added, ''Do what you want.''

''Well, I will.''

''Well, all right, then.''

I looked at his frowning face, the disgruntled mouth, and suddenly I laughed.

''What?''

''Are you always this difficult in 'real life'?'' I said with a touch of scorn.

The frown became a scowl. ''What do you mean, 'real life'?''

''Well, you certainly took enough pains to be charming on the *Kaulana*. And later, at the Hyatt. Mister Wonderful, weren't you? Where has all that gone? Was the entire thing a dream? A fantasy? Or just part of the scam?''

He looked as if I'd caught him out. ''I . . . no. No, there is no scam.''

''Ah. You truly *liked* me then. You were *attracted* to me.''

He hesitated, looking uncomfortable. ''Not exactly.''

''So you *weren't* attracted to me? You thought I was

ugly and not worth your trouble? Yet you . . . what? Pursued me all over town because of my resemblance to Nahiʻenaʻena, your midnight love? Oh, I get it. You thought she'd come to life, in the person of . . . *moi.*''

He stood, knocking his chair back impatiently. ''It's not like that. Why are you so damned . . .?''

''Smart? Hard to fool? Hell, I don't know. Must be in the genes. My *Hawaiian* genes.''

He threw up his hands. ''I've had it with you.''

''Great. Swell. Now will you drive me the hell home?''

We were on our way to his Jeep when the foreman, Kimo, pulled into the driveway in an old pickup. Coming to a stop a few yards away, he jumped out and crossed the distance to us at a rapid pace. This was the first I'd seen him close-up, and apparently the first time he'd noticed me. He was short, but taller than I, and had deeply set eyes beneath dark, bushy brows. He seemed to have a gentle quality about him, and I guessed his age at about forty. Our eyes met and held for a moment, and he addressed me in a courteous manner, with a nod and an ''*Aloha.*''

''*Aloha,*'' I answered back.

His attention turned to Dan. ''Sorry to interrupt, Dan, but there's a major leak in the roof of that utility shack, over in the far west corner. I can patch it up, but I think it'll need more than that if another storm like the last comes through.''

''It's that bad, huh?''

Kimo shrugged. ''If it was mine, I wouldn't let it go.''

''Do you have the supplies you'll need to fix it up right?''

''Some—not all. I think maybe you should take a look.''

Dan turned to me. "Sorry, Kate. He's right, I should check it out. That way, I can pick up whatever we need on my way back from Kihei. Do you mind waiting? It shouldn't take more than a half hour. I'll take you home the minute I get back—I promise."

He sounded as if he thought I might jump down his throat over the delay, so I deliberately surprised him by being okay about it. "No, it's all right. I know you have to take care of it. Go ahead."

"Thanks." He hesitated, then seemed to make a decision. "Make yourself at home meanwhile. You might want to check out the library. It's to the left off the living room."

I had intended to just wait in the Jeep. But the word *library* caught my attention. I am never one to forgo a good browse through a roomful of books.

I wandered back into the house and found it, a small room off a long narrow hallway much like the one on the other side, off the kitchen. The walls were a soft white, the track lighting perfect for reading. For the first time, I felt at ease here at Pua'lani.

Glancing around, I noted that the room was sparsely, but nicely, furnished. There were three comfortable-looking, white wicker chairs with brightly flowered cushions, one beside a window that was open, a slight breeze blowing through a sheer white curtain. Aside from a couple of rattan tables with lamps, and a small writing desk, the only other appointment was a life-sized statue of Maui, the Hawaiian demigod who had caught Haleakala, the volcano, with a fish hook and pulled it up out of the sea. Later, it is said, he climbed to the top of Haleakala and roped the sun, making it promise to keep reasonable and regular hours so that his mother could properly dry her tapa cloth. As depicted in this bronze statue, Maui was quite handsome. A fishnet was draped over his otherwise naked torso, all of it done in bronze.

I scanned the bookshelves, which were floor to ceiling, fashioned of koa wood that was polished to perfection, and looked quite old. The books' topics ranged from modern history to ancient lore, and from science to religions. One entire section held some of my favorite classic and contemporary novels.

A book on Hawaiian history stood by itself on one shelf, its vivid cover photo of the sunset on Haleakala catching my attention. Pulling it down, I thought I might just leaf through it a bit, rounding out my research for the next book—which, it seemed more and more, might take place on Maui. "Write about what you know," is the common prescription. It looked like I'd know tons about Hawaii by the time I left here.

I took the book over to the chair by the window and, sitting, started to open it to the table of contents. The book had a mind of its own, however. It seemed to want to fall open naturally at a place where a lengthy newspaper clipping had been folded and stuck.

Unfolding the newsprint, I found it was an article from *The Maui News,* dated Sunday, May 7, 1995. The byline was that of a Laurel Murphy with extensive quotes from Paul C. Klieger, editor of a new Bishop Museum report. At the top of the article were pictures of King Kamehameha III . . . and his young sister, Princess Nahi'ena'ena.

I couldn't help feeling a chill and looking about me for some sign of Nahi'ena'ena's ghost. It was just too much of a coincidence, finding an article about her this way . . . just as I was about to escape all this drama and head back to town.

Then I remembered that Dan Kala had specifically suggested I wait in the library. Had he known I wouldn't be able to resist the one book that stood alone, its resplendent photo of a setting sun turning the craters and cones of Haleakala to shades of pink, orange, lavender, and gray?

That seemed more likely than the presence of a ghost.

Kamehameha III, I noted, studying his image, looked quite dashing, in a white uniform with military-type epaulets and gold embroidery. Nahiʻenaʻena was lovely, with dark eyebrows, full lips, and a firm, rounded chin. At the same time she seemed, at least to me, to be pensive, if not a bit sad. Her coral and gold feather cape covered slight shoulders, and her long, dark, wavy hair was drawn back from her face and held there by a feather coronet in shades of coral and gold. In one hand she held what I knew from earlier research to be the symbol of Hawaiian royalty, a feather-tipped standard called *kahili.*

"*Mokuʻula,*" the headline read, "*A (hidden) treasure of Hawaiian culture.*" And in a sidebar, "*It was a place of royalty, of spiritual power, a place of the past where a king made a final stand against missionary and Western influences.*"

The article went on to tell about an island that existed in the town of Lahaina in the 1800s. "Mokuʻula . . . a 1-acre island set in a 17-acre freshwater fishpond, was one of the most sacred sites in ancient Maui . . . the site of a 19th-century royal palace of Kauikeaouli, Kamehameha III. It was considered a place of the highest *mana* (spiritual power), because the fishpond was the grotto of Kihawahine, a *moʻo* (giant lizard goddess) who was a powerful protector deity to the Maui chiefs, and through marriage, the Kamehameha lineage."

I scanned quickly through the article, captivated by the idea of this lizard goddess, and the term *moʻo.* Further along, I found that the *moʻo* were female guardian spirits who could possess living humans and assume human form. These *mo'o* frequently became guardians of particular families and lineages.

The article went on to say that the young princess Nahi'ena'ena, who had married her brother, Kamehameha III, in 1835, was thought to possibly have inherited the *mana*, or spiritual power, of Kihawahine, the giant lizard goddess. Kihawahine, who lived and died in the late sixteenth century, was the daughter of the great Maui chief, Pi'ilani. The article stated that Kihawahine was deified at death, and then took on the form of the *mo'o*, the giant lizard goddess. Thereafter, she took up residence in the 17-acre freshwater fishpond, on the shores of which Kamehameha III built his "getaway" palace.

Kamehameha III, I read, rebelled against the encroaching authority of the missionaries in the early 1800s. Hawaiians at that time were struggling to reassert their own traditional religion. Nahi'ena'ena, Kamehameha III's young sister, was said to be in terrible conflict over this as well. She was described as a princess with the "*kapu* of raging fire," and possibly an heir to the *mana*—spiritual power—of Kihawahine, the lizard goddess. Her mother, however, wanted both her children raised as God-fearing Christians.

Klieger, in his Bishop Museum report, wrote that Nahi'ena'ena's brother, Kamehameha III, carried the burden of being the *mo'i* (king) in a rapidly changing kingdom. The powerful women regents, the Christian Ka'ahumanu and her successor, Kina'u, had taken many of the prerogatives of rule away from the king, and had used the *mana* of the Christian *akua* (god) to fortify their positions.

A whole new set of prohibitions followed. "Sibling marriage among the *ali'i* (royalty)—once the highest mating possible to ensure the purity of royal bloodlines—was now considered incestuous. Plural marriages (*punalua*) were frowned upon in favor of monogamy, as were *aikane* (homosexual) relationships.''

Kamehameha III, according to the article, reacted to this usurpation of his rights as king by breaking all the newly introduced rules and following the old traditions. It was during this time that he ''cohabited (publicly) with his beloved sister, Nahi'ena'ena.''

The young princess, the article went on to say, was married in 1835—not only to her brother, but to a man named Leleiohoku, grandson of Kamehameha I. After the marriage she moved to Waikiki and became pregnant, in 1836. No one knew which of her two husbands had fathered the child, who died shortly after its birth. Nahi'ena'ena never recovered from the delivery and died on Oahu on December 30, 1836.

I set the newspaper clipping down in my lap as an unbearable sadness swept through me. It was similar to that I'd felt in the guest room upon first seeing Nahi'ena'ena's portrait—yet sharper, now, more immediate.

She was barely out of her teens. And she must have been desperately unhappy. Torn between one world and another, then losing her child that way . . .

Glancing back at the newsprint, I scanned it for more information, some inkling as to the feelings of the young woman, Nahi'ena'ena. There was nothing, other than what I might read between the lines.

The final *possible* mention of Nahi'ena'ena—or so it seemed to my imaginative mind—was that the *mo'o* lizard goddess, Kihawahine, was sighted in her grotto by the king's palace in 1838, when ''the chiefess Kekauluohi, an avid Christian soon to be appointed *kuhina nui* and given great political power, was nearly tossed into the waters by a giant lizard while she was canoeing to church at Waine'e.''

For some reason I saw Nahi'ena'ena—having finally moved on to a ''better world,'' her pain left behind—with just enough sense of humor to use her inherited *mana* from Kihawahine to assume Kihawahine's form as lizard goddess and play a trick like this.

Her sense of humor was something I did not question. I simply knew, somehow, that it did exist.

I looked out the window, aware that I'd lost all track of time and my surroundings. I wondered where Dan Kala was. Glancing at my watch, I saw that more than an hour had passed.

Well, I was in no particular hurry. And now that I thought of it, I was sleepy. Nahi'ena'ena's story had held me in its grip, and it was as if, in reading about her life, I had entered it and been wrung dry from it, the way one feels when caught up in a novel. As the minutes wore on and there was still no sign of my host, I yawned and stretched. Then, carefully placing the book beside me on the floor, I leaned my head back and closed my eyes. The lids grew heavy, and it was all I could do to keep them apart. I began drifting into sleep.

''Do you believe everything you read?'' a female voice said haughtily, jolting me awake.

I jumped. My eyes flew open, my head jerked toward the door. Automatically, I said, ''Who . . . ?''

There was no one in the room.

But surely I hadn't dreamt the voice. I'd *heard* it. Had it come from outside?

I rose and leaned close to the screened window, pushing the curtains apart and looking from side to side. The window was long, reaching from a foot above the floor to a foot beneath the ceiling. It gave me an adequate view. There was no one in sight.

The hallway, then? I walked to the door, calling out, "Is someone there?"

No answer.

Looking into the hall, I found it empty.

Was it one of those waking dreams, I wondered? Had I drifted off just enough to hear words from some other level of my consciousness—part dream, part imagination?

This place was giving me the willies.

I smiled, remembering that "giving me the willies" was a favorite expression of my grandmother's. I'd asked her once where it came from. "What's the willies, Gramma?" She admitted she didn't know. "It seems to fit, though, doesn't it? The *willies*." She had deliberately made her voice quaver, and shuddered. Then we both laughed.

And why was I thinking so much about her these days?

At any rate, I wasn't laughing now. There was something strange about this place, and I was half ready to believe, now, that Princess Nahiʻenaʻena really did haunt it.

With that in mind, I reached down and picked up the book with the article in it, thinking I might borrow it and learn more about Nahiʻenaʻena as a person. Walking through the main house I headed for the guest cottage. There I stood before the portrait of the princess and stared into her eyes.

"Are you trying to tell me something? And if so, what? And why?"

Was that you who said, "Do you believe everything you read?"

Just tell me it wasn't, that it was all a dream. I'll pick up my marbles and happily go home.

The eyes stared back, as fathomless as the sea.

Though their color was not blue like mine, but brown, I was reminded of Molikini—its clear azure waters host to a thousand tiny, silver fish, all of them silently running, dipping, coming and going, like so many secrets, never to be revealed. *Catch me if you can!* They slip through one's fingers like so much mercury.

I sighed and turned away. But the book, which I'd laid on the bed without consciously realizing it, had fallen open again. The news clipping fluttered, then stopped. I glanced toward the door. Was there a breeze? Not a whisper.

Looking up at Nahi'ena'ena, I imagined I saw her smiling.

Ah, so you still like playing games, do you? I sat on the edge of the bed and picked up the book. Suddenly, it began to shake and tremble beneath my fingers. Of its own volition, it flew from my hands and fell with a loud thud to the floor.

"Do you believe everything you read?" I heard in a loud, disdainful voice.

Chilled, I swung around to look at the portrait again. Now, instead of the laughter I'd seen in Nahi'ena'ena's eyes, I was drawn to her lips. A ribbon of sunlight lay across them. Did they move?

"No, I do not," I whispered. "What do you want? What are you trying to tell me?"

In the next instant I thought I saw motion by the corner table, slightly behind and to my left. I jerked around.

Nothing there. I wanted to run, then, but the thought was no sooner out of my mind than it felt as if needles were pricking the skin on my arms, legs, abdomen. Not goose bumps, but deep, painful pinpricks. I laughed nervously, rubbing my arms and legs. The pinpricks continued, striking my legs, arms, and torso in random places. *A pinched nerve*, I thought desperately. *I've been sitting too long.*

It was then that my wrists began to burn. I realized I was rubbing them, the way one will do an itch. But it wasn't an itch. It was worse. I looked down and saw that my flesh was red. A complete circle of scarlet had formed around each wrist. As I watched, the circles grew darker, more intense. The burning became an unbearable pain.

Frightened, I ran out of the guest room and into the house, skidding on a rug on the tile floor. At the kitchen sink, I twisted on the cold-water faucet. Holding both wrists under the soothing flow, I tried to stop shaking. Slowly, the redness subsided. Then, suddenly, the pain was gone.

I leaned against the sink, weak with relief. When Dan Kala came in moments later I was splashing water on my face. He took one look at me and said in a voice tight with worry, "What's wrong?"

"Just get me the hell out of here," I said. "Right now."

There was little conversation between us on the way to Kihei. I wasn't in the mood, and Kala was engrossed, it seemed, in his problems around the estate. I sat numbly holding my wrists, which no longer burned. Nor was there any sign whatsoever of what had occurred. I held them out of fear that the burning might come back, the way one will do when bewildered by pain that comes, then as suddenly goes.

As we turned onto South Kihei Road, he said, "I wish you'd tell me why you looked so pale and frightened back there in my kitchen."

"It's not important. I imagined something, that's all. You know how writers are . . . we live in our heads. Everything seems real in there."

"So you're saying you were working out a plot idea? That's all?"

"That's all."

He shook his head. "Well, I'm not buying it. But if that's the way you want it, so be it."

The truth was, I didn't want to talk about what had happened. There had been far too many strange things of late . . . the headache earlier, in Long's, the vision problems, the voices at Pua'lani. I could almost hear Gerard again, saying—when he'd accused me of forgetting things—"Good Lord, Kate, you're acting crazy."

The thing that bothered me most was that maybe he was right. Maybe I'd been going crazy, then . . . and maybe I was crazy now. Maybe I had a brain tumor that had gone into remission and was back now, in full force.

Maybe a lot of things.

Then too—there was always the possibility I'd actually been visited by a ghost.

Kala pulled into the driveway of the Hale Pau Hana and stopped the Jeep, coming around to help me out. I didn't want him touching me, and I shook his hand from my arm and stepped out on my own.

He shrugged. "I'll see to it your car is taken care of. It's a good tow company, though. You don't need to worry."

"Thank you."

"I, uh, told them you'd want it brought here to Kihei. To the rental company. That was right, wasn't it?"

Wincing, I thought about the expressions I'd meet up with on the faces of the rental clerks. The one thing they warn you about is not taking cars that aren't four-wheel drives onto isolated dirt roads. Good thing I'd had it insured.

"Yes, that was right," I answered. I was anxious now to get to my room and get some decent sleep. "Well, thanks for the ride. The clean clothes, the dinner. The bed."

"Any time," he drawled.

I frowned. "You know, with all your money, I'd think you might get those roads paved, so that your guests don't get stuck there against their will."

"My *guests*," he said, emphasizing the word, "are warned in advance not to drive those roads in a car that's no more than a motorized flea. Of course, *they* don't usually arrive without an invitation."

"Well, don't worry," I said coldly, slinging my purse over my shoulder. "You won't be seeing me again."

He gave an exaggerated sigh of relief. "The gods are with me, then."

With that, he climbed into the Jeep and slammed it into gear, and, without a backward glance, drove away.

After picking up an extra key in the office, I found that my condo had apparently not been either entered or disturbed during my absence. I checked my computer, to be sure, but it was as it had been the morning I'd left to go to Long's and then the Hyatt. I'd erased the words, *Ask him who he really is*, as they'd given me the creeps. They'd actually been written at the end of my current book, so I'd flipped up to the page I'd been working on last, left the computer in the resume mode, and hoped that next time I looked at it, the book was what I'd find.

It was. Words I'd written three days ago met my eyes. "Caroline flew to New York City, the gun carefully tucked away into her checked baggage. If Donald looked for it, he wouldn't find it. He'd be angry, of course. She didn't care. She . . ."

I'd left poor Caroline there. Left her for the sunset cruise on the *Kaulana*, and my own personal drama that had followed.

Well, she'd be good to get back to. Her life now seemed infinitely less complicated, and frightening, than mine had become in the past couple of days.

That would have to wait, however. I was exhausted. I put the air conditioner on in the bedroom, closed the curtains, peeled my clothes off, and flopped onto the bed. Never one to take naps, I decided this one was definitely called for. The air began to cool, my skin prickled as sweat dried on it, and when the room temperature was down to something that felt more like the seventies than the eighties, I nodded off to sleep . . . a restless sleep, laced with dreams of stormy weather, giant man-eating papayas, and Dan Kala dangling my lost car keys before my eyes. "*You'll have to stay now, won't you?*" he taunted, and somehow it seemed more a threat than an invitation.

I managed to sleep till nearly midnight. Then I awoke, hungry as a bear and ready to believe there was some rational explanation for my experiences at Pua'lani.

The wrists, for instance. I could have bumped up against some poisonous plant in the garden, and had a delayed reaction.

And the voices? Again, those odd things that happen between wakefulness and sleep. Not only that, but hasn't everyone, at some time or other, imagined they heard someone say something, when there wasn't anyone around at all? I used to tell my grandmother McKenna, "I heard somebody say something, Grandma. Honest I did. Somebody said my name." She would shush me and tell me it was all in my head. I knew in my heart it wasn't. But when one is a child and people don't listen, the child stops listening too. It's better than seeming odd.

Realizing I hadn't eaten since breakfast, and then only fruit juice, coffee, and sweet bread, I dragged my still-tired body out of bed and pulled on my robe.

Schlepping out through the dark living room, I took a moment to open the lanai doors and sniff the sweet scent of night-blooming jasmine that drifted up from below. There was a small, cool breeze, and I left the doors open to hear the pounding of the surf.

In the kitchen, I flicked on the lights, which felt so bright they hurt my eyes. Squinting, I launched a search for a frying pan just the right size for a single fried egg. It wasn't easy. This was the most thoroughly outfitted gourmet kitchen I'd ever found in a rented condo—which was great, I assumed, for real cooks. For someone like me, there was almost too much to hunt through. I found it, finally, right where one might expect it to be: nestled neatly inside other, bigger pans, inside a cupboard that had clearly and efficiently been set aside for pots and pans.

Silly me. I'd been looking in the oven, where grandma McKenna always kept her fry pans—still damp from their rinsing, as she didn't want to dirty up her dish towels.

I put the pan on the stove, took butter, an egg, and bread from the fridge, where I kept everything edible so that the ants couldn't get to them. *Talk about multidimensions.* Ants in Maui appear in split seconds, seemingly out of nowhere. You can set something on a perfectly bare counter without an ant in sight, and the very next second there they are—swarms of these tiny little red things, all over the place. The way they materialize is rather Star Trekkish, and lends a whole new meaning to the term "ant colony."

While the egg was sizzling I took out bread and

rested it cautiously on a plate on the stove, which was the one place I knew it would be safe for the few short minutes it took to put a sandwich together. Then I put water on for a cup of instant decaf. A few minutes later, my little repast ready to eat, I took it to the dining room table and sat at my computer.

Turning it on and opening it up, I found Caroline still in New York. Donald was about to find her at the airport, and there would be a scene in which . . .

In which what?

Let's see now . . .

The truth was, after a few moments I didn't honestly care.

Leaving a few spaces, I wrote instead, "Nahiʻenaʻena . . . Nahiʻenaʻena was sister to Kamehameha III, and wife as well. She had a child—but whose child? Her brother's? Her other husband's? She had a tragic life, but up to the age of fourteen, at least, a definite sense of humor. She loved to play. Her brother, in childhood, was her best friend. They often slipped away . . ."

With that, I stopped short, taking a sip of coffee and a bite of sandwich.

Where had that come from? How did I know these things? Were they, for that matter, real? Or was it only my writer's imagination at work?

That could be it, I thought. Often, in my novels, I have written about things I had no conscious knowledge of, but that turned out—when I finally did the research—to be absolutely correct. Where this kind of information came from, I never knew. A muse? A spirit guide? I always ask for help with my writing, be it for plot ideas, character tags, or just to get words on paper as quickly and easily as possible. At the end of a day, when I realize help has indeed arrived, I'm at times astonished. But always grateful.

It was with a certain sense of trust, therefore, that I set my sandwich down and allowed my fingers to hover over the keys till they began to move again.

"Nahi'ena'ena and her brother, Kauikeaouli—who had been appointed King Kamehameha III at the age of ten—were sent by their mother, the God-fearing Keopuolani, to separate missionary homes, to be reared in the Christian faith. They often slipped away to be together, and when the missionaries discovered this they became anxious about the possibility of what they called incest—although in Hawaiian tradition, such a physical union was the highest and most pure. The missionaries put pressure on Nahi'ena'ena to leave her brother . . ."

The coffee beside me grew cold, the bread stale, as pictures began to form in my mind: Nahi'ena'ena, at fourteen—the hormones either coming in or already full-blown. Feelings for her brother, her best friend, overwhelming her. Torn by the new restrictions, all the new prohibitions . . . everything that had seemed natural and innocent, now dirty and sinful. Wanting to be with the brother she loved, and yet . . .

My eyes closed as my fingers continued to type.

She is in the palace garden, for a prearranged meeting with her brother. Leaves rustle behind her. She turns. Her brother, now king, stands there—tall and handsomely dark, his figure well-built and strong. He has been silently watching her. Their eyes meet in acknowledgment of the love they feel, the sadness that surrounds them now, and this new, strange guilt that lies heavy on Nahi'ena'ena's shoulders.

There is an awkwardness lately in their moments together. No longer do they allow themselves to wrestle and play, as they did short months ago. Now when they touch there are feelings that are forbidden, feelings "of the devil," as the missionaries say. When

*their hands meet, making their flesh in all those won-
derfully tender and alive parts tingle, this is no longer
sacred . . . no longer a gift from the gods.*

Or so the missionaries say.

But how can that be? *Nahi'ena'ena wonders.* How
can something be sacred one day, and another, not?

*She smiles. Kauikeaouli does not care what the mis-
sionaries say. In fact, he will do anything he can to
irritate them. He does not believe in this new* mana.
*He thinks it is bad and will end in no good for our
people and our land.*

*Her smile turns pensive, and her brother steps for-
ward. Sitting beside her, he takes her hand.*

*"Why do you listen to them, Nahi'ena'ena? Why do
you let them cause your spirit so much unnecessary
sorrow? Their* mana *cannot be good, when it takes the
joy from people's hearts and turns it to fear."*

*With his other hand, he begins to gently, lovingly,
stroke her hair. "You are so much more than they are,
Nahi'ena'ena. You are the sun as it dips into the sea,
melting and turning to purest gold. Little sister, your
heart beats like that of the brightest bird. Let it find
its way to me."*

*His hand slides down to her shoulder, then her col-
larbone, and comes to settle, with no more weight than
the flutter of a butterfly wing, on her breast.*

*Nahi'ena'ena is covered now by a heavy cotton
dress, from neck to toe. The missionaries have pre-
scribed this for all Hawaiian women, as baring flesh
is said to be sinful. Even so, she draws in a ragged
breath. Through the cumbersome cloth her nipple
swells and hardens beneath her brother's touch.*

*She leans into her brother, pressing her hand over
his. Her lips tremble, then fasten on his. His hand
tightens, caressing the nipple, as his mouth moves on*

*hers. She gasps with pleasure. "Oh, Kauikeaouli . . .
I've missed you so much."*

*Her back arches as his free arm tightens around
her. Her mouth is at his ear. "Touch me there, in the
old way, Kauikeaouli. Touch me, please . . ."*

*His hand slides down. Her breath nearly stops. It
catches, and releases. She sighs, then shudders.*

In the next instant, she jerks away. I will have to
tell the missionaries, *she thinks, feeling hot with
shame.* They have said I must tell them everything.

*Frightened, she hides her eyes behind her small,
dark hands.*

*Her brother is shaken. He tries to collect himself,
but his tone is angry. "They force this shame upon
you, little sister. Why did they ever come to our
shores? Before this . . ."*

*He stands, drawing himself stiffly to his full height,
which by now is nearly six feet. "I loathe these people.
I will never—never, Nahi'ena'ena—let them into my
heart. Nor will I let them tell me what to do."*

*"Don't be angry with me, Kauikeaouli. Please
don't be angry. I don't know what I would do if you
left me."*

*Immediately, he sits beside her again. Taking her
into his arms, he consoles her. "I'm not angry with
you, little sister. I could never be angry with you. It's
them. I am angry at what they are doing to you—and
what they are doing to our people."*

*Gently, he pats her back, restraining himself from
other manner of touch, though he would give his very
life to be able to console her in the old way. Their
coming together has always been a joining of heart
and spirit, a special bond they alone had but can no
longer enjoy, with this great wall of Nahi'ena'ena's
guilt between them.*

He remembers his sister at ten, when their bond was

*in their playtime together. That was enough, then. She
loved to fool him, to play tricks on him, hiding things
and making him find them . . . hiding herself, in one of
the rooms of the palace, then jumping out to scare
him.*

*He, of course, would pretend to be taken by sur-
prise, though he'd come to know her hiding places
well. At times they would wrestle and roll about on
the floor, laughing and happy, content just to be together.*

*Then, not too long after . . . the new feelings began
between him and Nahi'ena'ena. The shyness when
they would touch, the sensation of melting, of loving,
of never getting enough of each other.*

*At first he held off. She was his sister, his playmate.
He didn't want that to change. But one day she
touched him . . . hesitant, yet curious to explore these
new feelings. "Don't you want to touch me too?" she
had asked— innocently, as if suggesting no more than,
"Would you like to take a walk?"*

*That was the way it was in those days, he thought
with some bitterness. Hawaiians were on the edge of
innocence, between a world where such relationships
were not only accepted, but preferred as the most
pure, the most sacred.*

*They came together, therefore, that day—he and
Nahi'ena'ena—naturally, as part of their play. Wres-
tling became touching. Touching became . . .*

Kauikeaouli sighs. Feelings for Nahi'ena'ena are
stirring in him again. Patting her on the back briskly,
he holds her off. "Go home, now, little sister. Go back
to the missionaries. Do whatever they say."

"No, Kauikeaouli! Please—I don't want to leave
you. We have so little time as it is. Can't we just be
together?"

She grabs his hand, pulling him up. "Come, Kauikeaouli. You hide, and I'll find you, just as we did when we were children.''

Kauikeaouli shakes his head sadly. ''We are not children, Nahi'ena'ena. We will never be children again.''

He does not say, ''Those who have brought words like sin and guilt to our shores have robbed us of our childhood.'' Nahi'ena'ena, however, knows this is what he means. She knows, as well—though she tries to deny it in her heart—that her brother is right. Life for them will never be the same again.

Sadly, she leaves him. He watches her disappear through the dense palace garden, the long, heavy dress clinging like an evil spirit to her skin in the humid air. A flicker of fear runs through Kauikeaouli. He almost calls out, ''Wait!'' as he senses, suddenly, that danger is about to befall his sister.

But then he shrugs it away, thinking, I imagine things that are not there. It is only that I want so much to look after her. Tears form in his eyes. With an impatient hand, he wipes them away.

Nahi'ena'ena walks slowly toward the home of the missionaries, with whom she has been placed for rearing in the new beliefs. Her feet drag, and perspiration drips from her hair and face, running in rivulets to her neck. The day is hot and humid; the long dress sticks to her flesh.

This is good, the missionaries say. It is good to suffer for God.

This is why she returns to them. Because she half believes now that it is good to suffer, though she doesn't yet know this ''God,'' or understand why he would demand this of her.

The reason she believes suffering can be good is that she has learned it has another purpose, one more *closely aligned to her own needs. If doled out in precisely the right amount, and in the proper manner, suffering can take her mind off her brother—and the feelings she has for him.*

The missionaries, of course, would never administer this kind of pain. Their form of punishment is well-meant, if faulty, and comes with the heavy, ridiculous clothes one must wear, or a declaration forbidding the hula and the flying of kites.

The other one, though—he knows how to silence the pangs of love. He is an expert at doling out pain.

For this reason, Nahi'ena'ena veers from the path to the missionary house where she lives, now, and takes instead a fork to the left, through dense papaya trees and shrubs whose thorns prick her cheeks. The walk is long, and her feet—bare now, as she has kicked off the tight, uncomfortable, mission shoes and left them under a tree—are scratched and bleeding.

She comes, finally, upon a small hut in a clearing. There are no windows on any side, only a door. It opens, and he stands there. She knows he has been waiting for her. He always waits, when she has been visiting her brother. He knows that eventually she will come.

With dread in her heart, Nahi'ena'ena steps forward into the clearing.

Pain. Terrible, terrible pain.

My eyes flew open and I found I was no longer at my computer, but huddled over, kneeling, on the kitchen floor. A blinding red haze filled my head, torment everywhere. Tears streamed down my face. The pain became centralized, it shot through my abdomen like a hot spear.

"Don't!" I tried to scream, but it stuck in my throat. "Stop, oh, please, stop! Help me, someone!"

Suddenly, it was over. The pain subsided as if it had never existed. For long moments I couldn't move, afraid that the merest twitch of muscle might bring it back. Then I tried a finger—lifting it less than an inch and bracing myself as fear swept through me.

No, it's all right. It's okay.

Sweat popped out on my forehead. I tried a foot.

Still okay. Slowly and ever so gradually, I eased back against a bottom cupboard, weak with relief, and stunned.

Dear God . . . what is happening to me?

The answer seemed obvious: I was going mad at last. This, on top of the incident with my wrists at Pua'lani, and the voices . . .

It was too much. I couldn't take my thoughts any further, couldn't lead them down a path that seemed too frightening to bear.

I reached up to the countertop, thinking to pull myself up, as I was still weak. My fingers closed over something metallic. Yet I'd left nothing on the counter, I knew. I had always kept it purposely bare.

I brought the object down to look at it. And with that one motion, the whole world turned mad. There was nothing I could count on now, nothing of which I could say, ''This is real.'' It would not have surprised me, even, if the sun had come up in the west.

What I held in my hand was my missing keys—the ones that had disappeared at Pua'lani.

I sat for a long while after that, trying to sort it all out. I sat on the chaise lounge facing the lanai and the sea, just as I'd done a few nights before. This time, however, I forced myself to stay awake—too afraid to sleep.

A quick check at my computer had revealed that I actually had written the scene with Nahi'ena'ena and

Kauikeaouli, just as I'd seen it. Apparently, I had drifted off into an altered state as writers often do—an experience not unlike the kind of "fictive dream" John Gardner wrote about, the hypnotic state writers fall into, in which characters come to life on the page and we raise our heads later to find ten hours have passed.

Why, then, did it end the way it had—with me on the kitchen floor? And why the pain?

That was the thing that frightened me. I recalled the very real burning in my wrists at Pua'lani, how I'd had to run water on them to get the burning to stop. Yet there had been no sign of injury afterward.

People, I knew, could imagine themselves into a psychological state where injuries occur. Some mental patients, through accessing a little-understood part of their brains, have actually raised welts on their skin, or made themselves bleed.

And there were those who, throughout history, had the stigmata—the bleeding holes in the hands, simulating the crucifixion of Christ. It is thought by some psychologists that the stigmata are self-induced, if unconsciously, through the power of the mind.

Was that the answer, then? Had I become so engrossed with Nahi'ena'ena in this short time, so sympathetic, I had begun to simulate her pain?

But why that specific pain? Why the wrists, and the abdomen? What terrible things had happened to Nahi'ena'ena in that hut? And was the man she met there responsible for them? Did he hurt Nahi'ena'ena, for reasons of his own, and in some way convince her that pain, as in all suffering, was good for the soul?

I couldn't know. And I felt frustrated by my lack of knowledge. Frustrated and afraid, still, for my own well-being. Whatever was going on, I had to get a handle on it and figure out how to get out of it.

When, finally, the sun rose, I knew what I had to do. Rising stiffly from the chaise lounge, I took one more brief look at Carolyn and Donald, still in the airport terminal. Their lives paled by comparison to Nahi'ena'ena's. They were not real.

My little princess was.

Turning off the computer, I packed it up in its carrying case, along with an extra battery. Then I took it into the hallway and set it by the door. In the living room again, I called the car rental company. I told them what had happened to the Sprint, ignoring the young clerk's "Oh, geez, another dumb tourist" tone. Then I asked him for another car, telling him specifically what I wanted.

It took him a minute to check the lot. "Give it a half hour," he said. "We'll pick you up."

In the bedroom, I packed all the clothes I had with me, which wasn't much—seven days' worth of shorts and tees, and a couple of good sundresses I'd found at Hilo Hattie's, for the signings. A pair of dressy sandals. Underwear.

Making sure the kitchen was clean, not a crumb in sight, I rang down to the front desk and told Mari-Lu I wouldn't be here for a while, possibly a few days. I told her where I'd be, but asked her not to give that information out, not even to my agent, if she called.

"I won't be needing clean towels, of course. Would you ask the maids not to bother?"

"Of course."

The cute blond guy from Kihei Car Rental arrived to pick me up. At the lot, I checked out the good, sturdy-looking Jeep I'd requested—not the most attractive one available, but one that already had a few dents. Perfect, given my penchant for potholes. An hour later I was in Huelo Point driving past the poor abandoned Sprint, which still hadn't been towed away.

I gave it a thumbs-up gesture and sailed on by, turning into the driveway at Pua'lani.

The Jeep's tires spit gravel. The brakes screeched to a halt in the drive. Ahead, I saw Dan Kala squatting at the edge of the pool, pulling a palm frond out of it. He looked up, tossed the frond aside, and rose. He began walking toward me, a curious expression on his face.

"I didn't expect to see you here today." His tone added, *I never expected to see you again.* "What's up?"

"I'm moving in," I said.

His eyes scanned the back of the Jeep, the packed bags.

"You're what?"

"I'm moving in," I said firmly. "What part of that did you not understand?"

CHAPTER 13

"And don't even bother to pretend you mind," I went on, pulling the bags from the Jeep and setting them on the ground. "You brought me here for a reason, and I intend to find out what that was."

He stood with thumbs hooked into the waistband of his jeans. His chin jutted out. "First of all, I did not bring you here. You came on your own. I thought we settled that before."

"A matter of semantics," I said crisply. "You *wanted* me here because of Nahi'ena'ena."

"I beg your pardon, but you are much more trouble than Nahi'ena'ena. I can't imagine why I'd want you around."

"Nevertheless, I'm staying. I've decided there isn't a better place on the island to work. And, I've got tons to do. Now, do I get the guest room again, or do you want to put me in that empty cottage over there?"

He shook his head. "You are the damnedest, pushiest . . ."

"Well?" I pressed the instant he paused.

"I should just send you home," he said.

"Oh, but then I might complain that you discriminated against me."

"Discriminated? That's ridiculous. And who would you complain to?"

"I don't know, the Chamber of Commerce? You are a hotelier, aren't you?"

He half smiled. "A *hotelier*. Come to think of it, I've never seen myself that way. But I suppose, in a way, I am."

"And this is listed somewhere as a public inn, right? See—you can't discriminate. It's against the law. I could have you closed down."

He laughed then. "I doubt that. However..." Reaching down, he picked up my bags, shaking his head again. "This may be the worst mistake I've ever made, but come on. The guest room it is."

"Perfect."

"*I'm back, little princess*," I whispered. "*Hang on.*"

Standing before the portrait once more, I willed Nahi'ena'ena to speak. She remained silent. Nor did I see any suggestion of the slightest change in expression.

Even so, there was something in me, a sense of inner timing, the sort of thing that lets one know when events are about to be played out and the only thing one need do is wait.

I found Dan Kala in the kitchen scrubbing vegetables for that night's dinner. "I've invited someone," he said. "You're welcome to join us. You needn't, of course."

"Thanks," I murmured between bites on a stick of celery. "What a gracious invitation. Who's coming?"

"Sharon Cole. She's a psychologist at the University of Hawaii on Oahu, and she's here visiting her family for a couple of days. I thought you might like to meet her."

"You think I need a psychologist?"

"She's a friend," he said simply, then looked away, turning the water on so forcefully it would have drowned out further conversation. Obviously, my companionship was not needed.

I poured myself a glass of guava juice and wandered back out to the guest room. Taking my notebook computer onto the lanai facing the sea, I set it on a table and sat down, opening it up. Carolyn, Donald, and the airport scene came on. Carolyn, despite their difficulties, was still secretly dreaming of marrying Donald, the handsome plantation owner, and living out her days in Mauian bliss.

I closed the file on them, leaving them hanging, and started a new one: *Nahi.doc*. With that one motion I made a deliberate effort to draw the royal pair back in. I had to know what was going on—not only with them, but with me.

Time began to expand. Yet, in the same instant, it stood still. I fell into that beloved space that writers fall into, the reason most write, as it's better than drugs or alcohol . . . a high without hangover, an affair without pain.

Without conscious effort, and with no real knowledge of where the information came from, I began to write once more about Nahi'ena'ena and her brother, Kauikeaouli, King Kamehameha III. I saw them in the palace garden as before, though this time they were younger, playing games together. I saw them at five and six, then at eight and nine, enjoying the companionship they'd had only with each other, as they were *ali'i*, royals, and forbidden to intermingle with "ordinary" Hawaiians.

Even as children they were tall, I wrote, as most *ali'i* were. There was a distinct difference in height between the *ali'i* and other Hawaiians, and I wondered where they had come from originally—even before the Marquesas, that is. I knew from earlier studies that they were said to have been descendants of gods. Some believed these gods to have come from another planet, to have "seeded" Earth with the original *ali'i*, and to have left instructions with them to cohabit only with their own, in order to keep the royal line pure. There were none of the medical side effects of such inbreeding that we've all been warned about today, presumably because the line was free, to begin with, from physical and mental weakness. It was only the eventual commingling, after the arrival of Captain Cook and others, that brought disease and genetic anomalies to the royalty and ended this "pure race of beings" for all time.

I recalled from my earlier research into Hawaiian history that there was nothing racist meant by the injunction not to commingle, or by the assignation of the word "pure"—at least not in current-day terms. Rather, the prohibition was meant to preserve the health and well-being of the people, in much the same way that Biblical warnings to not eat pork or mingle blood were brought to earth by "messenger angels". It's widely understood now that these warnings were meant only for the health of the people, due to diseases that were prevalent at the time.

So Nahi'ena'ena and Kauikeaouli had only each other, presumably, for most of their growing-up years. From what I've read, they loved each other's company. How, then, could these two spirited, open people *not* have shared a physical love as well, especially as it was not forbidden, but encouraged at the time? Surely that would have been a most natural outcome of their friendship and loyalty toward each other.

In my mind's eye I began to see more and more physical characteristics, as well as odd little character traits. Nahi'ena'ena had a way of touching a slender finger to the bridge of her nose and frowning when she was perplexed. Kauikeaouli tugged at his lower lip impatiently while pondering a problem, and Nahi'ena'ena laughed and teased him, saying that if he didn't stop, his lip would grow and grow till it was down to his knees.

These little gifts—these visions, if you will—flew faster and faster from my fingertips to the keyboard, creating a life on-screen like none I'd ever experienced in my writing before. It was as if a long-dormant well of information had been tapped, awaiting only the catalyst of my willingness to bring the details forth.

Time and space shifted. I know that now. I wasn't aware of it, however, that afternoon. One moment I was writing, "observing" Nahi'ena'ena and Kauikeaouli in the palace garden. Then, without my even noticing how or when it happened, something strange took place. I began to feel I was actually inside the palace with them, in a secret room only they shared.

I stood by their bed. Watching.

Gently, their fingers trailed each other's warm skin. Beads of perspiration formed above their lips and below their eyes, which were tender as they gazed at each other. There was no awkwardness, no embarrassment or shame. Playfully, Kauikeaouli touched his sister's breast. She giggled.

"Look, Kauikeaouli!" I witnessed. *"See how I am growing!"* Nahi'ena'ena's dark brown eyes look down at her chest. Kauikeaouli's finger traces a tiny nipple. It grows and puckers. Nahi'ena'ena shivers deliciously. "I wonder why it does that now. Do it again, Kauikeaouli."*

He does, but more slowly, and this time her eyes still as they meet his. She draws a soft breath, which ends in a smile and a sigh. Kauikeaouli knows what she is feeling. He has been feeling these things himself, for some time now. It is no longer as when they were

*children and could touch each other without thought.
In recent days they have come to crave this new kind
of touching, the richness it brings to their play.*

*There have been problems, of course. When their
mother discovered what they were doing, she sent
them to live in the homes of missionaries—separately,
and presumably only to be taught the Christian faith.
Kauikeaouli knew better, however. He knew that even
more than learning about the Christians and their Bible, his mother wanted her two children as far from
each other as possible, now. Keopuolani, who had become a devout Christian, had accepted the missionaries' belief that her children's love for each other
was a sin.*

*He turns back to his sister, his eyes brimming with
love.*

As I, Kate McKenna, stood in that secret palace
room beside Kauikeaouli and Nahi'ena'ena, I knew
that somehow things had changed for me. I was no
longer the author, imagining this scene, but somehow
truly living it. Nor could I avert my eyes from the
lovemaking. My presence in that room was so real, I
felt that if I were to cough or to make any noise whatsoever, they might turn and see me. My nerves tingled,
and my mouth had gone very dry. I was so aroused it
astounded me, and though I felt I shouldn't watch, I
was unable to move. As Kauikeaouli touched his sister's breast I felt he had touched mine. I shuddered,
desire rising so quickly it was impossible to stem the
tide. Nor did I wish to. I watched shamelessly, and
when it was over for the princess and her brother, my
own orgasm had been as satisfying as theirs.

It was in this condition that Dan Kala found me,
when he came to call me for dinner. I heard his voice
quite close by and opened my eyes to find myself on
the bed in the guest room, my computer forgotten on

the lanai outside. My left hand was on my breast, the right holding a strange, yellow silk scarf. Dan Kala stood in the doorway, a bemused expression in his eyes.

My face flamed. Moving my hand quickly from my breast, I wondered how much he had seen. For that matter, what had I actually done? Was the orgasm in mind only? And how had I gotten from the lanai to my bed?

Thoroughly confused, I struggled to a sitting position.

"Taking a nap?" he asked curiously.

"I . . . yes. Something like that."

"Sharon's here. She's looking forward to meeting you."

"Right. I'll . . . be right there." I stared down at the scarf in my hand.

"Something wrong?"

"No. No, nothing wrong." It was all I could do to smile reassuringly, and with that same bemused expression, he finally left.

Getting up off the bed, I took the scarf to the window, where the light was better. I already knew, however, what I'd see: a splatter of pink roses handpainted on the yellow background, and the designer's name— *Vera*—scrawled in one corner.

"Margo?" I said softly, my voice nearly failing me as fear swept through me. "Margo? Are you here?"

Of course Margo Reed-Lanier was not here—but *someone* had been. Someone had put that scarf in my hand, a scarf precisely like the one I'd bought my old friend for Christmas one year in college, at a time when we'd still been friends.

It wasn't the same scarf, certainly. That wasn't possible. The design was exactly the same, however. I remembered it because the colors were strictly Margo: yellow and pink, exotically "Spanish" I'd thought at the time, though now they seemed equally tropical and Hawaiian.

My thoughts swam furiously upstream and down, like so many salmon looking for a place to spawn. As with the "vision" of Nahi'ena'ena and her brother in my condo earlier, and the subsequent return of my car keys, there were too many questions now, and no answers at hand. Every conclusion seemed flawed. I ran the gamut once more of suspecting Dan Kala: Had he slipped into the guest room, found me sleeping—or worse—put the scarf in my hand, and then slipped out to stand by the door and call me for dinner?

For that matter, had he found me sleeping by my computer and carried me into the guest room?

Ridiculous. Yet how, then, did I get here? And how, earlier, did I get from the chaise lounge at Hale Pau Hana to the kitchen floor?

Even more: How did Margo Reed fit into this? Say she was somewhere here on Maui. Surely she would have no reason to play childish tricks. If anything, she'd always been far too blunt and forthright. If Margo had some issue to settle with me, she'd have presented herself, hands on hips, at my door. Or she'd call.

I remembered then that she had called—several times, up till a couple of weeks ago. I looked at the portrait of Nahi'ena'ena.

"Little princess, what's going on?"

In my hand, the yellow scarf seemed to take on heat. My palms began to sweat, and I dropped the scarf abruptly, disliking the feel of the silk against my skin. It fluttered to the floor, light as an autumn leaf.

Light . . .

Cold . . .

And dead.

Those were the thoughts that came to my mind. I stared at the scarf as it lay lifeless on the floor. A memory returned—not completely, only vague, hazy parts of it—something about Margo standing before me with that scarf around her neck, laughing. My eyes had fastened on the pink roses, and my fists had clenched. *Stop laughing! Stop laughing, dammit!*

I'd wanted to wrap my hands around her throat, to take that scarf and . . .

Frightened, I closed my mind on the memory, deliberately blocking the rest of it out. Nudging the scarf with my toe till it was out of sight under the bed, I turned to the closetlike bathroom in a corner to the right of the bed. There I combed my hair and washed my face, putting on a light dusting of powder and quickly running a lipstick over my mouth.

In the mirror I saw someone I was beginning not to know. My eyes were strained, and in them lurked someone I hadn't seen in years: a frightened, twenty-year-old woman, a straight-A student whose grades were beginning to slip, whose lover had accused her of forgetfulness, whose friend . . .

Stop it. That was long ago. You aren't that foolish, naive young woman anymore. You've learned to see through falsehood and betrayal. You've grown intelligent and strong. You've put the old anger—and fears—away.

But if that were true, I wondered, why did that twenty-year-old Berkeley student still hover behind my eyes, as if awaiting only the slightest chink to appear in my hard-won armor, before reasserting herself?

Why had she brought me here?

For the thrill. The adventure. I'd never been able to turn it down.

Which was how I'd become a writer. Who among

us, after all, knows where the next contract, or check, is coming from? And how it will all turn out?

Dealing with New York takes the instincts of a gambler . . . and a dysfunctional need to live on the edge.

CHAPTER 14

Dan Kala and his dinner guest were seated at the indoor dining table. Classical music played softly through speakers at opposite ends of the room. I recognized Beethoven, a romantic piano concerto. The table was candlelit around a flower centerpiece, as it had been when Dan Kala and I first dined here.

The woman seated across from him had dark hair, brown eyes that were large and luminous, a voice low and rich. Her hair was twisted into a full, loose bun at the nape of her neck, and through it had been wound a delicate stem of tiny white orchids. She wore a *pàreo*, white with bright blue flowers. It clung to her narrow waist and left her shoulders, which were broad and strong like that of a swimmer, bare.

She was a large woman, not heavy, but big-boned. Even sitting, she seemed quite tall. She wasn't classically beautiful—but there was a quiet presence about her that made her seem absolutely stunning.

Even as I thought that, she turned and smiled. "You must be Kate McKenna." She stood and extended a hand. "I'm Sharon Cole. Dan's been telling me about you."

I shook her hand, smiled, said, "Nice to meet you,"

and flicked a look at Dan Kala. "Has he really?"

She laughed. "Oh, nothing bad. He told me you're a writer. In fact, I'm almost sure you're the writer my sister's been raving about. She came home from a book signing in Kahului recently with an armload. Suspense, isn't it?"

"Yes."

Dan Kala poured wine into our glasses and touched Sharon's shoulder lightly, smiling down at her. "You two talk. I've got some things to do in the kitchen."

When he'd left, I sipped the cold white wine and asked, "Have you and he known each other awhile?"

She smiled. "You mean are we having a relationship?"

"No, I—"

Laughter bubbled up. "Never mind, it's all right. Dan and I knew each other growing up. Maui was more small-town twenty years ago, and everyone knew everyone else. My family still lives here on Maui, and I come over to see them as often as I can. My apartment and my job, however, are on Oahu."

I smiled. "That doesn't precisely answer my question."

"I know." She searched my eyes. "Does it matter that much to you?"

I flushed, looking down at my glass. "Of course not, not in the way you mean. I was curious, that's all."

Her expression was friendly, but no more forthcoming.

"I understand you teach at the university," I said, to put the conversation on a less personal plane.

She nodded. "I'm the only one in our family to have left the island to work. You may have met my brother, Kimo? He's Dan's foreman."

"Yes . . . as a matter of fact, I met him yesterday.

There was some problem and he came to ask Dan to look into it.''

Sharon sighed. ''There's always some problem, it seems. My brother works very hard, between Pua'lani and the taro fields. Have you seen them yet? They're just down the road, in Keanae.''

I shook my head. ''I haven't been there. I understand Keanae is lovely.''

She studied me. ''You've been quite busy, Dan tells me. With your writing?''

''I'm working at a few things. Is that all he said?''

''You mean,'' she said forthrightly, ''did he tell me what's causing that frightened look in your eyes? No. Would you like to talk about it?''

After an initial moment of surprise, I said, ''No.''

She nodded. ''Well, think about it. There's plenty of time.'' Setting her wineglass down she called out, ''Dan Kala? Get yourself in here with that food! We're hungry.''

''And you are a demanding woman,'' he called from the kitchen. ''Sit tight. I'm on my way.''

The easy banter made me wonder again if there was more than friendship between them. Sharon must have read my mind.

''Dan Kala is a complicated person,'' she said. ''There are times when he drives me mad. But I suspect you've discovered that?''

I set my own glass down. ''I'm not sure *complicated* is the word I'd use. But I do wonder sometimes if he's driving me mad.''

''Sharon is a student of Hawaiian history,'' Dan said, before taking a bite of the delicate whitefish he'd prepared. ''And something of a shaman, as well as a psychologist.''

"Really?" I buttered a roll. "That's fascinating. Tell me more."

"The shaman part is an honorary title handed down within my family," Sharon said. "Actually, I teach paranormal psychology, and that and mysticism often go hand in hand. There was a day, however . . ."

She set down her fork and touched her full red lips with a napkin. "My great, great, great-grandfather was a *kahuna*—a magic one, what people call shamans or medicine doctors these days. My grandmother, his wife, it is said, was a *mo'o*. Do you know what that is?"

"Vaguely. I read about the *mo'o* in an article in the library here. It said that Kihawahine, the daughter of the chieftain Pi'ilani, became a *mo'o*—meaning a guardian spirit, I believe?—when she died. I also read that Princess Nahi'ena'ena inherited her spiritual powers."

"Her *mana*, yes."

"But Kihawahine lived, as I remember, in the sixteenth century. How does one know these things? If there was no written language till the missionaries arrived . . ."

"Most Hawaiian legends are handed down through the chant," Dan said, relaxing back against his chair. "Traditionally, the way our people told their stories was very poetic, very lyrical. They didn't simply say, 'Isn't it a nice day?' but rather, 'This is a day of such beauty as that when my mother married my father and took into her heart the warmth of the sun, gracing her with the purest of love for all time.'" He grinned. "Or some such thing. I can't do it the way the old storytellers could. I'm afraid our schools didn't put much stock in the lyricism of the Hawaiian language when I was growing up."

"There is a revival underway, though," Sharon

added. "More and more Hawaiians are learning the language now."

"As well as the chant, and the old ways of story-telling," Dan said.

Sharon smiled at him. "When are you coming to my grandfather's classes in chant? You've already missed two."

"Sorry, I've been meaning to get there. I just sort of got sidetracked." He flicked a glance at me, and a quick look passed between him and Sharon. It was gone before I could decipher it.

"Tell me more about Nahi'ena'ena," I said, turning to Sharon. "What do you know about her?"

"Nahi'ena'ena? Well, you'd have to know the family background she came from. She and her brother, who became King Kamehameha III, fought their mother's efforts to raise them as Christians. They were traditionalists in the strongest sense of the word, and teenagers as well when all this was going on. It isn't surprising they rebelled."

"Yes, I read that. I've wondered, though, how Nahi'ena'ena must have felt—her mother wanting her to be one thing, her spirit crying out for another."

"Precisely. It would seem her spirit won out when she married her brother. But at what price?"

"What do you mean, 'price'?"

Sharon took a sip of water. "It's said Nahi'ena'ena drank heavily and dated several men in her late teens, before wedding her brother and Leleiohoku, in a plural marriage. As a psychologist, I can't help believing there was much more eating away at her than confusion over religion versus the old traditions. She clearly loved her brother, according to historic reports. Their relationship had been encouraged since childhood, and there were rumors early on that they were sleeping together. The missionaries, of course, were shocked.

But this was natural for Nahi'ena'ena and Kaui-keaouli. It was the way things had been for all time.''

"Do you think their physical relationship began when they were children?'' I asked, still wondering how near to fact the ''visions'' I'd had of the two of them together might have been.

"One can only guess. If so, I would imagine they were like a couple of little puppy dogs, simply playing at first. When they were children they spent time in both Honolulu and Lahaina, sometimes in the mission homes in which they'd been placed by their mother to be taught the Christian faith. There are rumors that they slipped away often to be together, and that during this period they were secretly wed according to their own tradition. When these rumors reached the missionaries, there was so much pressure put upon Nahi'ena'ena, she ran away from her mission home.''

"Ran away? You mean, back to the palace?''

"I believe so. I don't know where else she might have gone. Still, life couldn't have been easy for her there. It's said that she took a series of lovers—including an American sailor.''

"You're kidding.''

"No, not at all. Finally,'' Sharon went on, ''at the age of nineteen, she married her brother in that plural marriage. A year later she gave birth to a stillborn child, whose father she couldn't name, as she'd been sleeping with both husbands. Shortly after that, she died. One has to wonder if she simply couldn't bear her life any longer.''

It was difficult to picture the Nahi'ena'ena I'd seen in my visions as ending this tragic way. ''Perhaps her beloved brother turned to other women after the still-born birth of the child?''

"Oh, that seems almost a given. Kamehameha III

was known to have had several women over the years.''

"Poor Nahi'ena'ena. Poor Kauikeaouli, for that matter.'' I couldn't help thinking that as a book, this could be better than *Peyton Place*. ''Why do you think Nahi'ena'ena married him in the first place? If she knew about his other women, that is?''

"Well, of course, it was expected from the first that she and her brother would marry and maintain the purity of the royal line. And there were still many traditionalists in Hawaii who might have been pushing for the marriage, for political reasons. Also, by the time Nahi'ena'ena married her brother, women were being oppressed in Hawaii for the first time, because of all the Western ideas being introduced. They were considered incapable of political action, of being responsible for themselves or their property—and even forced to cover their bodies with long-sleeved, ankle-length dresses. The world had become a difficult place for Hawaiians, and for women in particular. It's possible even Nahi'ena'ena—especially as she'd succumbed, apparently, to despair and taken to drink—felt in need of the kind of protection marriage to her brother might offer.''

"Or,'' I said thoughtfully, remembering the way I had seen them together, ''perhaps she realized her only salvation, finally, was in marrying the man she loved.''

Sharon smiled. ''A romantic conclusion. But it may well be just as valid.''

"And if she married Kauikeaouli because she loved him, it's hard to believe she wouldn't have been jealous of his other women. That might have caused her to drink and to have affairs of her own.''

"You're quite right. Regardless of the acceptance of plural marriages in certain societies, there's always been the difficulty of that little green-headed monster getting in the way.''

"It's hard to imagine," Dan interposed, "how natural sex must have been in those days. It was all part of the spontaneity and liveliness of the Hawaiian spirit, until the missionaries arrived bearing words like *fornication*, *incest*, and *homosexuality*. Our people were thrown into confusion and conflict. It's said the most difficult task of the missionaries was in trying to convince our ancestors that sex was no longer a gift of the gods, but a tool of the devil.''

"And Nahi'ena'ena," I said, "was about ten—isn't that right?—when she was thrust into the midst of all those very enthusiastic newcomers, bent on delivering her from hell.''

Remembering the vision at Hale Pau Hana, I added, "I wonder if she worried for her brother, spiritually, and for that matter felt burdened by guilt over her relationship with him.''

"I do remember reading," Sharon said, "that there were missionaries she grew close to and liked as individuals. It's likely they worked on her to try to convert her brother.''

"And as you say, there were political games going on as well. On both sides?''

"Oh, decidedly. So many factions, but largely the Christians versus the traditionalists . . .''

"And all of them pulling both Nahi'ena'ena and her brother in conflicting directions.''

Sharon studied me. "You seem to have more than the usual tourist's interest in our princess. Are you thinking of writing about Nahi'ena'ena?''

"As in a novel? I'm not sure. For now, I'm just . . . caught up in her story, I guess.''

"I'd say it's a bit more than 'caught up,' '' Dan said quietly.

Sharon's dark eyes swung his way, then back to me.

"Has something been happening?" she said tensely.

I shrugged. Though I'd begun to feel comfortable with Sharon Cole, I still wasn't easy about discussing Nahi'ena'ena, and the experiences I'd been having, with Dan Kala.

As I thought that, he stood and began to clear the table.

"It was a wonderful meal as usual," Sharon said. "Let me help you."

"No, I can get it. You stay here and keep my houseguest company. I've got a few calls to return, and I'd like to do that before it's too late. You'll excuse me, Kate?"

"Of course."

"There's coffee here in the carafe. And help yourselves to brandy, if you'd like. You know where it is, Sharon?"

"After all the late-night discussions we've had over a snifter or two? No problem. Kate?"

I shook my head. "I'll stick to coffee for now." For some reason, I had the urge to keep my head clear.

Nodding, Sharon picked up the carafe and poured the richly scented brew into two cups. "Dan makes the greatest coffee in the world, don't you think?"

"I'm not sure I noticed."

Our eyes met. "You do like him, don't you?" she said.

Startled, I answered too quickly. "He seems okay."

A dark brow lifted. "Just okay?"

I wondered what she was getting at. Was she involved with Dan Kala—or not?

"I'm not really thinking of men that way these days," I said.

"Oh. Sorry. Women, then?"

I laughed softly. "No. I just have a lot of old stuff to resolve."

"Would you like to talk about it now?"

I almost said, *To you? Are you crazy? Absolutely not, I hardly know you.* But then I reprimanded myself: *This woman means me no harm. She's just being friendly. Relax.*

"There was someone in my life once," I said. "I found he couldn't be trusted."

She nodded sympathetically. "That's really difficult, isn't it? The feeling of betrayal."

"The worst."

"Did he leave you for another woman?"

I frowned, as this was a question I'd asked myself for years. Was Margo seeing Gerard before he and I broke up? Or did that start much later?

I decided to have a glass of brandy after all, and spotted it on a sideboard beside the table. Crossing over, I reached for a snifter. Pouring, I said, "I've never been sure. But that wasn't the reason we broke up."

Her eyes narrowed. "He didn't abuse you?"

"Physically? No. Verbally and emotionally? Yes, I believe now that he did."

"That can be every bit as bad."

Returning to my chair, I sipped the brandy, feeling it loosen my nerves, which had gone tight. "Yes. Yes, it can be just as bad." Staring off into the distance, I remembered the old accusations, the feelings of losing my mind.

Vaguely, I heard Sharon speaking. Coming back with a start, I said, "Sorry. I guess I wasn't listening."

She was looking at me curiously. "That's all right. I just wondered how long ago this was . . . and why it still weighs so heavily upon you."

That, too, was a question I'd often asked myself—

especially of late. Why was I still so angry, or bitter, that I couldn't even return Margo's phone call?

"I don't know," I said simply.

"Could it be . . ." Sharon asked, "that you still wonder if you were wrong—and he was right?"

Stiffening, I looked at her.

"I don't know," I said again, drinking the brandy in one deep draught.

She gave a light shrug. "Think about it, Kate."

Standing, she crossed to the sideboard. "I think I'll have a touch of that brandy now. Why don't we refresh yours and take our drinks outside on the lanai? It's lovely out there in the evening, and we can talk."

The sun was low over the hills now, the sky a masterpiece of hot pink and gold. We set the huge snifters on a table between two chaise lounges and settled in just as the last brilliant crescent of fireball disappeared. Soft lights came on in the garden, highlighting the coconut trees and shrubs. The sky still held its fuchsia tinge, while overhead a few bright stars appeared. For several moments we sat quietly, appreciating the view. Finally, Sharon spoke.

"I sometimes think life is like the taro plant, Kate. The entire plant is good. The leaves, for instance, can be used for many things. But the essence—the food that kept the Hawaiian people alive and healthy for so many years—comes from the root. The root produces the poi, which is rich in protein and carbohydrates, the building blocks of all life."

She smiled. "Bear with me on this metaphor, if you will. Today in Hawaii, as in life, there are too many of us at the fast-food stands. Too many eating the local favorite, the locomoco. You know the locomoco?"

"I've heard of it. I'm not sure what it is."

She grimaced. "Two scoops of rice, a scoop of

macaroni salad, a greasy meat patty, and gravy over the whole mess. Cardiac Alley, our medical people call it. Our people are dying young from heart disease and diabetes, and the only hope is that more will return to the poi.''

Her voice took on a stronger, firmer timbre, though it remained soft. Her words were that of someone with a mission, a desire to save. ''The gods knew our metabolisms. They knew the food given us would keep us strong, and for many years we listened to the old messages of the gods. Now we don't. Now we have discount stores with pizza counters, food that was brought to us from across the sea and is killing us off more surely than any nuclear bomb.''

I sipped my brandy and sent her a smile. ''You sound like an activist.''

''Oh, I am,'' she said firmly. ''I most definitely am. But to get back to you—do you see how nature parallels life?''

''I'm not sure. You're saying that I need to tend to my root? And cook up some poi?''

She laughed. ''That's it, exactly. We must focus on the good stuff, the root of all life that's been given to us by the gods—or God, if you will.''

''And this root of all life is . . . ?''

''Our own inner sense of what is right and wrong. We must learn to trust that, rather than dwelling on those things, and people, that don't nourish us. This way we will grow healthy and strong.''

I sighed. ''I know you're right. Still, it's rather scary—being responsible for one's own happiness and mental well-being.''

She nodded wisely. ''The truth can generally be recognized by the power of the emotion that attends it.''

I shook my head slowly. ''You are the damnedest shaman I've ever known.''

Sharon raised a brow. "How many shamans have you known?"

Laughing, I admitted, "None. I've just always had an image in my mind of someone standing on the side of a mountain chanting, or blowing tunes through a conch shell."

She grinned. "Oh, chants, is it? I can give you chants. What kind would you like? Rain? A good trade wind?" Her eyes narrowed, and her tone grew serious. "Or perhaps a raising of the dead."

I felt a chill. "No . . . I think I'll let the dead sleep."

"You may not have a choice much longer, Kate," she said quietly.

My gaze swung quickly to hers. "What are you talking about?"

"You're seeing things here at Pua'lani—are you not?"

"Seeing things? No . . . no, of course not."

"Oh, but you are. That's the haunted expression I saw in your eyes earlier. I mistook it then as fear. But it's more like confusion, isn't it? The 'not knowing.' 'Not understanding.' "

Staring, I felt silly, unsure. "I haven't told anyone . . . not anyone at all. How . . . ?"

Sharon's gaze wandered slowly about the terrace before coming to rest gently on me. "There are spirits here, Kate. They tell me things. And I know about Pua'lani."

I tensed. "What about Pua'lani?"

"Oh, it has quite a history. Long before Dan Kala bought it, there were stories of ghostly appearances. Strange happenings."

"Really? He didn't tell me that. He did say the people he bought the house from left Nahi'ena'ena's portrait behind on purpose. He thought they were afraid of it."

"And you? Are you afraid of our little princess, Kate?"

"No . . . not really. It's more . . ."

"Yes?"

"More as if there's someone else, something around her that makes me afraid."

"Ahhh . . ." Her breath came out in a long, deep sigh. "Something around Nahi'ena'ena. How astute of you to see that."

"Astute? Is there something you know, something you can tell me about this?"

"Only that I've long held the belief there were people close to Nahi'ena'ena at the time of her death who couldn't be trusted. For me, this is intuitive only. It came to me the first time I heard her story, many years ago."

I leaned forward, eager to discuss this with her now. "I think you're right, though. I could almost hear her saying to me, *Help me*. And, Sharon, the other morning, after I read Nahi'ena'ena's story here in the library, I fell asleep. I was wakened by a loud, clear woman's voice that said, 'Do you believe everything you read?' "

Sharon was silent a moment. Her eyes narrowed. "You heard this? Nahi'ena'ena actually spoke to you?"

"Well, someone did. And there was no one in the room but me."

She gazed at me with wonderment. "She's making contact, then. And you didn't run from it. Why not, Kate? Why weren't you frightened by this? Most people would be."

I answered thoughtfully, "You know, I've been asking that myself. Part of me thought I was imagining it at first. Then I felt frightened—but not of the princess. I feel sorry for her. And I felt drawn to come back here—to stay here, where, for some reason, I felt closer to her. To see the story out, I suppose.''

"That's very brave of you."

"Brave?" There was an edge to her voice, and my fingers tightened on the brandy snifter. "Do you think there's danger here?"

"What I think is that our minds can be tricked all too easily by spirits from the other realms. According to our tradition, these spirits can change form at will. They can even enter other forms . . . other people's bodies."

"Like the *mo'o*, you mean?"

"And the *kahunas*."

"Sharon . . . ? What is it?"

"I'm concerned about this other presence around Nahi'ena'ena, the one you said frightened you. Kate, as a writer, you open yourself to the unseen every time you sit down to write. Isn't that so?"

"I suppose. I know I'm not alone when I write."

She nodded. "Some call it a muse, others call it connecting with the ether, or with whatever energies that are out there. All through history the human race has been working with these energies. It's only in recent times, since science became king, that people have denied what they can't see. Only in recent times that they've either ignored or disbelieved the invisible." She smiled. "Of course, with quantum physics, even science is coming around to acknowledging the unseen now."

My answering smile was rueful. "Sometimes I think my muse is a frustrated suspense writer who died before she got the big one out, and she's living vicariously through me. There are times when I feel so driven, I ignore my own needs. But you . . ." I hugged myself, uneasy suddenly. "You see actual spirits around us? At this moment?"

"Not in body, all of them. Some are only a blur. One seems clearer than the others, however. I'd say she's young. And she seems in trouble."

I leaned forward. "Tell me. Where is she?"

"Just to your right. I see long, dark hair..." Sharon broke off. "The rest is in a mist, Kate. Tell me about this woman. Is it Nahi'ena'ena?"

"That's just it, I'm not sure. There are times these past couple of days when I'm certain I've seen Nahi'ena'ena. But I think this woman is someone else." I hesitated, then decided it wouldn't hurt to tell her more. "I've seen Nahi'ena'ena's brother too."

"*Kauikeaouli*? Kamehameha III? Are you certain?"

"Yes... Well, no. I mean, I don't know if what I'm seeing is real." I laughed, feeling awkward. "I can't even believe I'm sitting here thinking it *is* real."

"Can you tell me how it happens?"

"I'll try. I think it began a few days ago..."

I described to her my sensations at Long's, the morning I went to look for the missing film. "I had a terrible headache, and then it seemed like a movie began to play itself out in my peripheral vision. That's the only way I can describe it. There were people, I think, and some sort of scene. But I couldn't make it out, and then it was gone."

I told her about waking up here yesterday morning to find my car keys missing. And again about the voice in the library, then in the guest room... the "vision" last night of Nahi'ena'ena and her brother in my condo in Kihei, after which the keys mysteriously appeared on my kitchen counter.

The only thing I left out was the burning of my wrists here in the guest room, and the stomach pain I'd had in the kitchen in Kihei. Something made me hold back, reluctant to reveal that much. It was as if

the physical pain took the visions to another dimension
. . . either one where I was indeed crazy, and creating
these episodes in my body myself, or—if not—one
that was far too frightening to contemplate.

"Then, this afternoon," I continued, "I fell asleep,
over there in front of the guest room, working at my
computer. I 'dreamed' of Nahi'ena'ena and her brother
again. When I woke up . . ."

Again, I held back. I couldn't tell anyone how
aroused I'd been by that vision, how completely I'd
become part of that scene.

Sharon leaned forward intently. Around her eyes,
fine lines of worry appeared. "The vision earlier, that
you told me about—the one of Nahi'ena'ena going to
a hut in the woods after seeing her brother. You didn't
see what was being done to her? You said you saw
her enter the hut but not what happened afterward?"

"Not entering it. Walking toward it. But she had
been thinking about pain, and how it blots out desire.
I felt she was going there . . . I don't know, for some
kind of penance."

"And you had no clue as to who this man was, the
one in the hut?"

"No. I don't think he was one of the missionaries,
though. She seemed to be thinking of him as someone
apart from them."

"Really?" Sharon drew back, frowning. "Did he
seem Hawaiian?"

"It was hard to tell. In the vision, he was only a
vague figure in the doorway."

"And there was no one else in this vision? Only
Nahi'ena'ena, her brother, and this man?"

"In that particular one, yes. And only Nahi'ena'ena
and her brother in the one this afternoon."

"Ah. And are these the only visions you've had?"

I shrugged. "Something else happened, the night

before the headache and the visual problems I had at Long's. It was the night I met Dan Kala, in fact."

At that she seemed to stiffen momentarily, but she only said, "Go on."

I told her about the dream of a woman with long dark hair, a woman who'd become Margo.

"This Margo. She's a good friend of yours?"

"She was. I haven't seen her for a long while."

"You had a falling out with her?"

"Not precisely. She, uh . . . she married the man I told you about . . . the one I'd been in love with. But that was a long time ago."

"It still hurts?"

"Not the part about losing Gerard, I don't think. The relationship was over, and I was glad to be rid of him by then."

"So it's the betrayal of trust by your friend that hurt, more than the loss of the man."

This time I wasn't as surprised by her ability to go straight to the truth of things. "I suppose that's true. In the long run, losing Margo hurt more than losing Gerard." I smiled. "Good friends are hard to come by."

She smiled too. "While men are a dime a dozen?"

"Well, I wouldn't exactly say that." Laughing, I felt tension disappear.

"Do you know what this is all about, Sharon? Why am I seeing Nahi'ena'ena and her brother? I sometimes think I'm going mad. In fact, Gerard . . ."

She looked at me expectantly, but I shut my mouth and looked away. I wasn't ready to tell anyone that Gerard had finally accused me of madness for having "forgotten" so many things. Though people will claim they don't believe the things others have accused one of, there is a taintedness that lingers in the listener's mind, and even the slightest anomalies in one's actions may be questioned after that.

"Kate, things happen in Maui," Sharon said. "Surely you've noticed that you've been more intuitive since coming here?"

"Is that what it is? Intuition? I've sometimes felt my emotions have gone haywire here. For instance, when I first arrived I tended to cry at the drop of a hat. I'm not ordinarily like that."

"You may have been picking up either past or present energies from people around you. Jung called it tapping into the mass consciousness."

Though her voice was calm, she seemed worried.

"What are you thinking?" I asked, uneasy again.

"Just that, putting the effect of mass consciousness aside, what people think of as paranormal is often actually 'normal'—meaning, in mainstream talk, that it has a scientific basis. There are electromagnetic frequencies all over the globe, and for whatever reason, they happen to be quite strong on Maui. They also affect the emotions. Many people who visit here describe going through the kind of depression you mention, or at least some sort of emotional upheaval."

"But not everyone?"

"No, it seems not."

"Why is that, do you think?"

"I believe it's because people, like violins, aren't always tuned the same way. Nor are they tuned the same way each day. As for you, Kate, there's the added fact that you're part Hawaiian. I'd guess you've been open to these kinds of frequencies since birth, though you may not have tapped into them on a regular basis. Hawaiians have always been close to the earth and its movements and messages."

Her voice took on a lighter tone, that of the explorer, or teacher, one who loves knowledge for itself, rather than what it might sell for. "The research isn't all in on this, Kate. But we are entering a fascinating age. There are sounds, for instance—music, one might call it—that the earth generates, but that can't be heard by the human ear."

"Harmonic tremors? I've read about them."

She shook her head. "Scientists have known about ordinary harmonic tremors, the kind that come from volcanoes, for decades. But in Java, a team of scientists discovered tremor-type sounds that they felt were far too regular to be generated from the volcano. They described them as much like a musical instrument playing a single note, but rich in overtones. They also described what they called 'a regular pumping sound.' "

She smiled. "I wonder . . . and just to be fanciful for a moment . . . could this be the heartbeat of Mother Earth? The team who discovered this believed these sounds were stemming from a single source—a large, possibly cylindrical, gas-filled cavity inside the volcano. Imagine! A chamber for Mother Earth, to hold her heart—much like the chambers in the pyramids."

She looked at me then and chuckled. "Sorry. I tend to go on and on."

"Well, you've found a good audience in me. I'm all ears."

"Or are you merely being polite?"

"You're the shaman," I said, smiling. "You tell me."

She laughed. Swinging her legs off the chaise lounge, she sat facing me. "About those visions. You do feel comfortable with calling them that?"

"Sure, why not? I'm just glad to hear I may not be losing my mind."

Tenting her fingers, she leaned her chin on them, speaking in a serious tone. "Kate, I don't mean to mislead you. Often, these things are harmless. But until we understand what's actually going on, I'd advise caution.''

"Caution. In what way?"

Holding my attention with those worried dark eyes, she said, "There have been cases of a person being unable to come back. Also, cases of a person coming back entirely changed. With a different spirit, so to speak.''

I laughed nervously. "Are you talking about possession? Demons? I've never put much stock in such things."

"Then you should. The word *demon* came into use for a reason, Kate. People needed a word to describe the kinds of evil or mischievous beings they were running into throughout history. The gargoyles, the griffins . . . Personally, I see them now as spirits who are no different, in terms of morals and trouble-making, from the way they were when they existed as people on this plane. They've simply taken different form.''

She reached over and touched my arm lightly, then drew back. "Kate, it seems to me that up to now you've been standing on the fringes of this drama, whatever it is. You've been an observer. Further, watching Nahi'ena'ena and her brother seems a perfectly harmless pastime. But if you continue to allow their energies to come through you, matters could quickly get out of hand. Others could slide in through that portal you've opened for Nahi'ena'ena. Others who might not be so harmless.''

Where her fingers had lain on my arm, the skin still felt warm, as if bands of heat had passed from her to me. Even so, I was chilled. "Are you talking about Margo?''

"Perhaps. But I sense there are others too. Kate, why do you think this woman has appeared to you?

What are her motives? What is she trying to draw you into?''

"I haven't a clue. I've been half thinking I conjured her up because of my guilt over not returning her calls. You think it could be more?''

"Only you can answer that. But don't you think it's interesting that when I spoke of danger coming through others, you immediately thought of Margo? What is it you know—deep within, where your own truth resides—that told you this?''

I shook my head, confused. "I don't know. I really don't.''

"Then I would strongly urge you to find out—and not alone, but with a guide.''

"A guide?''

"For your own safety. I would be happy to refer you to someone. Or, I could work with you, if you like.''

I hesitated. "Just how would we do this?''

"There are many techniques. We would find the right one for you.'' Her face clouded over. "I warn you, however, this is not always easy. Or pleasant.''

"Sharon, you're beginning to scare me. Are we talking about an exorcism here?''

"Similar. The rituals to dispel demons go far back, to the beginning of time as we know it. They differ only slightly from culture to culture.''

"But I haven't actually seen any demons. No one's tried to harm me.''

She was silent.

I looked away, then back. "A while ago you said if I continue to *allow* these energies to make contact. How do you think I'm allowing it?''

"Largely by giving them your time and your focus. In coming back here to Pua'lani, I'm afraid you as much as issued an invitation, Kate.''

"All right, then, let's say I continue as I have been. What might I expect to have happen?"

"That's difficult to predict. However, if the situation accelerates, I must tell you I fear for your physical safety."

"Physical safety?" Dan Kala said sharply from the living room doors. "What are you talking about, Sharon?"

She looked up, and he came to stand beside her. "Why would you worry about Kate's safety?"

Sharon glanced at me. "I think you should tell him. Dan knows something about these things. He might be able to help."

He drew up a chair, facing us. "Help with what?"

I debated for several moments, whether to bring him in on this. Finally I sighed, thinking, *Why not?* "Nahi'ena'ena, that's what. You know, I almost wish you'd burned that damned portrait. Or tossed it over the cliff."

As I spoke the words, my brandy snifter, which had been resting in my hands, ignored, began to shake. Nerves, I told myself. *Look at me, I'm shaking.*

I managed to steady the glass only moments before it would have spilled warm brandy into my lap.

Still jittery, I gave Dan Kala an abbreviated version of what had been happening, and watched his face, trying to discern his thoughts. It was impossible. Dan Kala, I thought, is a man who either has no thoughts or is damned good at hiding them, as well as the truth. The latter seemed the more likely.

"I had no idea it had gone this far," he said.

"But you did know?" Sharon prompted.

"I suspected."

"You never should have let her return here, then."

"You could be right," he said.

"If it's multidimensional—"

"But we can't really know—"

"Will the two of you please speak to me directly?" I interrupted, annoyed.

Sharon gave a shrug, looked at Dan, then stood and walked to the large flat rock I'd fallen asleep on the first day here. She sat, drawing up her knees a bit and hooking her fingers around them. Though she was only a few feet away, I felt she had somehow removed herself from the conversation.

Dan turned to me. "Kate, it's difficult to tell what's actually happening to you. Are these things you're seeing just scenes from the past? Pictures frozen in time? Or are they truly happening right now—or even in the future—in some other dimension? One thing I do know is that more and more I hear stories from people who claim to have slipped between dimensions. Sometimes it happens for only a brief millisecond—a person gets a flash that doesn't seem to belong to him or her. Something like those little pictures one gets in that twilight zone just before falling asleep."

"You mean the kind that seem like dreams, yet not dreams."

"Right. And as to that, what are dreams? It's widely believed that we actually do slip over into other dimensions when we dream. Other 'realities,' one might say. Sometimes people seem to have much longer dimensional slips. We may even find in the future that mental patients who seem delusional are only living in another, very real, but strange-to-us dimension. I'm not saying this is true—only that conceivably, it could be."

"And what about me? Are you thinking I might be delusional?" I studied his face to catch the truth before a pacifying answer could be devised. There was nothing there, however, other than a slight narrowing of the eyes.

"Not delusional in the traditional meaning of the word," he said. "I believe what you're seeing is real—at least to you. I have to believe it, Kate." He shrugged. "I've seen it myself."

My gaze swung up to meet his. "You've seen Nahi'ena'ena? But you told me—"

"Not Nahi'ena'ena. But I've seen the tricks. Things disappearing, then coming back. And sometimes in the night, when everything is still, outside and in . . . I have heard voices. Not directed toward me, as yours seem to have been. But I hear them."

Oddly this seemed reassuring. I began to relax. "You hear them too," I said wonderingly.

"I do."

I studied him, then tensed again as it came to me with a shock: "Your interest in me, that night in Hecock's. It was more than curiosity about the physical similarity to Nahi'ena'ena. You wanted me to come here! My instincts were right about that. You hoped she'd make contact with me."

He looked away, obviously uncomfortable. "Not immediately. I wasn't sure at first what I wanted. But it's true I had hoped *something* would happen—"

"Shame on you, Dan Kala!" Sharon interrupted. "You of all people should have known what could happen. To have deliberately brought Kate here and placed her in possible danger—"

"Now, wait a minute," he flared back at her. "That's not the way it was."

He turned to me and steadied his voice. "When I left you at the Hyatt that first night, I had no idea you'd find out where I lived and show up here. I swear that's true, Kate. That's why I left you there the way I did. Once I'd had a chance to think it through, I knew

I didn't want to drag you into any of this."

"It's also true," I said with an edge, "that you didn't exactly break your neck to get me back to Kihei. You could have driven me home when my car broke down, instead of keeping me here overnight."

He seemed unable to meet my eyes.

"What kind of game are you playing, Dan Kala?" Sharon asked softly. "What is it you're not telling us?"

He turned silent, gazing moodily out over the sea.

Sharon stood, her mouth forming lines of disapproval. Taking a deep breath, she addressed me. "I have to be going, Kate. But first, there's something I need to talk to you about. Would you walk me to my car?"

"Sure." I stood and she linked my arm with hers.

"You're going to tell her?" Dan asked as we turned to leave the terrace.

"I have a feeling that if I don't, you never will," Sharon said in that same disapproving tone. "Really, Dan, I don't understand what you're doing—not at all."

Again, he looked away.

"So, what is it?" I asked as we walked around the pool toward the drive. Dan's cryptic remark, "*You're going to tell her?*" was heavy on my mind, and I couldn't imagine what was coming. It seemed that all kinds of machinations had been going on behind my back.

"Kate," she said, "Maui is a small world. And I didn't come here only for dinner tonight. There's something I need to tell you. I'm just not sure how you're going to take it."

Immediately, I had one of those flashes of insight, the kind that sends a tremor to the belly, a clue that life as one has always known it is about to change.

"My brother, Kimo," she continued, linking her arm once more through mine, "thought he recognized something about you when he saw you earlier. At first he wasn't sure what it was, and since your photograph has been in the newspaper several times when you've signed books here on the island, he thought that might be it. Before I came here tonight, he talked with me, however, and we put two and two together."

"Two and two?"

"I don't mean to shock you, Kate, and I hope you don't mind my bringing you this news, but it turns out we know your family."

"My family?" I said, puzzled.

"The Kalamas?"

I shook my head, not understanding at first. Then it dawned, and with it did come shock. "You mean my *mother's* family? They're here, on Maui?"

She smiled. "Just down the road, as a matter of fact."

"But I thought . . . I suppose I thought they might be gone now . . . like my mother."

"Oh, I assure you, they are very much alive."

My family. People who looked like me, perhaps. Who might even think like me.

I sent a questioning glance to Sharon.

"They're very nice people," she said reassuringly. "Your grandmother still holds to many of the old traditions. I think you'll like her."

"My grandmother? I have a living grandmother? My mother's mother?" It was almost too much to hope for. "But how do you know this is my family?"

"I talked to them before I came here," she said. "They know all about you. They've been waiting for you, Kate."

CHAPTER 15

"What do you mean, waiting?" I said, confused, still facing her on the drive.

"Oh, they've known about you for years, your grandmother said. They thought you didn't want to know them, and they never would have forced themselves on you. They're much too sensitive for that."

"I can hardly believe this," I said, pushing my hair back with a shaky hand. "It's too much of a . . ."

"Coincidence?" She smiled.

"No. No . . . I don't believe in coincidence."

"Nor do I. I believe your meeting was meant to occur, Kate. I'm not certain I know why. Perhaps simply to heal old wounds?"

I was still having difficulty taking it all in, but her last words made sense. "Yes. That may be it."

"Are you willing to meet them, then?"

I hesitated for only a moment. "Of course. Of course—I'd like that."

"Good." She nodded her approval and we began walking to the car again. "Your grandmother, your aunts, uncles, and cousins are all looking forward to meeting you. Your grandfather . . . well, I should tell you up front, he can be difficult."

"Difficult? In what way?"

"He's a man of the old ways. Descended from *ka-hunas*, as my own father is. You'll see. It's always better to form opinions for ourselves, don't you think?"

I wasn't all that certain at this moment, but didn't press the point.

"I've already spoken to Dan about this, and he's agreed to drive you to their house tomorrow. It's not too far. Just up the road, in fact, but a long walk in the heat. They asked if you might come tomorrow evening, around six. Is that all right? Everyone will be in from the fields by then."

"The fields?"

"Taro. Your aunt Deborah convinced everyone to come home from Oahu years ago, and work the land again. It's a family endeavor now."

"How, uh . . . large a family?"

"Oh, dozens. They're all about."

She must have noted my small prickle of uncertainty. Touching my cheek in a gentle, reassuring way, she said, "It'll be all right. You'll see."

We stood beside her white Geo, turning our eyes skyward a moment to appreciate the stars, which were brilliant under an ink-blue sky. Sharon looked back at me suddenly. "I'm so glad we met."

She gave me a hug, and I remembered to hug back, letting her feel my breath on her cheek, in the non-*haole* way.

After a moment she pulled back, her brow furrowed. "Kate, give me a call in the morning, and we'll set up an appointment to meet in my office at the university to work on a few things. Meanwhile, I can't stress enough that you need to protect yourself from further happenings of the kind you told us about. What you've experienced so far could well be only a first approach, a gentle nudge, asking you to open up more. Look at it this way: You are standing outside a movie house now, and every once in a while someone opens the door so that you can see a small slice of the film inside on the screen. You stand outside trying to decide whether to go in.'' Her hands gripped my shoulders, gently but firmly. ''Kate, if you do decide to go inside and watch this particular show, you could get so caught up in it, you might—at least for a time—lose your own vision of reality.''

''Are you saying I might become delusional—even if I'm not, right now?''

She studied me. ''There's that word again. *Delusional.* Is there some particular reason you've become focused on it?''

I gave an elaborate shrug but couldn't meet her eyes. ''Not really.''

Sharon dropped her hands. ''My dear new friend, I do not for a moment believe that's true.''

At my halfhearted protest, she held up a hand. ''No, no, I won't push. Let me simply say for now that my own personal belief is that *everything* happens in the mind. Visions, dreams, alternate realities . . . ghosts, demons, hobgoblins. I think we create them in our minds—or allow them entry into our minds—and then outpicture them, so to speak, much the same as holograms. So perhaps in certain meanings of the term 'delusion'—hallucination, say, or mirage—all this might be called delusional. But it certainly is not insane.'' She smiled. ''That's what you were really asking, wasn't it?''

''Yes.'' I smiled back. ''I'm afraid this is all a bit much for me. I've always put these sorts of things into a little compartment called the 'supernatural,' and since I didn't believe in the supernatural, I pretty much dismissed them. Or thought of them as being insane.''

"Kate, the longer I live, the more I know for a fact that there is no such thing as the supernatural—at least, not in the old meaning of the term. There are only very normal, very natural, energies that as yet are largely misunderstood."

She slid behind the wheel and turned the ignition on. "Therein lies the problem," she said as the engine purred and warmed. "Our lack of understanding. That's why I feel I must say again that if you continue to put yourself in the way of these things we do not fully understand, you may not be able to stop what happens. I urge you not to fool with this. You must take it seriously, my friend."

"I will," I said, holding my hand out to touch hers on the wheel. "Thank you, Sharon. *Mahalo.*"

"*Aloha*, Kate." She looked beyond me, and I turned to see Dan walking toward us from the house, though he was still some distance away.

"I would also be very careful about beginning a relationship right now," Sharon said in an odd tone.

"Oh?" I couldn't hide my surprise. "You mean with Dan Kala—or with anyone?"

"Well, it is Dan who has been put in your path," she answered enigmatically. And to him, as he approached, "I wondered if you'd deign to say good night."

He gave a shrug and said, "Well, it wouldn't be the first time, would it?"

"No," she agreed with a sigh as he stood with his hands in his pockets, still holding himself apart from her. "We have had our moments."

She slid the car into gear, saying, "Take care of your houseguest, Dan. If anything happens to her, I will hold you personally responsible."

On the surface it might have been the kind of light,

parting threat that no one takes seriously, ordinarily. But there was no lightheartedness in her tone. And, noting the lines of worry around her eyes, I was doubly glad that I hadn't told her about the physical pain I'd experienced during and after the last two visions. Her concern—however well-intended, and however friendly—had already begun to feel a bit like an invasion of privacy, an intrusion upon the things I'd come here to do.

"Thanks for the great dinner," I said, yawning as I walked beside Dan Kala back to the house. "And the company. I'm really tired, though. If you don't need help cleaning up, I think I'll turn in."

Even under the dark sky, I could see him studying me. "You're a guest. You don't have to do chores while you're here. But are you all right?"

"Absolutely. I'm fine. There's just been a lot to take in. Nahi'ena'ena. A new family. My life seems peopled, suddenly, by strangers."

At that he fell silent, and I realized how my words must have sounded. "Not that you're a stranger, exactly," I added by way of an apology.

He didn't respond, and we rounded the swimming pool, a cool mist from the hand-hewn waterfall dampening my face and arms. Water trickled softly over black lava rocks, and the sweet, heavy scent of lush blossoms was strong.

"You have a lot of plumeria here, don't you?" I said, more to lighten the mood than anything.

"Plumeria? Not so much. There is a stand of it out at the far end of the garden."

"That's the only one? And it carries this far? I've been noticing that scent since I arrived here, and I would have thought—"

I broke off as he stopped walking.

"What is it?"

"Are you smelling plumeria now?" he asked, tilting his head and sniffing lightly at the air.

"Yes, of course." I smiled. "Don't you?"

"Not at all."

"But it's so strong! Your nose must be off from cooking with all that garlic."

He stared at me. "Kate? How long has this been going on?"

"What do you mean? How long has what been going on?"

His voice hardened. "Don't play games. How long have you been noticing that scent?"

"The plumeria, you mean? My goodness, you make it sound like I'm having a secret affair." But my laughter was shallow, I knew that. I was feeling uneasy, suddenly.

"You detect it when Nahi'ena'ena's around, don't you? *Tell* me," he insisted, grabbing my arm.

"Well, what if I do?" I snapped. "What difference can it possibly make to you?"

"What *difference*? Kate, don't you get it? Your vision is already involved, with these things you've been seeing. And now, it seems, your sense of smell. How many more of your senses has Nahi'ena'ena taken over?"

"I don't know what you mean," I said, pulling away.

"*Think*, dammit. Have you *felt* anything? Have you actually felt anything?"

I hesitated too long this time. "You mean physically? No . . . no, of course not."

He made an impatient sound. "You're lying."

"Oh, for heaven's sake! Why ask if you're not going to believe me? And answer my question. What difference does it make, anyway?"

"The difference is in how far this has all gone. Sharon was right, you know. Kate—"

He ran a hand through his hair in a gesture of irritation. "Sharon was right. This could get out of hand."

My voice tightened. "But you knew that all along. And the truth is, you half hope it does—don't you?"

"No," he said, glancing away. "No . . . of course not." But there had been that moment of hesitation in his voice.

"You thought I might be your key to Nahi'ena'ena," I said angrily. "Your passageway through to her. And you didn't really care too much about what might happen to me."

He stared, his eyes cold. "You paint a very black picture of me. Is that what you honestly think?"

"Of course not. I think you're Sir Galahad. And why wouldn't I?"

He opened his mouth to speak, then shut it. Turning on his heel, he strode into the house.

I should have been contrite, I suppose. Felt guilt for egging him on. Any other time I might have. But the soft, sweet scent of plumeria drifted across the path, and after a moment I smiled—following it like a siren call, back to the guest room.

CHAPTER 16

In the guest room I went directly to a small cabinet for candles and holders, which I knew were kept there for use in a power outage. Leaving the front door open to the sea, I pulled the miniblinds up so that all three glass walls were exposed. Slowly and deliberately I lit each of the candles—two dozen minus one—placing them around the room on the bureau, chairs, on the floor along the glass walls, and one on either night table, illuminating the portrait of Nahi'ena'ena. When I'd finished, the room looked as if it had been prepared for a ceremony.

Why I did this wasn't clear. I only knew that the moment I'd entered the guest room and looked at Nahi'ena'ena's portrait, I'd felt directed, as if some inner voice sent instructions for every movement. For that matter, the directions had begun long before—out there in the garden, with the scent of plumeria and the swift, sure knowledge that Nahi'ena'ena was about.

When the next instruction said, "Flowers—find flowers," I followed it unquestioningly outside, to where ginger blossoms grew beside the lanai. Along with the bright red blossoms I found a few white orchids, as well, and made a bouquet. Pausing there under the stars, I held the flowers to my breast, feeling happier, suddenly, than I had for a long time. I realized then that the entire night, all through dinner and the conversation afterward, this was where I'd longed to be. Sharon's warnings drifted away on the soft night air.

The urge came to make a sound in my throat, a sound like a chant, a chant that would rise up to those stars and bring Nahi'ena'ena down to me. A part of me knew how incredibly odd this might seem to anyone watching. Another part said, "No, this is the true reality. This is the way it was meant to be."

Drawing in a deep breath, I felt it expand the diaphragm, then push against the lungs. A thrill ran along my spine as the tone rose up to my throat and was released in a soft, high, sweet pitch. That one note seemed to ring on and on, even after it had left my lips. And though I had never had a particularly good voice, I somehow knew that the chant I felt forming in my heart would rise to become one with the stars, one with the sky and the universe, and therefore one with all that was perfect and good.

I lifted the bouquet of flowers as part of my gift, and felt as if my body were lifted with them, off the ground. My chant continued. My vision shifted. All about me, the world began to shimmer. I turned my eyes toward the guest room and saw the myriad candles, and beyond them the portrait, but knew I was separated from them now. I stood on some other plane, and all was peaceful here on this plane. All was right.

I was with my child.

My child. Looking down at my arms, I was not at all surprised to see that they cradled a baby. The flowers were gone, and in their place was a tiny bundle, a face no larger than a newborn's, fists drawn up to the mouth, the eyes wrinkling in a soft cry. Lovingly, I brought the child to my face and whispered, "Hush, sweet baby, hush . . . it's all right. I've got you now."

Before me then appeared the same gauzy form of several nights before, drifting slowly toward me. *Nahi'ena'ena*, I thought—though I couldn't be sure. The hair was long and dark, the arms stretching out. The figure drew close. For one brief second it became Nahi'ena'ena, her eyes wild, frantic. "My baby!" she cried. "My poor baby!"

As I watched, the form changed, splitting in two. The figure beside Nahi'ena'ena, vague at first, became more and more distinct, the arms forming from a mist, and then the face . . .

Margo's face. Just as before.

"Help us, Kate!" she implored, her gray eyes filling with tears. Her hand went to that of Nahi'ena'ena's, as if in joining. "For God's sake, help *me*, Kate. He tried to kill my child!"

A shock rolled through me. Understanding nothing, yet overtaken by grief myself, I looked down at the baby in my arms and saw there were now two. The second child lay like a transparency over the other, while two very different and distinct outlines had formed.

"Who?" I asked, though my voice was but a cracked whisper on my tongue. "Margo—what can I do?"

She opened her mouth to speak. "Be careful," she began, stepping forward. "Don't let him . . ."

In the next instant a cold wind struck me, knocking me nearly off my feet. Another voice came, from the other side of the veil—a jarring, dissonant note that broke into this reality and shattered it like glass, into a million pieces. A powerful *whoosh* of air surrounded me, sucking me into its vortex, holding me in place. And though I reached a hand out to Nahi'ena'ena and

Margo, they were wrenched away. The two women merged into one, then abruptly disappeared.

My arms felt suddenly empty. Weightless. I looked down to see that the babies were gone, and that at my feet was the bouquet of flowers. A hand reached down and picked it up.

"It looks like you dropped these," the intruding voice said. "What on earth have you been doing now?"

In my confusion and disorientation, it took me a moment to understand that I'd stepped back into my usual space and time. It was Dan Kala who held the flowers. Dan Kala speaking. I took the bouquet with shaking hands and looked at him numbly, unable to form words.

"What on earth have you been *doing*?" he repeated, his gaze boring into mine.

Anger rose then, bringing me back swiftly. I felt spied upon, invaded. More ... I felt a terrible loss, with Nahi'ena'ena and Margo gone. I wanted Dan Kala away from here immediately, out of my sight. I wanted them back.

"For God's sake," I lashed out, "don't I have any privacy here?"

"You have every right to privacy," he said irritably. "You do *not* have a right to burn down your room." He gestured to the candles. "I was standing out by the cliff when I saw flames through the hedge. It occurred to me that you just might be on fire."

"Don't be ridiculous! It's only candles, and I'm watching them. They're fine."

"I'm not so sure about that. In fact, I think there's something damned odd going on here. You looked like you were a million miles away. And why have you got the place lit up like some damned cathedral?"

I started back into the guest room, stumbling a bit,

my legs like lead. "If you're so bloody worried about the cost," I flung over my shoulder, "I'll pay you for the damned candles! And if you don't mind, I'd like to be left alone now. I am a paying guest, after all."

He followed me inside and folded his arms, raising a brow. "Oh, really? A paying guest, are you? I don't recall having seen any cash change hands."

Angrily, I reached for my purse, on the bed. "You want cash? You've got cash." I dropped the flowers and pulled out a handful of bills. "Here, take this. It's all the cash I've got, but I'll write you out a check in the morning. Just tell me how much you want."

"Never mind," he said just as angrily. "I don't want your money, that's not the point. And why do you have to be so confounded difficult all the time?"

"I'm not being difficult! I just want to be left alone."

"I can see that. It's the reason *why* you want to be left alone that troubles me."

I tossed the money onto the bed and took a defensive posture, hands on my hips. "See, that's what I don't get. I'm a guest here, that's all. I'm somebody you don't even know. Why should anything I do trouble you?"

His jaw clenched. "You are the damnedest . . . I don't know why I even bother with you."

"Which is precisely what I've been saying. Now, will you please go?"

"Gladly." He stomped out the door without looking back.

For some time after Dan Kala left, I sat on the bed, shaken and confused. Not over him, however. With his departure my thoughts had swept like a tide back to Nahi'ena'ena and Margo.

Why had the two appeared to me together—not

once, but twice, now? And why had Margo said, "He tried to kill my child"? She had taken Nahi'ena'ena's hand at the same time, seeming to bond with her. But *why*?

Had Margo been pregnant, and had something happened to her baby? Was that why she'd called me so many times? For sympathy? A friendly ear?

Or was there another, darker, reason?

Fear raised the hairs on the back of my neck. Gerard had been abusive emotionally—but was he capable of more? I had always assumed that marriage to Margo must have changed him for the better. What if that wasn't true?

My head hurt, and I felt as if I had a hangover of sorts, though I had drunk very little alcohol at dinner. *It's the vision. I'm feeling ungrounded, out of balance. Not as comfortable now, "out here," as in that other world. It would be so good to go back there, to call them in again . . .*

I remembered those first moments of lightness, feeling as if I had crossed over to a plane where all was peaceful and good. I remembered the baby in my arms, comforting it, and how wonderful it felt to hold it safe.

Then I recalled Sharon's warning: "If you decide to step inside and watch this particular show, you might lose your own vision of reality."

This time the warning stuck and, reluctantly, I focused my thoughts, instead, on my past, and Margo— the pain I'd felt when she had told me that she and Gerard had married. I'd drawn away from her then, and in my heart I knew I was pulling away for good. Even when the Christmas cards came, I shoved them into an out-of-the-way place—reluctant to throw them away, as that would be giving them too much power, saying too much about the hurt I felt. Still—I didn't have to look at them, did I?

Finally, when the calls started to come a month ago, I wasn't able to stuff my anger down anymore. And for some reason I didn't fully understand, that terrified me. I'd run to Maui, hoping to forget Margo, Gerard, and perhaps even myself . . . the person I'd been when I knew them both.

But Margo had tracked me down, she had come to me for help, appearing to me over the miles from Seattle.

I laughed softly at this premise, which suddenly seemed ludicrous. Yet—if she hadn't been able to reach me by phone . . .

There were stories of people connecting through their thoughts. Close friends, relatives, twins. A kind of telepathy. Was that what this was? This thing about a baby—this plea?

Or had I imagined the entire vision, from start to finish?

I would have to phone Margo.

Glancing at the clock on the nightstand, I realized it would be after two A.M. in Seattle. If I called now, and Margo answered in her usual, grumpy, middle-of-the-night voice, only to tell me she was fine and what was I doing, imagining things again, I wasn't sure how I'd take it.

Looking down at the bed, I was stunned to see that the flowers I'd dropped there had not merely wilted, but gone entirely dry. Touching a petal, I felt it crackle beneath my finger, as if it had been picked months or even years before. Some force outside myself seemed to direct my hand over the bouquet, as if to bring them back by sheer force of will. The flowers remained only flowers, prematurely dead. I lay down beside them and closed my eyes. Before I knew it, sleep overtook me.

Sometime around dawn, I was awakened by a sound nearby. Raising my head, I saw that the sun had only begun to touch the sea from the east. The sky to the northwest was still a deep royal blue. The room was dim, the candles burned to a nub. Off to my right, where the path and a ribbon of garden wound around to the driveway, a movement caught my eye.

Jerking upright, I stared into the gloom. A flash of white, like that of a man's shirt, disappeared into the shrubbery. My muscles tensed. *Someone had been watching.* Then my feet hit the floor. Within seconds I was through the door, running across the lanai, scrambling over the flowers, pushing the branches aside.

A dead end pulled me up short. Less than ten feet through the shrubbery was nothing but solid wall. The wall was adobe, at least eight feet tall. Too high to reach the top or see over, it began at the cliff and ran to the front of the property, I remembered, out by the road.

Looking both ways, I saw no one between here and the short distance to the cliff. Turning toward the road, I searched an area of several square yards of shrubbery, in case whoever had been here had made his way through it to a waiting car.

There was nothing. No one. Not even the sound of crashing branches that my own foray had caused. Whoever had been out here was gone.

I shivered. Dan Kala, spying on me again? He could have run along the path to the front of the house, entering by the main door.

But . . . Dan Kala, lurking outside in the dark? On his own property? More likely, he'd come barging through my door.

Furthermore, the person I'd seen didn't behave like an irritable innkeeper, checking on burning candles. Every instinct told me that my intruder had been up to no good.

Going back into the guest room, I locked the door securely behind me and lowered the miniblinds, closing them tight. On my bed still lay the bouquet of flowers and, hardly surprised now, I saw that they had decayed even more since I'd fallen asleep. They were little but powder, and when I touched one, it came apart completely, fluttering into a pile of dust.

For a long while I lay on the bed beside them and thought about that, chilled to the bone. At last, light began to creep through the tight slats of the miniblinds. Glancing at the clock, I saw it was nearly seven. Ten, in Seattle.

I got up and sat at the small table by the door and, without opening the blinds, looked through the little address book I'd brought with me. Though I'd never returned Margo's calls, I'd written down her number out of habit.

Dialing, I listened as the phone rang on the other end. It was midmorning. Would she be there? Or might she be outside in her garden, or working out at the local gym?

Dear God . . . why doesn't she answer?

I hung up, finally, deciding to try again later. Hugging myself against a sudden, overwhelming depression, I made my way to the shower.

CHAPTER 17

I saw almost nothing of Dan Kala that day, which did not disturb me. I did wonder if he had heard me outside in the early dawn, and yet, though I could have sought him out at breakfast and questioned him about the incident, the idea never once occurred to me. It was only later that I asked myself why this was, and why I instinctively held back from taking my host into my confidence—even about such an important matter as a possible intruder.

Throughout that particular morning and early afternoon I kept busy at my computer, becoming more and more deeply entrenched in the story of Nahiʻenaʻena and her brother, Kauikeaouli. I did not sit on the lanai this time, but inside the dark guest room with the blinds pulled tight, wanting no intrusion on my thoughts. I started at seven, and when next I raised my head it was after two in the afternoon. My back hurt, and my head ached. I had forgotten to eat, and though my stomach was queasy, I was loath to stop for food even now.

Instead, I scanned my real food—the pages I'd written. Most of them had sprung from my imagination, it would seem . . . and yet, did they? In my heart I knew

the words had been given to me. All the time I had
been writing, I'd been "living" with Nahiʻenaʻena
and Kauikeaouli—not in a vision, as I'd done before,
but the way it was when I wrote any book. The information simply came.

It was then I saw that I'd written nearly fifty pages,
an astounding number for one day. I knew then, that
I was truly becoming obsessed.

And what of it? I told myself. Most novelists are
obsessed. If we weren't we would never finish a book.
It takes getting lost in it, putting all else aside: friends,
lovers, relatives, holidays, dinners out, television. All
must take their leave, at least for a time, in service of
The Book.

That one stopped me cold.

This thing about novelists was true. For most of the
good ones, anyway.

Therefore, why was I not working my fingers to the
bone at this moment on the book I'd contracted for—
the one about Caroline and Donald? Why was I ob-
sessing instead over a princess who had died more
than 150 years before—who had long been cold in the
ground?

For the first time in my career, I'd set a work-in-
progress aside to become even more beset by something else. I would need a damned good excuse for
turning this one in late—something better than "The
dog ate my manuscript." A surfing accident? Struck
down by a rampaging Hobie? Stung by a poisonous
pufferfish?

My moment of uneasy humor was short-lived as I
realized that I'd spent the day only in writing—and
that Nahiʻenaʻena had not once made an in-person appearance. Nor had Margo.

Was I losing them? I worried. Had I told too much
the night before to Sharon and Dan? Were my visions

like books, in that once one has talked about the plot, it's sometimes impossible to write it, since all the energy one had for it is gone?

No, that can't be. They *had* come since then: last night. I eased back, relieved. It must be a simple matter of focus, now. If I intend for it to happen, it does.

And if that's true, I can be there in moments, in that other world, right now. I can talk to Margo—Margo, whom I'd forgotten completely for most of the day . . .

A saner, more rational voice offered the reminder: *There's a more direct way. Call her. Call Margo now.*

Turning my computer off and setting it aside, I picked up the telephone receiver, punching the redial button. Again, the ring went on and on at the other end of the line.

Well, that might not be so odd. As I recalled, Margo had written on the back of one of those Christmas cards that she and Gerard traveled frequently. They could be anywhere—in France, even, at one of the Laniers' châteaux. Not having had the opportunity to be the mistress of one of those châteaux—or even to visit one—I did not have a phone number. Further, I remembered that the numbers had been unlisted, at least when I was with Gerard.

There was one other thing I could do. Before leaving San Francisco, I'd hired an answering service to screen my calls and inform me immediately in Maui of those from my agent and editor. Records were to be kept of all other calls, but I wasn't to be disturbed for them. I would contact the service for that information on a regular basis.

Connecting with the service on the mainland, however, I found that there had been no calls from Margo in the past two weeks. It seemed clear she had given up on me—and was, most likely, traipsing around Paris and drinking fine wine.

A tiny wave of bitterness swept through me. It did not last long. It did, however, leave an aftertaste, and it might have been that aftertaste that caused me to feel relieved that Margo hadn't called again. I put the vision of the night before behind me, shrugging it off determinedly as a product of my overly vivid imagination.

Noting, then, the time, I remembered there was something important I had to do today. Something around six. What was it?

With a sense of shock, I remembered: *I'm meeting my family. My Hawaiian family. How could I possibly have forgotten something as important as that?*

My mind did not seem to be functioning on all four cylinders these days. I kept drifting in and out.

As I crossed to the closet to choose clothes, my feet dragged. Everything in me wanted to return to my computer. To Nahi'ena'ena. There just wasn't time.

In the Jeep on the way to my family's house in Keanae, I found it increasingly difficult to keep up my end of the conversation. There were too many things to think about, and so much else to be worked through.

"About last night," I heard Dan Kala say as if from a distance, "I want you to know I understand how you might feel you want to keep some things to yourself. I . . ." He hesitated. "We all have things we don't tell others, for some reason or another. At any rate, I'm sorry if I've crossed some invisible boundary line. Whatever's going on with you, you're right—you're a guest, paying or not." He sent me a brief smile. "The rest is really none of my business."

"Thank you," I said, for lack of any other ready response. Then, "You know, I've looked at all this from every angle, and even though I do believe in synchronicity, it still seems odd . . . my meeting you that way, then coming to Pua'lani. The way you kept the portrait of Nahi'ena'ena, and the visions I've had . . . all of it coming together at the same time that way.''

His glance was sharp. ''What are you getting at?''

''I guess I'm wondering if there's been more to our meeting than it seems. If some outside force had a hand in it.''

He shrugged, and his expression became distant.

''What is it?'' I said. ''What's wrong?''

Shaking his head, he tried a smile that didn't quite make it. Swerving, he barely missed a mongoose on the road. ''I guess I'm just a bit worried about this dinner tonight.''

''You? Why?''

''I don't know. Aren't you nervous about meeting your family?''

My family. For the first time this day, I really thought about that, and was suddenly scared to death. Would they like me? And would I like them—this mother, father, sisters, and brothers of my mother, whose name was Luce? Meaning, in Latin, ''light''?

Not a typical name given by Christian missionaries. Were they Catholic, then? The Catholics had arrived soon after the others.

Yes . . . that fit. My father had been Catholic. Back in the days when he had married, the days of stricter religious mores, he'd have married, most likely, a good Catholic girl. My grandmother McKenna, in fact, raised me in the church till as a teenager I'd rebelled against all rules—including those of religion—put down my foot, and refused to attend Mass anymore. This led to quite a struggle between us for a while.

My father, having come from an earlier, more ''obedient'' generation, would most likely not have married and taken home a non-Catholic girl.

It seemed strange to me that I'd never thought about all this before. Never having known my mother or father, and without any memories to keep them alive, I'd thought of them very little. I did, of course, wish often that they'd lived, and that I'd had a mom and dad like most of the other kids in school. Sometimes I even made up fantasies about them: They'd been handsome and spirited, full of life and the living of it—drinking and dancing the night away, like characters in a *Great Gatsby*-type novel. At times I became depressed that I'd never known them, these fantasy creatures, never had a chance to be raised by them and, of course, to grow up more like them.

My grandmother, however, did not encourage me to feel sorry for myself. And despite our little power struggles—as we were both rather bull-headed and strong in our opinions—she had been good to me. I'd therefore never felt too much of a loss.

The question now was: Would my mother's family understand why I hadn't looked them up before?

Did I understand it, for that matter?

"Where does that lead?" I asked, pointing to a narrow road on our left with rounded rocks on either side of its entrance in the shape of the menehune.

"It goes to the cliffs," Dan Kala said. "There's a shortcut leading from it to the point, and to Pua'lani, but it's a bit overgrown with bamboo. Kimo uses it sometimes when he walks from his house to mine."

"And the menehune?"

"I believe they've been there for centuries. There were once ceremonies on the beach at the foot of this cliff, I'm told, back in the days of the *kahunas*, before they were outlawed by the missionaries and the new political order."

"There aren't any *kahunas* now?"

"Oh, they're around." He smiled. "More than ever, I'd say, though many of them are doctors now, as well as teachers and so on . . . people who have learned about the earth's energies, and how they work."

"And they use these energies for good? For healing?"

"For the most part. Of course, there will always be those who align themselves with darkness rather than light."

My thoughts moved back to Margo, and then Gerard, and all the months I had allowed him to hold that mysterious, dark influence over me. There had been brief, terrifying moments when I'd come to doubt my own sanity: *Is he right? Am I crazy? Losing my mind?*

And finally: *If I'm not, then he is. Otherwise, why would he do these things to me?*

I sighed. "How well do you know my family?" I asked, focusing on them as we pulled into a tree-lined drive a few minutes later.

"I don't know them well at all," Dan Kala answered. "I've known *of* them, of course, since I bought Pua'lani a few years ago. I knew they were friends of Kimo's, and taro farmers. They and Kimo have helped each other out in the fields in times of bad weather, or when either family has needed additional help to bring in a crop. But I'm gone a lot on business. I haven't had as much time as I'd like to meet my neighbors."

We rounded a curve in the drive, and my family's house appeared, surrounded by deep front and side lawns that were lush and green. The house itself was old Hawaii—not the kind of tract home that mushroomed after World War II, but not new and luxurious like Pua'lani, either. A large white farmhouse with a verandah on three sides, it sat in the middle of several acres surrounded by ginger flowers, wild orchids, banana trees, and a vegetable garden that was rich, it seemed, in everything from corn to beans.

A small girl with large, dark eyes stood on the verandah. The Jeep came to a stop a few feet from her. She watched us climb out, then turned to the screen door and called in, "Gramma, Gramma, she's here!" in a voice that seemed a mixture of curiosity and nervous excitement. I wondered if her tummy fluttered as much as mine. Who might she be? A second cousin?

A tall, thin woman appeared at the door, stepping out onto the porch. Her hair was dark and pulled back into a bun at the nape of her neck, much the same as I often wore mine. She wore a plumeria lei and the traditional "postmissionary" dress: high at the neck, with a long, narrow skirt. I'd learned that Hawaiian women still dress this way for special occasions, and felt honored that she would dress this way for me. For my own part I had worn a crisp cotton sundress, sleeveless, and with a low back but high neck, out of respect.

As the woman came down the steps toward us, I could see that her face was lined, and she was older than she had at first appeared. Her bearing, however, was young and straight. *Majestic* is the word that came to mind. Her eyes had the gentle, almost dreamy look of a mystic.

She held out both hands. "Katherine?"

I licked my lips, which had gone dry. "Yes. I'm Kate."

"Kate . . . I've always loved that name. I'm your grandmother. Marie."

Awkwardly, I took her hands and held them. Without warning, tears sprang to my eyes. Despite my efforts to gulp them back, they overflowed, and my grandmother enfolded me in her arms and held me for a very long time. I could feel her breath at my ear, and against my cheek.

She drew back, reaching for the lei and removing it from around her neck, then placing it around mine.

"*Aloha*," she said softly. "*Aloha nui loa*, Granddaughter."

"*Mahalo*," I said. "*Mahalo*, Grandmother. Thank you." I wiped at my eyes.

"You look so much like Luce," she said. "I am so happy to have you home."

I knew, suddenly, that I was even more happy to be here.

CHAPTER 18

"We're a bit early," Dan apologized, after introducing himself.

"I'm glad," my grandmother said, smiling. "Everyone's still in the fields, and we can all get to know each other before dinner. Would either of you like something cold to drink? I have iced tea . . . or, if you'd like, a glass of pineapple wine?"

Dan shook his head. "Not for me, but thanks. I think I'll leave you two to talk while I run over to Kimo's place for a minute." He smiled at my grandmother. "If that's all right, Mrs. Kalama?"

"Of course. Do run along."

A few more pleasantries were exchanged, and we watched him drive off in the Jeep.

"Let's go around to the kitchen," my grandmother said, taking my hand. As I walked beside her through the side garden toward the back of the house, the lavish fragrances and colors were almost too much; I had a sense of unreality that made it somewhat difficult to keep my balance. My grandmother seemed to sense this, keeping a firm but gentle grip on my arm.

The small girl from the verandah earlier ran ahead of us. Her name was Noelani, my grandmother said—

No-ay-lah-knee—which meant "Mist of Heaven."

"Our people are beginning to give their children the old names again," she added, "which makes me quite happy. There is so much poetry in them."

Noelani turned out to be extremely shy. She uttered barely three words to me, though she kept casting glances my way and smiling.

"Her mother is Lu," my grandmother said. "Deborah's daughter. I watch over her while Lu works her own kiosk at the Ka'ahumanu Mall. She has a lovely artistic talent, which she uses to make handpainted bells, like wind chimes."

"They sound wonderful. How many sisters and brothers did my mother have?" I asked.

"Three sisters . . . two brothers. Not all of them can be here for dinner tonight, but they do want very much to meet you. Your aunt Deborah will be here, and your two uncles, Robert and James. Several of the *keiki* will come for dinner, of course. Even the younger ones work in the family taro fields when school is out, though of course we don't work them too hard." She smiled, and her dark eyes twinkled. "Just enough to give their little spirits a chance to connect with the land."

"*Keiki*?" I asked.

"Children. They all want to meet you, Kate."

She must have noted my crestfallen expression at the thought of being faced with a crowd. Squeezing my hand, she said, "Don't worry. You'll find them easy to take. They'll be kind to you at first out of respect for your mother. Then they'll be kind because they love you . . . as I already do."

I didn't know what to say. Again, tears stung my eyes.

It was, perhaps, my grandmother's ready acceptance of me that was overwhelming. Only a day before, I'd been—I had thought—alone in the world. I'd become accustomed to being alone. And though I'd longed at times to be part of the kind of big family gathering that seemed planned for tonight, it was intimidating as well. It was difficult, in fact, to return my grandmother's words of love, though I had already begun to feel love for her. It was impossible not to respond to so kind and gentle a woman.

Aside from that there was something else—a sense that I already knew my grandmother, and had for a very long time.

Our walk took us over an emerald green lawn surrounded by shrubbery and flowers in such startling reds, pinks, oranges, and golds, they made me blink. I couldn't help thinking that this was precisely the kind of garden Caroline, in my suspense novel, dreamed of being married in. It was almost as if I'd seen it beforehand, in my mind.

"Your grandfather takes care of all this himself," my grandmother said proudly. "He talks to the plants as he works, and they give back every ounce of his love by just growing and growing. We can hardly keep them down."

This didn't sound like a man who was "difficult," as Sharon had described him. "Will he be at dinner?" I wondered.

My grandmother hesitated before answering, "Yes . . . yes, I think Keoki will join us." Her tone, however, indicated that she wasn't entirely certain.

I wondered if he was avoiding me. "Where is my grandfather now?"

"Keoki has been with the rest in the taro fields since early morning. As you may know, we Hawaiians are very hardworking, though we loathe nine-to-five. We tend to prefer our own businesses, where those who

don't mind working nine-to-five can do that for us.''
She smiled.

"And Deborah?" I asked. "Noelani's grandmother?" The child had disappeared, giving us both
a quick smile and running into the house.

"Oh, you'll like your aunt Deborah, I'm sure. She's
your mother's younger sister—divorced, I'm sorry to
say. She is, however, the one who talked us all into
working the land again. Before that, we were a family . . ." She hesitated. "Well, let me simply say that
life as we had come to know it was causing separa-
tions between us. We'd become scattered. Luce's leaving here and moving to the mainland, just when she
was about to bring new life into the world . . ."

She paused and turned to me, touching my cheek
gently. "You, Kate. You have no idea how much we'd
looked forward to having you with us."

"I'm sorry, Grandmother. Why did she leave? What
happened?"

Her dark eyes searched mine. "You don't know?
No one's ever told you?"

"Not a thing, other than that she married my father,
became pregnant with me, and they decided then to
live in California. My grandmother McKenna didn't
talk about them much. She didn't believe in dwelling
on the past."

My grandmother's eyes were gentle. "Perhaps, too,
she did not want you to think ill of her?"

"I don't understand. Why would I?"

We began to walk again, slowly. "There is absolutely no reason why you *should* think ill of your father's mother, my dear. However, she might have
thought you would. It was your grandmother Mc-
Kenna, you see, who insisted your father return home
and bring Luce with him. It was she who insisted that
her only grandchild be raised in California. Luce

didn't want to leave her home, but your father felt he
must obey your grandmother's wishes.''

"I'm sorry," I said again. "I didn't know."

"Well, it's an old story, one that we here in the
islands are familiar with. After World War Two, our
women left in droves with their navy husbands. What
disturbed me most, however, was not so much the loss
of your mother from my life—though that was difficult enough—but my fear for her well-being.''

I looked at her. "Fear? You had reason to think
she'd be unsafe in California?"

"Oh, not in the way you might mean. Your father,
though there was never time to get to know him very
well, seemed a good-hearted enough man. No, I worried more for Luce's spirit, and that she might become
homesick for her family and the islands. I knew that
if my daughter's *mana* were to leave her, it would be
only a matter of time . . ." My grandmother sighed
and shook her head.

"Till she died, you mean? Are you saying you think
my mother died because she lost her spirit?"

I cast back in memory and could recall only a shad-
owy figure in a bed, a woman with long dark hair, ill
for what seemed a very long time. I was three, then,
and allowed into her room only occasionally. I remembered having to stand on tiptoe by the bed to see her.
Later, I heard the word *cancer* spoken by my grandmother to a friend, who had asked about my mother's
illness.

"She had cancer . . ." I said now. "That was what
killed her."

"Ah, but cancer is a disease of despair, Kate. You
see?"

A disease of despair.

As my grandmother said those words, I thought not
only of my mother, but of Nahi'ena'ena. When read-

ing of her death shortly after giving birth to a stillborn child, I had wondered if she'd succumbed to despair.

"Do you blame my grandmother McKenna, then, for my mother's death?" I asked. "For forcing her to leave her home?"

My new grandmother stopped walking and gave me a quick hug. "Oh, my dear child, there is nothing to blame anyone for. Your mother made her choice, and that was her right. As for your grandmother, it was natural for her to have wanted her family with her. We Hawaiians, too, are very strong on *ohana* . . . family. Therefore, even though we grieved for our own loss, we understood why your father's mother did as she did. As for your father, we could only admire him for honoring her wishes."

"Yet you do think my mother's illness stemmed from despair because she missed her family?" I pressed.

"I can only judge by her letters to us. Would you like to read them while you're here?"

"My mother left letters?" It was almost too much to have hoped for—that I might now come to "know" my mother through the written word, which had always meant so much to me. "I would love to read them," I said.

My grandmother squeezed my shoulder, and we began to walk again. "Then you shall. Why don't we go into the kitchen now, and have some tea?"

Skirting a stand of thick shrubbery, we came upon a backyard, where the scenery changed so drastically, I had to struggle to hide my surprise. Here, among well-tended flowers and small blossoming trees, were rusted frames of several old cars, scattered mechanical parts, and a messy pile of empty soft-drink cans. The difference between this and the front of the house was like night and day.

"My youngest grandson," my grandmother said with a sigh, noting my surprise. But she followed the sigh with a light cascade of laughter. "Deborah's son—Damien. He's named after Father Damien, a true saint, who worked with the lepers in Molokai. I'm afraid *our* Damien is still 'finding' himself."

She gave a light shrug. "I honor his path, while not necessarily applauding it. I do request that he confine himself to the backyard, and that at least once a week he clean up everything but the cars. Also, he must dispose of his trash properly, so that it does not offend Mother Earth."

Again, a sigh. "Unfortunately, I couldn't find him to request that he clean up today. I suspect he's with his friends at Hookipa, surfing."

She bent down to pick up an empty can, dropping it into a recycling pail nearby. "My grandson is good for me. By creating this little island of chaos in the midst of my lovely home, he reminds me not to become too smug in the lovely things I have acquired. He reminds me of what life is for every one of us— nothing perfect or without flaw. At times I come out here and sit, just staring at all this and thinking. Then I look up to where the mountain meets the sky, and I see the astounding pink of a setting sun as it tumbles out of sight, or hear the soft chatter of hundreds of little mynah birds settling in for the night. In those moments I know I have nothing to complain about. Nothing at all."

Following her gaze, which was tender and dreamy, to the rim of mountain, I could see that setting sun as if she had painted an image of it in oils.

"I didn't know I had a grandmother who was a poet," I said, smiling. "I think I like that."

She put an arm about my shoulders and hugged me. "And I am fascinated with your books," she responded with that ever-present smile. "I've read every one of them, Kate. Does that surprise you?"

"Not at all," I said, laughing. "Nothing you might do or say could surprise me now, Grandmother."

I was wrong, of course. I spoke too soon.

In the cool kitchen with its blue-and-white-checkered curtains and screened windows along an entire side, I sat at a long wooden table and sipped iced tea that had been laced with mint from my grandfather's garden. A pot simmered on the stove, while a large ceiling fan sent a spicy hint of gingered pork drifting past my nostrils, making my stomach growl.

Taking a slice of mango from a plate set before me, I bit into it, enjoying the cool, sweet taste. The last morsel was just going down when my grandmother caught me unawares.

"Tell me about our little princess, Kate. I understand she's been visiting you."

My hand paused on the way to a napkin. I sat back and said cautiously, "Sharon told you? What on earth made her think she had the right to tell anyone, even you—?"

My grandmother shook her head. "Not Sharon."

"Who, then? I don't understand."

"Well, my dear, one might say I got it straight from the horse's mouth."

CHAPTER 19

"You've seen her too?" I said, bewildered. "Nahi'ena'ena?"

"Only in my mind. Sometimes, when I've been in prayer, I've seen Nahi'ena'ena's face as if in a dream . . . and when I see her, you are there too, standing behind and slightly above her. Like a guardian angel, Kate." She reached for my hand. "That's how I knew you would come."

I sat back, astounded. "I'm sorry, Grandmother. I just don't get any of this, not at all."

She smiled. Releasing my hand, she took a napkin and handed it to me. "Well, when you think of it, Kate, it's not so odd. Our family goes way back to Nahi'ena'ena's. There's a very strong tie."

I couldn't hide my surprise.

"Oh, we weren't in the royal line," she said. "Far from it. But if one traces my line back—and therefore yours, as well—one finds an ancestor, a young woman who served Nahi'ena'ena from childhood to adulthood. Her name, the stories tell us, was Melika."

"Melika." The name resounded within me as I spoke it. There was a strange familiarity to it. "What more do you know about her?" I asked.

"Melika was, apparently, only one of many such servants to Nahi'ena'ena, though the stories tell us she held the honored role of midwife when Nahi'ena'ena's child was born. A sad story . . . you may have heard it?"

"Yes. The baby was stillborn, and Nahi'ena'ena died shortly after that."

My grandmother nodded. "There may have been other midwives or servants involved in the birth. Melika, however, was said to have been the one most versed in the use of roots and herbs for medicinal purposes. According to the stories that tell our family's history, this was a gift handed down to us through the generations. Every woman in our family was trained in and practiced the old ways of healing, right up to this generation. Right up to you, Kate. Unless . . ."

I shook my head. "I once took St. John's Wort for an entire month for insomnia, but that's about all. It worked like a dream."

"Ah . . ." she said. "One cannot get away from one's roots, Kate . . . no matter how hard one might try."

"Grandmother, I've never deliberately *not* wanted to know my family. It's just that I never deliberately pursued it, either. I've always been so . . . busy."

"Or, for some reason you've never understood," she said wisely, "perhaps you were deliberately holding back?"

"I suppose that might be it," I admitted reluctantly.

Her tone was gentle. "Perhaps something in you knew what you would be faced with here on Maui, Kate."

"Nahi'ena'ena, you mean? You think my being here is somehow predestined?" As I said the words, I went cold, despite the hot day. "Surely you don't think Nahi'ena'ena's been sort of . . . hanging around, waiting for me?" I tried to laugh, but it didn't come out quite right.

"Not for your arrival only. For matters to come together . . . the right people, at the right time."

"And those people would be?"

"Well, you, certainly. Perhaps someone in our family. *Your* family, now." Her eyes studied me, and for the first time I thought I detected a flicker of worry. "As for Dan Kala . . ."

I frowned. "What about him?"

"Kate, Sharon has told us a bit about how you came to be at Pua'lani. You don't really believe it's coincidence you met Dan Kala and ended up there? At a place where Nahi'ena'ena has been known to appear in the past?"

"No . . ." I agreed. "I don't believe it's coincidence. I just don't know, yet, what it *is*. That's the hell of it." I looked at her. "Sorry."

"And how do you *feel* about Dan Kala?" she asked.

I shrugged. "There are times when he's okay. Most of the time he's insufferable. A pain in the neck. If it weren't for Nahi'ena'ena, I wouldn't stay at Pua'lani a moment longer."

My grandmother shook her head. A brief sadness crossed her face. "Granddaughter, do you know what Nahi'ena'ena's spirit is most noted for?"

"No. But I suspect you're about to tell me."

She reached across the table for my hand. "My dear child, our little princess is most noted for bringing together star-crossed lovers who in some way harmed each other in the past."

After the initial surprise there was little time to ponder that, as assorted relatives began to arrive for dinner. My new family came tramping into the kitchen *en masse*: my aunt Deborah, dark and thin, almost stringy, but with beautiful eyes. The two uncles sent quick, curious smiles and ''Aloha''s in my direction. After that came children of varying ages, piling around me as if they already knew me. There were introductions, and some of the cousins offered hugs, though others held back shyly. The younger *keiki* names, many of which were Hawaiian, escaped me in the confusion. All told, I counted nineteen people in the room, plus Dan Kala, who arrived on their heels and stood off to the side, arms folded, quietly observing as he leaned against the wall. A worried frown creased his forehead, and again I wondered what he was thinking, and why he hadn't wanted to tell me the night before about my family.

My grandmother had gone to the stove to ladle out rice, her dark hair now damp from perspiration, a few gray strands falling over her brow. She paused as another man entered the room—a man whose obvious age told me he must be my grandfather. A small silence fell. It seemed that the others held their breaths, waiting to see what might happen.

At first glance Keoki Kalama looked to be the opposite of his wife. Where she was tall and majestic in bearing—still quite youthful—he was short and seemingly ancient. Where she was open and accepting, he held himself in, peering at me through eyes that had so many folds of wrinkles around them, I wasn't sure if he was narrowing them at me or not. If I were a betting person, I'd have bet on the former, however.

''Keoki?'' my grandmother said, wiping her hands on a towel. She took my hand, leading me over to him. ''This is our granddaughter. Luce's daughter . . . Kate.''

I smiled and held out my arms as if to hug him, as I had my grandmother—but met empty air. My grandfather did not meet me halfway, and after a moment, my arms fell to my sides. I tried not to let my disappointment—and embarrassment—show.

"Keoki!" my grandmother admonished her husband.

Drawing himself up to his full height, which was still shorter than mine, he met my eyes with obvious reluctance. Finally, he stuck out his hand.

"*Keoki!*" my grandmother said more vehemently. "You act like a *haole*! And to your own flesh and blood!"

But he was adamant. He would not touch me, other than to shake my hand. I settled for that and reached out.

The dry, withered fingers surprised me with their grip. I felt a strange vibration run up my arm. Since there was no carpeting or any other apparent reason for static electricity, I had to believe my grandfather's energy had caused it.

But what was that in his eyes? Was it anger—or fear?

That it might be fear seemed to come from some level of knowledge beyond my normal consciousness.

I looked at my grandmother, who shook her head. She turned to her daughter, who, with my uncles, was washing her hands at the sink. "Deborah?"

My mother's younger sister—under fifty, I guessed, despite the threads of gray in her short dark hair—finished drying her hands and came over to me quickly and hugged me.

"*Aloha nui loa*," she said, grinning. "Welcome, Kate. We've been wanting to meet you for a very long time."

My grandfather stood off to the side, scowling.

"Well, now . . . let's all sit down and eat," my grandmother said, in the awkward but soothing manner of women everywhere whose husbands are being embarrassingly difficult.

Everyone sat. The dishes of steaming, fragrant food were passed, and the aunts, uncles, and *keiki* began chattering all at once.

"Tell us about California!"

"How long have you been here on the island?"

"How long have you been a writer?"

"Where do you get your ideas?"

"Tell us about Aunt Luce. Do you remember her at all?"

"How long can you stay?"

"Why don't you stay here with us? There's plenty of room, isn't there, Grandmother?"

And so it went, until finally my grandmother laughed and said, "Enough! You'll wear the poor child out. Let her eat her dinner in peace."

"I don't mind," I said. "I'm just very, very happy to be here."

I meant it, and my eyes met Dan Kala's across the dinner table. Then, as if drawn by my grandfather's strange, uncompromising energy, we both looked at him. He had been eating his dinner slowly, almost ceremonially, as if every morsel was sacred. He hadn't said a word and had barely looked up, in fact.

In that instant, as we glanced at him, he did. His eyes, nearly swallowed up by the vast amount of leathery wrinkles, fastened on me. In a slow, deliberate motion he set his fork down beside his plate.

"The child is a bastard," he said in a voice so sharp it sliced like a knife through the room. "A bastard, plain and simple. No one even knows who her father is."

CHAPTER 20

A terrible silence fell. The entire family, and Dan Kala, paused with their forks to their mouths and stared—first at my grandfather, then at me.

My aunt Deborah was the first to speak.

"Kate, are you finished? Why don't you and I take a little walk?"

She stood, and I looked at her numbly, unable to move. Getting up, Deborah came around to my chair, taking my hand. "Come, it's a lovely evening. Let's go out and watch the sunset."

I noted that my limbs moved, though I could barely feel them. They seemed disconnected from any other part of me. As we left the kitchen I saw that Dan Kala sat in the same position, still staring at my grandfather. I couldn't fathom his expression. The only thing that registered was that he hadn't once looked at me.

"You mustn't mind my father," Deborah said reassuringly. Her arm was about me, and she patted my shoulder as we walked. "He's an old man. Not senile, understand. Still sharp as a tack. But there are times when my father simply drifts into another world. He has that *kahuna*-like ability to see into the past, you know. Not always, but often, and at the most inopportune times. Now that I think of it, I doubt he was even thinking of you, and I'm sure the others have realized that too.''

''But—''

She paused, taking me gently by the shoulders. ''Kate, Jack McKenna was your father, there's no doubt about that. He and Luce were married in Honolulu, and she brought him here afterward to meet us. They were extremely happy together. And Luce was *delirious* with happiness when she found she was pregnant with you.''

Her words warmed me, and I was grateful for them. ''I guess it's just that what my grandfather said stirred up some old fears. I've always wondered why my father ran off after my mother died. I was only three at the time, and the only thing my grandmother told me about it, later, was that my mother's death broke his heart.''

''But you asked her where your father had gone?''

''She said she didn't know, and I believed her.''

We turned onto a narrow path lined with tall papaya trees and a ground cover of tiny blue flowers I couldn't name. When a fine rain began I was reminded that we were actually in the rain forest here.

''Do you want to go back?'' Deborah asked. ''It will probably stop soon . . . we could wait it out over there.''

She nodded in the direction of a white wrought-iron bench beneath a tree heavy with glossy green leaves, the branches bent like those of a weeping willow, nearly to the ground.

''I'd actually like to be alone a few minutes, if that's all right. I appreciate your kindness, Aunt Deborah—''

''Please, just call me Deborah.''

"Okay. Thanks. But do you mind if I just sit here by myself awhile?"

"Not at all." She scanned my face. "Kate . . . you're not still upset?"

"Not upset. But I do feel a bit awkward. All those people . . ." My smile was rueful.

She laughed gently. "Those people are your family now, Kate. You needn't feel embarrassed. But I know what you mean. When we're all together, we can be quite an intimidating crowd."

She turned to go, then came back for a final hug. "Please don't decide about your grandfather yet. Give him time. He's a good man, at heart. Let him tell you why he behaved the way he did. I imagine his reasons will surprise you."

I wanted to believe what Deborah said, but couldn't forget the reluctance with which my grandfather had greeted me. There was more going on here than met the eye, and I thought that Sharon and Dan could both have told me more. I wondered, not for the first time, why they hadn't.

As I sat on the wrought-iron bench beneath the limbs of this ancient tree, gazing around at this beautiful garden, I knew I should feel relaxed and at peace here. Yet the longer I sat the more depression set in, and the more clouds of darkness surrounded me.

My thoughts went back to my mother and her death. For the first time in years I remembered a day when she had reached out a hand to me as I sat beside her on her bed. The hand frightened me with its terrible lack of weight, the bones standing out in sharp relief, the flesh prematurely wrinkled and hanging loose over the knuckles. Young as I was, I knew my mother was dying, and as she touched me with that skeletonlike hand, I feared that if I were to look up from it, I would see only a skull.

"Don't be afraid, Kit-Kat," she whispered then. "I won't leave you. I'll always be with you. I swear."

Later, standing at the side of her grave, I recalled those words with much bitterness, wanting to cry out, "You lied! You said you wouldn't leave!" Instead, I took the anger and grief inside and held it there.

I could only wonder, now, how much those desperate emotions had tainted my life and relationships. Perhaps being here with my mother's family would help, I thought. Perhaps I should move here to stay . . .

It was while I pondered these things that I began to have a sense of being unsafe—specifically, this moment, under this tree. Stiffening, I looked around. There was not much to see beyond the low-lying branches . . . only hazy lights emanating from the front of the house, slanting out and across the verandah and down the four or five stairs. The rest of the garden was dark, aside from wispy gray shadows cast by a full moon. The rain had stopped. The sky was clear. Still, every nerve in my body tensed, as if for flight.

"Hello?" I called out tentatively. "Is someone there?"

No answer. Nothing but a sound—a crackle, as of twigs snapping underfoot. Troubled, I thought of the early-morning intruder at Pua'lani. The feeling was strong, suddenly, that someone was watching.

I turned on the bench to look behind me, straining my ears to hear even the slightest sound. For several long moments I sat that way, on the alert.

Nothing.

I began, just a bit, to relax. But then something touched my foot—bare except for the strap of a sandal. I jerked to my feet and screamed, as, looking down, I saw that the entire ground around me was covered with tiny lizards. There were dozens, possibly hundreds, and I couldn't move in any direction without stepping on them. Several slid over my feet then, and one ran up my leg, under my dress. Letting out another yell, I jumped up onto the bench, pushing at the one beneath my dress, shaking it and the lizards on my feet free as best I could—stomping and kicking to get them away.

It was thus that Dan Kala, followed by the others, found me.

"Is this some new kind of dance I don't know about?" he asked in a tone of mild amusement.

My family crowded around. "Are you all right?" Deborah asked worriedly.

"We heard you scream," my grandmother added, reaching out. "Kate, what happened?"

I brushed my hair back from my face. "Be careful," I said, shakily. "Don't come close. There are lizards—geckos—hundreds of them, right there." I pointed to the ground.

Dan ignored my warning and walked over to me, his eyes scanning the spot where the geckos had been. There wasn't a sign of them now.

"You must have frightened them off," he said, dubiously. "Can't say I'm surprised."

I looked beyond him to where my grandfather stood, half in moon-shadow, his expression solemn and thoughtful.

"You were afraid of these geckos?" he asked in a tone that told me he questioned my sanity.

I looked away, embarrassed now. "They startled me. There really were hundreds," I added lamely. "They ran over my feet."

"Geckos are good luck," my grandfather responded, as if to a child. "Your mother undoubtedly sent them to protect you."

All eyes turned to him. "What are you saying?" my grandmother asked. "You think Luce was here?"

My grandfather only looked at me.

"I . . . I *was* thinking about her," I said, "just before this happened. Then something made me afraid."

"You poor child," my grandmother said. "What were you afraid of, Kate?"

It all seemed so ridiculous now. "I don't know. I just . . . thought I heard something."

"You're all right now, though?" Deborah asked.

I nodded.

She smiled and made a shepherding motion to the rest of the group. "Why don't we all go inside, then? My father"—she looked at Keoki—"has something he would like to speak with you about, Kate."

I hesitated, my eyes warily on the ground.

"Oh, for heaven's sake," Dan Kala said impatiently. "Here." He held out his arms, and despite my protestations, scooped me up and carried me over his shoulder, out from under the tree. When we reached the path to the house, he set me unceremoniously down.

"You know," he grumbled, "you are the most high-maintenance woman I've ever known."

The younger cousins laughed, though not derisively. They were enjoying the show. Only my grandmother did not smile. Rather, she looked at Dan Kala, then at me, and frowned.

CHAPTER 21

I walked beside Deborah back to the house, feeling tense about this thing my grandfather "wanted to talk to me about." I cast a questioning glance at my aunt, who remained silent, but took my hand in a firm, reassuring grip.

Once inside, everyone gathered in the huge living room. Screened windows across the front looked out onto the verandah, while ceiling fans sent a light breeze wafting from corner to corner. Cushions on the rattan sofa and chairs were white, splashed with pink flowers and large green leaves, and on the floor was a dark green mat of the type often seen in beach houses, or country vacation homes. It was clear the younger children had been playing there; toys were scattered everywhere.

As we entered through the front, a young man of about seventeen came from the back. He carried a surfboard under one arm. In his other arm were various rags and a large can of what appeared to be some sort of cleaning material. He had a narrow face with high cheekbones, like Deborah, and a thick shock of unruly dark hair

"Damien," Deborah said with a trace of irritation,

"where on earth have you been? You were supposed to have been home in time for dinner."

He tossed her a look but was silent as he crossed the room in the opposite direction to set his surfboard upright against the wall. On a patch of floor that was bare and obviously worn from similar activity, he set the rags, then squatted to open the can.

Deborah's mouth tightened. "Damien . . . this is your cousin from the mainland. I would appreciate it if you would come here and greet her properly."

He shot a dark look my way, but didn't budge.

"Damien!"

I wondered what his problem was. It seemed obvious he wanted nothing to do with me. Was it only that I'd interrupted his fun at Hookipa?

"That's okay," I said, smiling, in an effort to keep the peace. "I don't like to be interrupted when I'm working, either. Damien and I can get to know each other later."

That won me the briefest of glances. My grandfather at that moment demanded attention by clearing his throat. I turned to see that he sat now at a library-sized table in a corner, with a thick book before him. Behind him were bookshelves from floor to ceiling, and in the corner itself was a statue of the Sacred Heart. A bouquet of flowers and a large red votive candle rested at the foot of the statue. The candle had been lit, and around the neck of Jesus had been hung a plumeria lei.

Dan Kala stood across from my grandfather at the table, looking as if he'd rather be anywhere but here. I saw that a chair had been pulled out in readiness for me. It seemed I didn't have much choice, and if there ever was a set-up, I thought, this was it. They must have been talking about this—about me—all the while I was in the garden alone.

Going along with the royal command for the moment, I crossed over and sat. A lamp with a brown woven shade hung over the table, casting harsh light on my grandfather's face. The wrinkles seemed deeper than ever. But there was strength in those eyes. And something else, something that surprised me, as it had earlier—fear.

"Your grandmother tells me you have been visiting with our princess," my grandfather said without preamble.

"Visiting?" I answered carefully. "That's one way to put it, I suppose."

"And what precisely is your interest in Nahi'ena'ena? Are you writing a book about her?"

I was a bit put off by the clipped tone but decided to let it pass. "No ... At least, I don't think so. I am writing down my experiences of the past few days. I haven't thought about it as a book yet."

The eyes narrowed. "And if you were to write such a book, what kind of book would it be? A novel? Or would you write the truth?"

"I try always to write the truth," I answered testily. "Even in my novels. But then again," I pressed, "what is truth? Yours may not be the same as mine."

For the first time, I sensed I'd caught my grandfather's full attention. Seizing the moment, I continued. "I think Nahi'ena'ena is trying to tell me something. I think there's something she wants me to do for her."

There was an instant of silence, after which he made a scoffing sound. "What could a *haole* possibly do for a Maui princess?"

"It appears to me," I said firmly, "that I must not be a *haole* anymore. If I'm your granddaughter, that makes me one of you."

My grandfather's gaze searched my face and held there. I stiffened myself not to weaken and look away, though if he'd rejected me in that moment, I think I would have run.

My grandmother came to stand behind her husband, massaging the narrow shoulders. "It will be all right, Keoki. It *will*. Luce's child is with us now. Can't you just be grateful for that? Can't you welcome her, as Luce would have wanted?" She looked over at me. "Look at her, Keoki, it's Luce sitting there facing us. It's Luce speaking through her voice, and it's Luce in her eyes. Would you turn your own daughter away— as well as her grown child?"

Through the dry, narrow lips escaped a deep breath, ending in a sigh. With that sigh seemed to come years of anger and grief. They were nearly visible, to my mind, hovering for a moment between us like a cloud. Then my grandfather spoke.

"You are in grave danger here, Luce's child. It would have been far better had you never come."

CHAPTER 22

A heavy silence fell. The sun dipped low behind the western mountains, and the room darkened around us. I was aware of my shy uncles excusing themselves to check on something in the fields. Deborah disappeared upstairs with Noelani, whispering that she would tuck her in, and the various cousins wandered off to find other entertainment. Damien came to sit on the floor beside my grandfather, his back propped against the wall. He still did not look at me, but concentrated on cleaning his nails with a rather lethal-looking fish-gutting knife.

Dan Kala seated himself beside me, while my grandmother took a chair across from me, next to her husband.

I faced my grandfather. "What is it?" I said, my voice sharper than I'd intended. "What is this about?"

His glance fell briefly on the book before him. With a delicate gesture, he smoothed the thin pages with his hand. Then he looked back at me, and I saw the distress in his eyes.

Just say it, I thought, *just say it, for God's sake*. I knew in that instant that he'd read my thoughts. My grandfather sighed, but began.

"When the missionaries came, Granddaughter, they recorded many of our family histories, first from the stories that had been handed down, and then from actual events they themselves witnessed. Included in this book is the history of your grandmother's family and mine, including certain incidents that took place at the time Princess Nahiʻenaʻena and her brother, Kamehameha III, were married. This written history confirms what I was told as a child." He paused. "It is for this reason that I feel you should not have come."

My first reaction was one of surprise that this man—whom I had at first nearly dismissed as a short, wizened old grouch—now spoke in such a scholarly, well-educated tone. With his last words, however, the atmosphere in the room seemed to change and become dark.

"The point is, I did come," I said softly. "And now that I'm here, you might as well tell me the rest."

His gaze met mine and held. My grandmother reached over and pressed his arm. "Tell her, Keoki," she murmured. "She has a right to know."

"Yes, do go on," I said with a shade of irritation.

It was with obvious reluctance that he began again. "According to the stories, during the time Nahiʻenaʻena and Kamehameha III were married, an ancestor of mine—who was known only as Komohu—was said to be close to the royal court. There is little known about Komohu, as to his background. We do have it as fact, however, that he became a most powerful *kahuna anaʻana*, and was greatly feared for those powers."

"An evil *kahuna*?" I asked, remembering this phrase from my reading.

"Unfortunately, that seems to be so. The one other thing we know about Komohu is that he is said to have committed a terrible deed during this time, and for this reason was banished from the court." My grandfather hesitated, then looked at me. "Nothing, I might add, seems to have stopped Komohu from perpetrating his foul deeds upon innocent victims . . . right up to this time."

"Are you saying he harms innocent people? Even now?"

He reached over and covered his wife's hand. "I—your grandmother and I, that is—believe that to be true."

I sat back, folding my arms and narrowing my eyes. "Tell me what this Komohu has done. Or what you believe he's done." Evil *kahuna* or not, he certainly had my grandfather hornswoggled. And that was half the battle, wasn't it? Instilling a belief in evil, and thereby creating a door for it to walk through?

My grandmother spoke. "Keoki and I had no idea what was really going on, Kate, till the day we married. On our brief honeymoon we sat together on the beach and told each other stories . . . family histories . . . and we read this book, which had been handed down through Keoki's family, and given to us the day we wed. Understand, there are many family histories in this book. Keoki's family either hadn't read my family history, or simply never made the connection between his line and mine. If they had . . . it's quite possible we might not have married."

"Connection?" I said. For a moment I was afraid she was going to tell me that she and my grandfather had turned out to be closely related. That turned out not to be the case, however.

"I told you about Melika, my ancestor," she said, "the one who was Nahi'ena'ena's midwife? She and Komohu, Keoki's ancestor, were said to be the two closest people, at one time, to the royal pair. That, of course, would be before Komohu was banished from the court.''

"I see. So your two ancestors knew each other. Go on, Grandmother.''

"We believe, now, Kate, that the day we married— for reasons we don't understand but feel certain go back to that time—we set into motion certain forces that have brought harm to both our families. Seemingly, for all time.''

I fell silent, thinking. Hornswoggled or not, this was heavy stuff. And who was I to discount it—I who not only had visions night and day but had been declared crazy by a former lover?

"What kind of harm?'' I said finally.

"Death and misfortune for both our families,'' my grandfather answered, his voice heavy. He looked at my grandmother, and something I could only call intense love seemed to pass between them . . . the kind of love that lasts through things like death and misfortune. I couldn't help but feel envious.

"When you say death, are you referring to my mother's?'' I asked.

"That, of course,'' my grandfather said. "Losing our beloved daughter at such a young age was part of it. There has been much more, however. In my own family there have been any number of suspicious deaths in the years since your grandmother and I wed. As to our financial fortunes''—he shrugged—"every other year, our taro crops fail, whether from disease or too much rain.''

"But surely, Grandfather, with the weather all over the world changing so much, that could be attributed to natural causes.''

My grandfather glanced at Dan Kala. "If so, my neighbors do not seem affected by these natural causes,'' he said pointedly.

Dan evaded his eyes. "It's true, my crops haven't failed in the time I've been here," he said reluctantly.

"And yet, it seems you have the same weather—not to mention less help—than I."

Shifting uneasily in his chair, Dan didn't respond.

"Let me get this straight," I said. "Grandfather, are you saying you believe this Komohu has placed a curse on you? And if so, why? What would be his motive?" As a writer of suspense, I knew that motive was everything. It was where mayhem began, and where it ended.

"As to motive, we can't possibly know," my grandmother answered. "However, it might be more accurate to say that if there is a curse, it's been on *my* family—and that it only became Keoki's problem when he married me. Kate, in my line the suspicious deaths or accidents go back much further—at least to the days of Nahi'ena'ena and Kamehameha III. As for more recent time, the day your mother was born I nearly drowned in the *tsunami* that struck our shores in 1946. I remember it so clearly . . . it was April first, and your mother always made a joke of having been an April Fool's baby." Her face clouded over. "Kate, if I'd lost my life that day, neither your mother nor you would ever have been born."

"What happened?" I said, intrigued. At the same time a thread of fear ran through me.

"Oh . . . I was young. And I wasn't thinking. Like many other spectators, I had walked to the bottom of the cliff, amazed and bewildered as to why the entire harbor had suddenly become devoid of water. There was no television on Maui in those days, no on-the-hour news reports . . . and it all happened so fast. Few of us knew what it was, you see. We didn't know that *tsunamis* sucked the water away from the shore, then barreled it all back in at terrifying speeds and heights. When this indeed happened, some believed God had sent the world a warning, a sign.''

''And you? What happened to you, Grandmother?''

''I was paralyzed with fear when I saw that mountain of water coming toward me. I was nine months pregnant and burdened by all that excess weight. It seemed impossible, I thought, to run fast enough to get away. Then suddenly, at the last moment, I felt as if I were being lifted by unseen hands. I somehow found myself at the top of the cliff, unharmed, and right after that I was whisked to the emergency hospital. Your mother was born . . . and what had been a moment of horror became a miracle.''

Fixing her gaze on me, she added, ''Kate, that *tsunami* left fourteen dead, including seven tiny children between the ages of three months and four years. Many infants were swept out to sea and never found. That I was spared . . . well, you can understand why I believe very strongly, now, in the power of divine intervention.''

I was deeply moved by her story. ''Yes, of course I do. Grandmother, how many other incidents have there been in your family?''

''Far too many, I'm afraid. Numerable unexplained accidents and financial misfortune throughout the years. The worst, however, were the early deaths. My younger brother died of a mysterious virus during World War Two. Two aunts died at a very young age. And then, Luce . . . she was only twenty-one, you know.''

''No . . . I didn't know,'' I said, surprised. *Twenty-one.* I'd been thinking of my mother all my life as being older, when in fact she was little more than a teenager when she left here. And pregnant with me.

I still didn't know if I bought this story about an

evil *kahuna*, though. The doubt must have shown on my face.

My grandmother said with dignity, "We've lived with this a very long time, Kate. It seems a reasonable—if not the only possible—explanation. According to our history, *kahunas* have been known to do such things, destroying families, careers, and even fortunes, for all time."

"I'm sorry, Grandmother." I seemed to be apologizing a lot today. "It's just . . ."

An evil kahuna . . . and a family curse? Could it be true? Or only superstition? Trouble stalks certain families all the time. Most of them don't have medicine men to blame it on, though.

"Okay, let's say this Komohu is responsible for a curse," I said. "There's something that still doesn't fit. If Komohu was *Grandfather's* ancestor, why was *your* family line cursed before *his*? And where does Melika come in—if at all? I mean, I suppose she might have just been around, and perfectly innocent—but if I were writing this mystery, I'd be sure they were connected somehow."

My grandmother sighed. "These are questions we have asked ourselves since the day we first put all this together. There's simply no answer, Kate. The only thing we know for certain is that everyone in our combined families has been plagued by an unusual amount of tragedy, to a lesser or greater degree."

I met her worried eyes. "And now you know," she said gently, "why your grandfather was reluctant to greet you. Keoki did not mean to be unaccepting of you. He simply believes you are not safe here."

As she spoke the words "not safe," it became full-blown, then—the fear.

"What do you think is going to happen?" I said, my eyes going warily to my grandfather.

"I think, Granddaughter, that one of these days when your spirit is most vulnerable and unprotected, Komohu will come after you—just as he came for your mother and the others. For that matter, I fear that he already has."

We sat looking at each other silently for several moments after that. Our thoughts were interrupted finally by the ringing of the phone. Deborah came from upstairs. "Dan, it's for you. Kimo. You can take it in the kitchen if you'd like."

He thanked her and left to answer the call. Deborah slid into the seat on my right, sending a questioning glance from one to the other of us, and finally to Damien, who still sat on the floor, his back against the wall. He gave a dismissive shrug and looked away. Deborah's mouth tightened.

"What's going on?" she asked her parents. "Have you told her?"

"Oh, they've told me, all right," I said. "I'm just trying to take it all in." I rubbed my bare arms, feeling chilled.

"My father," Deborah said gently, "is particularly worried about you because of your visits, as he calls them, with Nahi'ena'ena. He believes you are opening yourself to the gravest possible danger this way."

I looked at my grandfather. "Is that true?"

He shrugged. "In allowing yourself to be carried back into that time, you will almost certainly cross paths with Komohu. If you had stayed away from Maui—if you had never come to these shores—the outcome might have been different for you."

"You mean, I might not have drawn Komohu's attention to me." I thought then of the pain I'd had during the visions. Pain that somehow, in my heart, I could not attribute to either Nahi'ena'ena or Margo. I remembered how I'd come out of some of those visions afraid.

Komohu? There was no way to tell.

"Well . . ." I said heavily, "there must be some way to break this curse."

Everyone looked at me. No one responded, and I knew I hadn't been the first in the family to think this, or to find that it wasn't so easy a task.

I sat back, feeling drained suddenly. "You know . . . if I hadn't already had those visions, I don't know if I'd believe any of this. Now . . ." I gave a shrug. "Tell me more about this Komohu. Why do you think he was banished from court? Have you any clue?"

My grandmother looked uneasily at her husband, then at me. "No one can know for certain, of course. But from the stories handed down through our families, we believe Komohu . . ." She paused. "We think it's possible he murdered Nahi'ena'ena's child."

"*Murdered?*" I couldn't hide my shock.

"There have been rumors throughout the years," my grandfather said. "In the minds of some of our people—certainly not all—there has always been a mystery surrounding the death of that child. Some believe he may have been murdered at birth, to prevent him from carrying on the royal line. As you may know, there was a great deal of political intrigue surrounding the royal court at the time Nahi'ena'ena and her brother, Kamehameha III, married. There were those among our people who turned against the royal pair because they were committed to maintaining the old Hawaiian traditions. A great deal of money and power were offered to certain persons in or surrounding the royal court, provided they would turn against Nahi'ena'ena and Kauikeaouli, and align themselves, instead, with church and political leaders. The plan being, of course, to bring about radical change."

"But, *murder*?" I said. "Of a baby? A child?"

"For a *kahuna ana'ana*," my grandfather pointed out, though it clearly pained him to say it, "stopping a child from breathing at its birth would have been a comparatively simple matter. In those days there were *kahunas* of varying powers, just as there are now. Some were mere charlatans, while others could control the elements, such as the wind and weather. Some were healers, and some the opposite. The *kahuna ana'anas*, for instance, were experts in the practice of the death prayer. Komohu was one of the latter, we are told, though his evil side was apparently hidden for quite some time. He eventually fell out of favor with Nahi'ena'ena and her brother. No one is certain why this happened. The rumors, however, persist."

"But that's horrible." Something began to nag at my mind, then. A seeming contradiction.

"Grandfather . . . Grandmother . . . what if your suspicions about Komohu are right? And what if the curse didn't come from Komohu? Nahi'ena'ena was said to have had powerful *mana*. What if it was she who cursed both your families, out of revenge for the murder of her child?"

My grandmother frowned. "I don't see . . ."

"Because they acted together! The midwife—your ancestor, Grandmother, and the *kahuna*"—I looked at my grandfather—"who was yours."

My grandmother covered her mouth in horror. "I can't believe . . ." But a flicker of doubt crossed her face.

"What is it?" I said.

"Melika. The stories tell us she disappeared . . . the same night Nahi'ena'ena gave birth to her stillborn child."

* * *

"I will not run, Grandfather," I said moments later. "It seems to me that whoever is in charge of this curse, whether it's Nahi'ena'ena or Komohu, they've pretty much got me already. The only way out now is to stand up and fight."

My grandfather searched my eyes. "Have you any idea what you might be letting yourself in for?"

"Oh, I think I have some idea. Abdominal pain, headaches, wrists that burn for no apparent reason . . ."

Everyone's eyes fastened on me with something like horror. My grandfather leaned forward anxiously. "Are you saying it's begun?"

"That would be my guess."

With everyone's eyes on me, I told them about the time I'd awakened on my kitchen floor, my stomach in agony, just after Nahi'ena'ena had gone to the hut in the woods—apparently seeking pain. And then about the burning wrists. "But it was all right," I added quickly. "It didn't last. It went away."

My grandmother paled. "Oh, Kate, this is too much. You must stop these visions now!"

"She won't be able to stop them," my grandfather said quietly.

My grandmother turned to him. "What are you talking about, Keoki? This is Luce's child we're talking about. There must be a way—"

"Sharon," I interrupted. "She might help."

They looked at me.

"She said she would work with me. Dispel the evil spirits, so to speak." I tried a smile, which failed.

At that point, Dan came back into the room, clearly distracted. "Mr. and Mrs. Kalama, everyone—I'm sorry, but I have to leave. A transformer blew in that last rain, and we've got to clear the wires before the next storm. Kate—''

"Don't worry about me," I said. "I can walk back. It's not that far."

There were several arguments to that, and I finally gave in for the moment and accepted that someone from the house would drive me.

"She'll be in good hands," Deborah assured him.

Dan nodded—seemingly relieved to have me off his hands. "All right, then. See you back there."

We watched him leave, and I thought about what my grandmother had said: *Nahiʻenaʻena is known for bringing together star-crossed lovers who have harmed each other in another life.*

Dan Kala? And me? No way in hell.

Turning back to the table, I said, "Well . . . where were we?"

"Where we were," my grandfather said sternly, "is that you worry me, Granddaughter. You do not seem to be taking this danger as seriously as you might."

"Grandfather, it isn't that I'm not afraid. I am. But running isn't my style."

"I think we should contact Sharon right away, before she goes back to Oahu," Deborah said. "I'll call her later on tonight, if that's all right with you, Kate? She had tickets to take her parents to the county fair tonight. Otherwise, she might have been here."

"Thanks," I said. "Would you ask her if we can get together in the morning?"

In truth, I wasn't entirely sure about this "exorcism" thing. But it seemed to belay my grandparents' fears.

"Meanwhile," Deborah said, "Kate, I can't help wondering . . . is there anyone new in your life, anyone who has made contact with you lately, whom Komohu might have pretended to be?"

"Pretended to be?" I remembered, then . . . *kahunas,* like *mo'os,* could change shape and form.

"No, I can't think of anyone new."

No one but Dan Kala.

The thought entered my head like a shot, and I brushed it away just as quickly. Dan Kala might be a pain, but—

"I just wondered," Deborah said, and sighed. "Look, regardless of where these visions are coming from, and who's involved, please remember, Kate, that you are dealing with a very real energy. And the mind is a delicate thing. There could come a time when you would come back from one of these visions no more than a shell—or so filled with pain you can no longer function."

This was what Sharon had said. "You seem to know a lot about it."

"Only because I've worked as a volunteer at a mental health clinic in recent years, and I've been with patients who are filled with a rage to murder. I've actually become ill from their energy. I've also been with mothers who have lost children, and been deeply depressed myself for days thereafter—even though I was trained, as a volunteer, to distance myself from their grief."

She reached over and touched my hand. "Sometimes it's impossible to distance oneself, no matter how hard one tries, Kate. You have no idea how you might return from your next sojourn into that other world."

"So what you're saying, is—don't go there."

"Exactly. Protect yourself in every way possible, at least until we can bring Sharon in on this."

"Grandfather?" I met his worried eyes. "I would guess you might know how to protect yourself from these things—at least to some extent."

He didn't answer.

"Teach me," I said. "Tell me what to do."

He shook his head.

"Why not?"

"You're a child in these things. It would take years."

"Well, I haven't got years. All I've got is right now. Teach me."

Again he shook his head. "What I suspect is going on may be only the tip of the iceberg, Granddaughter. There may be much more. And to take action without understanding the full picture could be more dangerous than taking no action at all. I believe your first instincts were right. We'll talk to Sharon."

"I must say on this point I agree, Keoki," my grandmother said, standing. "Meanwhile, the hour is late and our granddaughter needs her rest. Kate, I've been thinking. You must stay with us tonight. I'll sit beside you, and I won't leave you for an instant. In fact, we can read your mother's letters together. Would you like that?"

I felt deeply touched by her caring, and grateful. I was anxious, as well, to read my mother's letters.

But some stronger, deeper instinct drew me back to Pua'lani. It was something I could not define. Nor, upon thinking about it, did I desire to.

I stood beside her. "Thank you, Grandmother. But I need to go back to Pua'lani tonight. My computer's there, and I'd like to write all this down before I forget it. It's important I do that, I think. Sometimes writing things out exorcises them as well. Besides, Dan will be there . . . I won't be alone."

She studied me for a long moment, then took me into her arms. "Whatever you think best."

I drew back, looking into her eyes. "Somehow, you don't seem as worried as the others. Why is that?"

"It isn't that I'm not worried. I am. It's that I'm trying to have faith that God will protect you, Kate. God, and whatever protected me from that *tsunami* . . . and brought you and your mother into our lives."

Deborah came and gave me a hug. "I'll drive you home. No, on second thought, Damien, why don't you drive Kate? It will give you two a chance to get to know each other."

I could see that she was anxious to make him do something—*anything*—friendly, so that I wouldn't leave with a bad opinion of her son. On the other hand, I could also see that Damien had a hungry eye on his surfboard in the corner. All I needed at this point was a sullen chauffeur, especially one armed with a fish-gutting knife.

"Nonsense," I said. "It's a beautiful night, and to be perfectly honest, I'd really rather walk. It'll help to work off the tensions so I can sleep tonight."

"But, I—"

"You worry too much," I said, smiling and pressing her cheek with mine. "Look, it's wonderful to have a family. I can't tell you how much it means to me to have found you. But I'll be fine. I'm a big girl, now."

I didn't mean it to come out the way it sounded— as if to point out that they had missed their chance to nurture me as a child. But it was true that I'd taken care of myself for a good ten years, and I wanted them to know that I could do so now. That way, they might not worry.

My grandmother seemed to understand. Crossing to a mahogany sideboard with several drawers, she opened one and pulled out a small package tied with blue string.

"Your mother's letters," she said, handing them to

me. "Take them with you, Kate. You might want to read them tonight."

I looked down at the slim bundle. "There aren't very many," I said, trying to keep the disappointment out of my voice.

My grandmother looked into my eyes. "She wasn't with us very long."

Blinking tears away, I said my good-nights, hugging everyone in turn. This time, even my grandfather gave me a stiff hug back. It wasn't a happy hug, however. Those old eyes were still heavy with concern, and the embrace was more like one a person gives another when saying a final good-bye.

CHAPTER 23

Although the rain had stopped, the night was darker than I'd anticipated it might be. Clouds hid the moon, and I was grateful for the flashlight everyone had insisted I bring along. Following the road north, the sounds of night insects and birds were all about me. Their screeching set my nerves on edge. With my grandfather's warnings about his *kahuna* ancestor still fresh in my mind, I couldn't help peering anxiously into the dense, overgrown thickets on either side. There were few cars, but one slowed as it passed me, and that increased my agitation. I looked back, prepared to run if it stopped, but it only speeded up again and moved on. I laughed softly, thinking what a nervous bunny I was. A truly powerful *kahuna* would surely not show up in a car.

Near Pua'lani, I remembered the path that wound through the bamboo forest, which Dan had pointed out on the way to my family's home earlier. *A shortcut*, he had said, *but a bit overgrown*. Debating, I wondered how overgrown it could be. My feet had begun to hurt in the thin sandals, which, though low-heeled, were not as comfortable as those I wore every day. Thinking of the car that had slowed, I decided finally that it might be better to be out of sight than here on the road, where anyone might drive by and see me—including, possibly, stoned teenagers out looking for a rowdy night.

But the path, which seemed so wide and clean at its beginning, narrowed once I was well along it. The thick bamboo met over my head in an arch, forming an impenetrable tunnel. Mosquitoes were dense here; I could feel them biting every inch of my flesh. Swatting them away as best I could, I knew I'd pay for this decision.

Pausing, I thought I heard a noise, a footstep, behind me. Turning swiftly, I strained to see through the dark. Very little moonlight made its way through that snarled ceiling, and the small flashlight reached only so far behind me along the path. I could only listen, and after a few moments when no other sound came to my ears, I moved quickly on. Once I nearly dropped the flashlight, as my fingers were wet from fear. My back, shoulders, and legs were on fire now from the mosquito bites.

At last a path branched off to the left. Noting that the flashlight was dimming, I wasted no time turning that way. *It has to lead to Pua'lani*, I thought. *Or at least to the road*.

Seemingly, however, the path went on and on. For no logical reason I could think of, I began to run. The bamboo tunnel narrowed in spots. Wiry strands of new growth scratched my face and bare arms. *Be careful, be careful*, kept running through my mind. I didn't know if the words were my own, or if they came from somewhere, or someone, outside me. Finally it didn't matter. I just ran. My muscles, instead of loosening up, became tighter and tighter, my movements jerky, as in a nightmare.

It was with great relief that I saw the bamboo widening ahead, then the sky, the moon now shining on the red tile rooftop of Pua'lani. The path led me straight to the garage. Rounding it, then the pool, I ran for the main house, wrenched open the front door and called for Dan. Leaning against the closed door I focused on slowing my breath, which was coming in huge, harsh gasps. I found I was shaking all over. Even now—here—I couldn't rid myself of the illogical notion there was danger nearby.

Calling out again, I realized that Dan wasn't home. *He must be with Kimo, still. Damn.* The last thing I wanted was to be alone here now.

With more courage than I felt, I forced myself to open the front door and look out, if only to satisfy myself that my fears were ungrounded, that I was being foolish, silly. The ornamental lights were on around the pool and along the drive up from the road, their low wattage casting more shadows than light. I saw no one. Heard nothing.

Still feeling shaky, I went through the house to the French doors, and out onto the lanai. The Malibu lights were on here, too, hugging the ground around the bushes, the extent of their illumination largely decorative. I glanced toward the guest room. Only darkness through the shrubbery, no sign of life there.

Crossing the lanai to the guest room, I opened the door and went quickly to turn on the light beside the bed. Involuntarily looking at the portrait of Nahi'ena'ena, I whispered, "What's going on here? Why am I feeling this way?"

My little princess didn't deign to answer. Her expression remained inscrutable, and in truth, I was relieved. After hearing my grandfather's stories about the evil Komohu, I wasn't all that eager to converse, just now, with spirits from other worlds. In fact, as I sat on the bed to scratch the mosquito bites that had become a raging fire in my flesh, I no longer felt so comfortable here in this room.

My energy, I knew, was out of whack. Unstrung. Further, my leg and side muscles were cramping now from the run. I couldn't sit still. Beginning to pace, I scratched the damned bites, with one eye on the shrubbery between me and the main house. I wanted to know when lights came on in the living room, indicating Dan had come home.

Finally the tension, and the itching, got to me. *I'm too isolated from the front of the house here*, I thought. *What if Dan comes in and goes straight to his room without turning lights on? I might miss him.*

Irritated with myself for too much angst and too little action, I pulled my swimsuit from a drawer, went into the bathroom to put it on, grabbed a towel, and headed around the side of the house to the pool. Dropping my towel onto the wooden deck, I dived into the deep end and swam briskly, doing several laps till my nerves had been soothed and calm took over. Then I turned onto my back and floated, gazing up at the stars, letting myself be carried around the pool by the movement of the water. When the gentle tide carried me to the waterfall, I dipped a hand under it, enjoying the mist of the fine spray. It was so relaxing there I nearly fell asleep. It seemed as if hours passed.

"You look relaxed," a male voice said, jolting me back to life.

I didn't open my eyes, but continued to float. "I am," I said. "How about you? Did you get that transformer fixed?"

"Transformer?"

"Yes, isn't that what Kimo—"

My eyes flew open as I realized with a start that the voice wasn't Dan Kala's. Twisting my head around, I saw no one beside me. I began to tread water.

"Who—who's there?" I was ashamed to hear my voice quaver.

"My, how quickly they forget," the voice responded with mild amusement.

I saw him then—on the deck beside the waterfall. It took several moments to believe my eyes. Then all kinds of emotions swept through me: confusion, wonderment—old anger, perhaps. Even fear.

Gerard Lanier squatted on the deck at the edge of the pool, dipping his hand into the water to sample it, a familiar lazy grin on his face. He was dressed in long khaki pants and a white dress shirt, the sleeves rolled up to the elbow. His skin was darkly tanned, his teeth flashing white in the dim light.

He hadn't changed a bit.

A thousand memories came rushing back: the first day we met, the first time we made love, the way we said good-bye . . .

And all the good and terrible moments in between.

"What in the world are you doing here?" I said, gripping the edge of the pool, as I was feeling quite weak now. Glancing around, I searched the shadows. "Margo?"

"Margo's not with me, Kate. I'm here alone."

"Alone . . . But why? Gerard, how in the world did you know where to find me?"

In my dazed state, this was all I could think to say. For it seemed as if he must in fact have tracked me down and found me here. The feeling I had was one of astonishment mixed with an odd anxiety. Why Gerard Lanier had popped up after all this time, and just when I'd been thinking so much about him, was beyond my comprehension.

Smiling in the old cocky, self-assured way, he offered a hand to pull me out. I hesitated a long moment, then took it. A thick, gold bracelet gleamed against the dark wrist. I recognized it as one I had given him years before. *A token of love.*

He pulled me up onto the deck beside him. Sitting, I wiped my face, shook out my hair, and stared . . . unable to believe he was here.

"You look like you're seeing a ghost," he said, grinning.

"I think I am. Where in the world did you come from? What are you doing here?"

"Well, to answer your first question, I came from the mainland. As to what I'm doing here, I had business with one of the vineyards on Maui."

"That's not what I meant," I said, gathering my wits about me. "What are you doing *here*? At Pua'lani?"

He drew his long legs up and sat Peter Pan-style, arms looped around them. "Margo told me you were in Maui. She asked me to check things out, see how you were doing. She's been worried about you, Kate."

"But Margo couldn't have known I was here."

"On the contrary. She had your address in Kihei— the Hale Pau Hana. I called there and they told me you could be reached out here for the next few days."

"They told you that? But they weren't supposed to tell anyone where I was."

"Well, let's say I offered an incentive."

"You bribed the desk clerk?" I said, appalled.

"No, a maid. She got me the information."

The same old Gerard, I thought, buying his way through life. I shouldn't have been surprised. Even so, I couldn't help staring. It had been so many years . . . I'd have expected a few gray hairs at the temples, a few lines around the eyes. But there was nothing, no sign that Gerard had aged at all. His skin was smooth, his manner still as offhand and boyish as when we'd been at Berkeley together. There was not one indication that this man had been through difficulties over the years, that he'd ever suffered a setback, a disappointment, a heartbreak.

But then Gerard Lanier had always been this way. Throughout the time I'd known him, nothing ever seemed to bother him. He went through life oblivious to other people—or their travails.

"So, what are you doing here, Kate?"

"I, uh . . . I'm working on a book. And on vacation."

He smiled. "I've been following your career. I'm so proud of you, Kate. You've been quite successful."

I didn't answer. It always irritates me when people who haven't worked for my success or even supported me in getting there, say they're proud of me—as if they had something to do with my development.

"And your personal life?" he said. "What about this guy you're with here?"

I blinked. "Guy I'm with? I'm not with anyone. What are you talking about?"

His eyes flashed, and for a brief split second I saw the old jealousy. "I'm talking, my dear sweet Kate, about the guy who owns this place."

I laughed, but without mirth. "You mean Dan Kala? How do you know about him?"

He wiggled an eyebrow, like an old-time villain. "I have my ways."

I was supposed to smile at that, I knew. And there was a time when this kind of attention would have made me feel loved and flattered. Now, I was merely annoyed. No—more than annoyed. I felt closed in on.

"I'm not *with* Dan Kala," I said irritably. "This is an inn, and I'm a guest."

"That's all?"

I frowned. "Gerard . . . what about Margo? Why

isn't she with you? There hasn't been any answer at the house."

"Margo . . . ah, Margo, Margo, Margo." He sighed. "Must we talk about her?"

"Yes," I said, uneasy now. "We must."

"My dear Kate, I'd forgotten what a good little detective you are." He chuckled. "Once you get an idea in your head, you never give up. Well, the truth is"— he threw up his hands dramatically—"Margo's left me, Kate. Moved out. I haven't talked to her in weeks."

I couldn't hide my shock. "*Left* you? But you said she told you where I was."

He grinned. "Actually . . . I fudged a bit. Margo didn't tell me you were here. I found your Maui address on a letter she was getting ready to mail to you. She left it behind."

I remembered then how Gerard played with the truth, as if words didn't matter, had no meaning in themselves. This was something I had come to understand finally: that when he accused me of not remembering correctly, more times than not it was he who had been at fault, for telling me differing stories at different times. Funny how I'd forgotten that.

"But you're right, Kate," he said, with mock remorse and a grin. "I should have told you the truth right off. It's just hard, sometimes. I never know how people are going to take things."

I shook my head, thinking how well off I was without this man. I must have been blind at twenty—and stupid.

"Gerard, no one knows how people will take things. Most tell the truth, even so."

"My little Jiminy Cricket." He touched my chin, then traced my lips. "Nothing's changed, has it?"

I pulled away. "Actually, quite a lot has changed."

His voice lowered to a sensual timbre I remembered all too well. "Not for me. I never got over you, Kate. I'm on my way to France, tomorrow. I wish you'd come with me."

Humiliatingly, my nerve endings tingled, for just a brief second, with all the excitement of that young, naive college girl I'd been when first meeting Gerard. It was with more strength than I'd known I had that I narrowed my eyes and spoke coldly.

"You are unreal. I haven't seen you or even heard from you since that last day at Berkeley. Now you show up here as if nothing ever happened, and you come on to me as if it were yesterday? What the hell are you up to, anyway?"

His mouth tightened. "I'm not *up to* anything. I just thought you might have missed me as much as I've been missing you."

"Oh, please. Just tell me what happened between you and Margo. And where is she? I want to talk to her."

"I don't know why you care," he said in a loud voice. "She turned on you, after all."

"Turned on me? You mean by marrying you? Oh, and so you had nothing to do with it?"

"It was *Margo* who chased after *me*, Kate. I admit, I was weak. I was still not over the relationship with you—"

I shook my head, turning away to pick up my towel and wrap it around me, knotting it at my waist. Standing, I said, "Look, I don't think I want to hear this after all. I just want to talk to Margo. I've been worried about her."

"Worried? Why?"

I wondered if I should tell him. Then I thought, *What can it hurt?* "Because she was calling me. A lot. And we never connected." I shrugged. "Besides that, I've been having . . . premonitions about her.''

"Premonitions!" He laughed. "Kate, I can assure you, Margo's fine. She's staying with her family, that's all. And I've been traveling. The house is closed up.''

He rose and stood looking down at me. "Margo and I are getting a divorce, and she's all right with that. Believe me—whatever these premonitions of yours are, I can assure you there's nothing to them.''

He smiled. "Look, I'm leaving in the morning for France. Come with me. I've got the corporate jet, and if you're so worried about Margo, we can stop off in Seattle. I'll take you to her, and she can tell you herself that everything's all right. After that . . .'' He drew a finger down my nose, as in the old days, and lowered his voice to that sexy half-whisper. "We can do all the things we used to dream about.''

"You are absolutely insane,'' I said, moving back.

He grinned. "Insane to still love you?''

"Insane to think I'd just pick up and go away with you after all these years.''

He gave an elaborate shrug and glanced at his watch. "Well, think about it, at least. You've got just about eight hours.''

The audacity astounded me. "Gerard, I don't care if I've got a lifetime. I am absolutely not going anywhere with you.''

I turned to leave, but he grabbed my arm. I looked down at his hand. The gold bracelet on his wrist glistened in the torchlight, and I remembered then when I'd given it to him—after an argument, as a make-up gift. He had grabbed me in much the same way during that argument. His hand had left a bruise. I had reasoned, illogically, that the argument—and the bruise— were my fault. I was the one to "make up.''

I looked up at him now, wondering what I'd ever seen in Gerard Lanier.

"I'm going in," I said angrily.

His eyes turned hard, bright. "It's this guy, isn't it? You're in love with him."

"Gerard—for God's sake, I hardly know him."

"You can't fool me, Kate. I've seen you in love. I know what you're like. And that smile on your face when I first saw you floating there in the pool was for a man."

I laughed—and that was a mistake. The hand on my arm twisted, burning my skin.

"There are things you don't know about this new boyfriend of yours," he said angrily.

I tried not to answer that, but couldn't help myself. Yanking my arm away, I said, "What the hell are you talking about?"

"I've heard about him. He's not for you, Kate."

"Oh—and you are?" I rubbed my still-burning flesh, turning away. "I've heard enough. Good night."

"Kate, listen to me. You can't get close to that guy. He's bad news."

I turned back. "Funny—that's what people told me about you."

He flushed. "Well, they were wrong. But I'm not wrong about this. Stay away from Dan Kala. You've got to come with me, Kate. I *insist*."

This time my laughter was outright mocking. "You *insist*?" I wasn't so sure any longer I was even talking to the Gerard I once knew. This was a different Gerard, one whose bad qualities had worsened, if possible, over the years.

"I'm telling you, you don't know the whole story—" He reached for my shoulder.

"Let go of me, dammit!"

He held fast. "It's for your own good, Kate. You've got to leave here."

I looked into his eyes and saw something there now that truly frightened me. "What's wrong with you, anyway? Let go of me! Right now!"

I broke away and Gerard stepped back, though his face was dark with rage. At the same time a stiff wind began to blow. It whistled through the trees and flapped curtains at open windows of the main house. Shingles blew off the roof of the garage, rose to dizzying heights, and slammed into the ground. As I watched, amazed, the wind picked up speed, nearly knocking me over.

A light in the main house caught my eye. An orange light, flickering gently at a curtain, then bursting into—

A roaring, blossoming, flame.

"Fire!" I screamed, beginning to run. "My God, the house is on fire!"

Next to the front door I spotted a garden hose. Wrenching the faucet on, I pointed the hose at the window that was aflame. The narrow stream wasn't meant for putting fires out. The flames only grew.

Dropping the hose, I ran for the door and yanked it open. My only thought was to call 911. However, in the kitchen I ran straight into Dan Kala, hanging up the phone.

"The line's out," he yelled. His face was smudged with soot. "The wind is spreading flames through the house. Help me close the windows!"

I nodded and took the hallway to the right, while he took the one opposite. The wind was roaring through the eaves by now, and I could hear more tiles blowing from the roof and clattering to the ground. Racing from bedroom to bedroom, I checked each one

quickly, slamming down every open window, then
yanking every door shut behind me. I started back
down the hall. It was then I remembered the library.
All those beautiful books.

By the time I got to that end of the hall, flames
were already licking at the bookcases. I grabbed up a
throw cover that had been laid over a chair and began
to beat them out. The heat scorched my face and
hands. It singed my hair. A blast of wind, followed by
a huge *pooof* of flame, nearly knocked me down. I
held the cover like a suit of armor in front of me,
fending off the flames as I ran toward the window to
shut it.

The light curtains at each side of the window were
by now on fire. With my bare hands, I grabbed at
them, pulling them down. It was then I saw Gerard.

I hadn't been thinking of Gerard when I ran toward
the house, but some part of me assumed he'd be right
behind me, helping to put out the fire. Instead, I saw
him standing now in an open grassy area facing the
house. Facing me. His blond hair lifted in the wind,
framing his face with a golden glow. His white shirt
flapped madly about him, and his arms were upraised.
At that moment the wind picked up speed. I forgot
Gerard, slamming the window down.

Then I saw that Dan was beside me, throwing buckets of water on the carpet and curtains. The fire on the
bookshelves was out, and I pointed to an overstuffed
chair that had started to blaze. He dragged me off the
carpet and together we yanked it off the floor, tossing
it over the chair to smother the flames.

Within seconds, all was quiet in the library. Every
flame was out. We ran into the living room, where the
curtains had gone up like a torch. Together we jerked
them down, scorching our fingers in the process. Dan
was wearing boots. He stomped on the curtains. I was

in bare feet, so I went for cushions on the sofa, pulling them over one by one and dumping them down till the last flame was out.

We paused, then, out of breath, and looked around. "The other side?" I asked, wiping sweat from my face.

"It's okay. The windows were closed over there."

I realized suddenly that I felt shaky, and stumbled to the dining room table, slumping into one of the chairs. Dan fell into an opposite chair, leaning forward on the table and rubbing his face tiredly.

"I think we caught it just in time," I said.

"Yeah. It looks like mostly smoke damage."

"And curtains can always be replaced. We were lucky."

He looked at me. "I can't believe how you saved those books," he said.

I shrugged.

"I couldn't have done it without your help."

"Well . . . I'd have hated to lose them."

I noted then that there were flowers on the table, and votive-type candles in small crystal holders. The candles were unlit now, but a scent of burning wax hung in the air, along with the pungent smell of ash and smoke.

"This is where it began," Dan said. "When the wind came up, it blew the curtains in so far, they caught fire from the candles. I was in the kitchen. I didn't see it at first." He shook his head. "This has never happened before, in all the time I've been here."

"It was odd, wasn't it? It came up so quickly . . ."

I remembered Gerard, then, that image of him standing in the garden, arms upraised. Was it a gesture of jealous rage, because I'd refused to go with him to France? Or because I'd run to help Dan?

And where was he now?

"Hold on a minute," I said. I got up and went to the front door, scanning the area between there and the pool, then beyond it to the road. Gerard was nowhere in sight. Slowly I closed the door, and on second thought locked it. For a moment I leaned against it, oddly afraid.

I shook the fear off, though, calling it absurd. I was upset still from the fire, I told myself. Gerard was gone—off to France in the morning. Further, he'd run like the coward he was, leaving Dan and me to fend for ourselves.

Why hadn't I seen what he was, years before? Well, I'd seen it since, and if I'd needed any confirmation, tonight was it. Gerard no longer cared about Margo—or me. But then, he never had. For him, we had been a mere game.

I went back to the table and sat across from Dan.

"Give me your hand," he said, wetting a napkin with water from a drinking glass.

"Why?"

He sighed. "Just give me your hand."

I saw then that he was looking at the burns I'd gotten when tearing the curtains down. I stuck my hand out and he took it, carefully wiping away dirt and soot. "Yours are burnt too," I said. "Mine aren't as bad. Let me do yours."

He acquiesced, and I took a clean napkin and began, being cautious not to hurt the injured skin. "Have you got any aloe vera?"

"I think there's a plant on the kitchen sink."

I remembered seeing it. "I'll get it," I said.

Coming back with a broken piece of the plant, I rubbed the juice from it on his burns, then my own.

"Does that work?" he asked.

"It helps burns to heal. We might not blister this way."

"And how do you know that?"

I looked at him and shrugged. "I don't know." But a woman's face flashed before me—an unknown woman, with short, dark, curly hair.

He was silent, watching me, then, "What were you looking for—when you looked out the door?"

"Oh, nothing."

He gave me a skeptical look.

"No, really. I was looking for an illusion. An old illusion—one that no longer exists."

He shook his head. "You are one very bizarre lady."

I laughed, and it felt good—a release of tension. Forgetting Gerard, I said, "Talk about bizarre . . . what were you doing with all these candles tonight?"

There were so many of them, the table looked much like the guest room had, when I'd lit so many.

He seemed embarrassed. "I, uh, lit them for you."

My eyes widened in surprise. "Me?"

"I thought you might like to have a drink with me, to, uh . . . celebrate finding your family. And I lit the candles because I know you like them . . ." His voice trailed off.

"Because you know . . ." I couldn't think what to say, except, *Amazing what a little competition can do.* "Tell me . . . did you go to all this trouble because you saw me at the pool with a man?"

"A man? No . . . I did see you at the pool when I came in, but you were alone. You looked so relaxed I didn't want to disturb you." He frowned. "There was a man?"

I smiled, unsure whether he was telling the truth or just playing it cool. "Never mind."

He shrugged, but looked unsure and awkward, like a small boy about to ask his teacher if he could erase the blackboard for her. "Well, then, uh . . . we probably shouldn't light the candles again. But would you like a drink?''

I met his eyes, and in that instant it felt as if I were shedding a life . . . maybe two or three.

''Oh, what the hell,'' I said. ''It's been a dreadful night. Why don't we skip the alcohol, and just cut right to the chase?''

CHAPTER 24

The smooth cotton sheets felt like satin—a wet, dripping, satin glob between us. It was morning, and Dan Kala's bedroom was so hot you could fry an oyster in it.

I yawned and smiled. "Pardon me, but your tongue is in my ear."

"Ummm. I noticed that too."

"I wonder, do you think you might move it just a bit?"

"More than I have, you mean? Happy to oblige. Like this?"

I sighed. "Oh, yeah . . . just like that."

Several moments later he drew away. I wiped perspiration from my neck and chest with the damp sheet, as Dan reached over and flipped the window air conditioner on. Then he lay back on the pillow and gave a lazy sigh.

"Heaven."

"Bliss," I agreed. "You get a gold star, in fact."

"I do? And just where are you going to stick it, Madam Schoolmarm?"

"Right here," I said, indicating a point on his body that, for the moment, stuck out the most.

He laughed. "But no one will get to see it there."

"I will," I said, kneeling over him and taking care of matters at hand.

Later, he lay back against the pillows and sighed. "I didn't know it could be like this."

"Uh-huh. You don't have to say that, you know."

He looked pained. "I don't? I thought that was what all women wanted to hear." He turned and half lay on top of me, nibbling my ear.

"That doesn't mean they believe it." I fell silent, then, enjoying the moment.

"Tell me about your past loves." He smiled into my eyes. "And make them sound like real jerks, so my ego won't be bruised."

Thinking of Gerard's impromptu appearance the night before, I didn't smile. "That wouldn't be hard."

"To make them sound like jerks? Or to bruise my ego?"

"The former. Let's just say I haven't always had luck with men."

He grew serious and lay back with his head propped up on his hand. "So tell me."

"No, I want to hear about you. You never talk about yourself."

"Well, I will. But you have to tell me first."

"Oh? And why is that?"

With the tip of a finger, he tapped my nose. "Because that's how it works."

"Says who?"

"Says I. And I'm the innkeeper here. I could put you out in the cold."

"Ha! What cold?" I swung my foot over in front of the air conditioner, to cool it off. A shaft of icy air traveled up my leg. It felt delicious. "I'm waiting," Dan teased. "Time to reveal all."

''Yeah, well, believe me, you don't really want to know.''

But I could see that he did, and after a few moments more of hesitation, I did reveal all. It wasn't a pleasant story to go back into, so I tried to tell it in shorthand . . . the things I'd hoped for and believed would happen with Gerard, and the way they fell apart under the weight of his betrayal and accusations. The accusations were the worst of it, I said—his questioning of my sanity. I stumbled over the telling of that, but with gentle prompting and words of encouragement, it became easier as I went along.

''I've never told this to another man,'' I said when I was done. ''In fact, I've never told it to anyone, except—''

''Yes? Except who?''

I shook my head. ''It doesn't matter.'' I couldn't bring myself to tell him about Margo—and that she had betrayed me too.

Dan sat up, turning his back to me, and putting his watch on, but not before I saw his eyes fill with anger. ''The man was a bastard, to treat you that way. You're better off without him.''

You're damned right about that, I thought.

I stroked Dan's back and could feel the tension in it. ''You don't have to be angry for me. I'm okay now. Really.'' Sitting up, I leaned over him, circling his neck with my arms. ''It's your turn, now.''

''My turn?''

''To tell me about your past loves. Hey, don't even think of backing out on that! We had a deal.''

He took my hand, kissed the palm, and turned to take me in his arms, rolling us both back down on the bed.

''Well, now, let's see . . . there was Mary Ann in first grade, and then Suzannah in the tenth . . . now

Suzannah, she had the most wonderful deep violet eyes, and to say she was endowed, well—'' He nuzzled my breasts.

''I don't think I want to hear about Suzannah after all,'' I said.

Long moments later he eased his mouth back from its second loveliest resting place—on mine—and sighed. ''I never really thought this would happen. You women are a tough lot.''

''You'd better believe it.''

I pushed till he rolled off and I was on top. ''The problem is that most men don't know that. They think we're easy. We're not, you know.'' Pushing myself up, I swung my legs to the side of the bed.

''Hey, where are you going?''

''Away.'' I took my swimsuit from the floor, where I'd dropped it the night before, and pulled it on.

''Wait a minute. Why do I feel like I'm being dumped?'' He drew the sheets up to his chin. ''Am I?'' he said. ''Did you use me? Was I only a one-night stand?''

I laughed. ''No, you were not a one-night stand. I'm going to get us some juice and coffee.''

''*You're* waiting on *me*? Wow. I thought it was supposed to be the other way around. Doesn't the handsome hero in your books always bring coffee to the woman in bed?''

''Who says you're a handsome hero? Now go shower. When I get back, I want you looking alive.''

In the kitchen I put the kettle on for the Melitta drip, stuck the filter in the cone, placed it on the pot, and found mango juice in the refrigerator. While I waited for the water to boil, I walked around the living room thinking that, in daylight, the smoke damage looked pretty bad. Not to mention the drapes that lay on the floor, right where we'd left them the night before. It would take a lot of work to clean things up. Smiling, I noted that I'd mentally included myself in the work crew—or more precisely, someone who'd be around long enough to be part of it.

I then went outside to take a quick shower, leaving my swimsuit on. Afterward I stood drying off, inhaling the fresh morning air. The sun was shining, the birds were singing, and I allowed myself one small cliche . . . the one about "God's in his heaven, all's right with the world."

It certainly felt that way. I was even a bit grateful that there hadn't been a peep out of Nahi'ena'ena for nearly twenty-four hours now. It occurred to me briefly to wonder what she was up to—like a child in her room who'd been much too quiet. But this wasn't a day to focus on worry. For the first time in years, I felt whole.

Of course I knew one didn't need a man to feel whole. But that wasn't the kind of whole I meant. More a coming together of bits and pieces that had been apart far too long. I knew, of course, that the night with Dan had started out partly as a reaction to Gerard's having shown up, hoping to run my life again. Sometime in the night I'd also known, however, beyond a shadow of a doubt, that *this was the way it was supposed to be*. It felt so different from Gerard, or from any man I'd ever been with. I'd found that "one" at last, it seemed—that other me.

Shivering happily, I wrapped an oversized towel around me and went into the guest room to strip off my suit and pull on shorts and a tee. I glanced at Nahi'ena'ena, but if she had any secrets to reveal, she was mum on the subject for now. Making my way back into the kitchen, I sniffed flowers in pots along the terrace—noting more than ever their heady fragrance and bloom.

Did I look as lush as they, now, I wondered? Was my color as lovely, as vivid? I couldn't resist a quick glimpse into a mirror over a small table by the door.

Ohmigod. My half-washed-off makeup was a mess—the mascara so smudged I resembled nothing so much as a zombie from *Night of the Living Dead*. If I'd had any fantasies of how sexy I'd appeared upon waking up, how like a ravishing and ravished Demi Moore or Sandra Bullock, they were dashed in that split second.

Running to the kitchen, I turned the burner off under the teakettle, which had no whistle but was boiling up a storm. Pulling down a paper towel, I wet it and scrubbed my face with liquid dish soap and water, then ran back to look in the mirror to see if I'd got it all.

Not bad—except that my face was now red and raw from all that rubbing. Licking the tip of one finger, I wiped leftover bubbles of soap from the corner of my mouth. My hair, too, was a sight—plastered to my skull from the shower, a mass of kinky knots.

A comb. I need a comb.

Looking down at the little table, I saw it had a drawer. Might there be one there? These tables with mirrors over them were often used for one specific purpose: to check one's hair and makeup before answering the door.

I grabbed the tiny brass ring and pulled the drawer out, feeling it catch, as if the wood had warped. Slowly I eased it the rest of the way.

My breath caught.

And then it seemed I had no breath at all.

There, on top of a folded piece of paper that appeared to be a letter, was an old photo—of me.

Standing stock-still, I felt confusion overtake me.

Then fear. What was Dan doing with this? What the hell was going on?

Grabbing the photo up, I recognized it as one Gerard had taken while we were together at Berkeley—nearly ten years before.

I picked up the letter beneath it. The return address at the top was in Paris, France. The return name: "Philippe Lanier."

Gerard's father.

I leaned a palm on the wall to steady myself. My other hand shook as I scanned the letter. The message was brief: "A check will be mailed to you immediately upon receipt of information as to the current whereabouts of Kate McKenna."

CHAPTER 25

"What the hell is this?" I threw the photo and letter at Dan. "You make me sick! It was a game all the time, wasn't it? A game with me the mouse and you the cat. And I played right into it." My voice was loud and angry. It shook. "How could you *do* it? How could you go so far as to make *love* to me? Well, forget that. It wasn't love—it was only sex to you, wasn't it? And you made it part of the game."

His face paled. He sat up quickly in the bed. "Did you read it?" he said, with a nod toward the letter, which had fallen on the floor.

"Of course I read it! I may be a fool, but I'm not entirely an idiot."

He ran a hand through his hair. "I'm sorry. I meant to tell you long before this, I just kept putting it off—"

I was still shaking, and I wanted to get out of there. But I had to know. "Just tell me who precisely you are, and how the hell you got involved in this."

"If you read the letter—"

"If I read the letter, which as you already know, I did, I know that Gerard's father hired you to find me.

Therefore, I already know the *what*. Now I want the goddamned *why*."

From the kitchen came the sounds of metallic ticking as the teakettle cooled. That, and my wet hair dripping onto my bare shoulders, were all too hurtful a reminder of the peace I'd felt only minutes ago. It was all I could do to stand there as Dan Kala climbed naked out of bed and walked to the closet to take out a pair of jeans. I looked away as he pulled them on. Turning my back on him, I stood at the window, staring blankly at the view.

"This is the way it happened," I heard him say from behind me. "And I swear this is the truth. A couple of weeks ago, one of my clients—Charles Gormely—called me. He's been a business associate of Philippe Lanier's for years, through one of those obtuse European conglomerate tie-ins. Charles asked me to help out his old friend—to do a little 'detecting' job as he called it, saying it was a natural extension of the investigating I do for my clients. I turned him down, at first. I told him it wasn't my cup of tea. But less than twenty-four hours later Philippe Lanier phoned from France and begged me to find you. He said that you and his son, Gerard, had been in love, and that Gerard had never gotten over you. He said he hoped that if you and he got together again, it might help settle him down. Put him back on track."

"*Back on track?*" I said, outraged. I swung around to face him. "The last thing I need in my life right now is a Gerard who's 'back on track.' "

I shook my head disbelievingly. "So you've been spying on me from the first. And lying too."

"No. I haven't lied. Not purposely. When I first approached you and we had dinner, I was trying to figure out if I actually wanted to tell Gerard's father I'd found you, and where you were."

"Oh, well, everything's fine, then. That really lets you off the hook."

"No, it doesn't. But I swear I never told Philippe Lanier I'd found you. As for Gerard, I was specifically told not to pass the information along to him, but directly to Philippe. And to let him advise Gerard."

"Wait a minute. I don't get it. You haven't told Philippe you found me?"

Then was Gerard telling the truth, I wondered, when he said he'd gotten my address off a letter from Margo to me?

No. The whole damned thing was too damned pat. Dan Kala had provided him with that information and was being paid a pretty penny for it.

"How much?" I said coldly. "How much did they pay you?"

"For God's sake, Kate, it wasn't the money! Look, at first I was curious. No—the word might even be suspicious. It seemed to me there was something almost sinister about Philippe Lanier's request, though I couldn't say why I felt that. Then when I found you, it put me in a difficult position. I didn't want to withhold information from a client. On the other hand, I liked you. I didn't want to put you in any danger."

"What do you mean, danger?"

"That's the hell of it, I don't know what I mean. It's something I sensed in the tenor of my conversation with Lanier. Then there was the secrecy he insisted upon. There was something about it I didn't like."

"Yet you took the job," I said bitterly. "I trusted you, and you—" I turned away, blinking tears from my eyes. "Dammit, why did you do it?"

His voice was heavy. "Let's just say I was intrigued. Can we leave it at that?"

I swung back. "No, we cannot. So you were in-

trigued. So you checked into the Hyatt, pretending to be there on consulting business—''

''No. That was true. I was meeting with clients there, at the same time I'd been looking for you.''

''Two for one—lovely. And you found me—easily enough, I assume, because I'd been doing autograph signings at bookstores around the island, and they were publicized in the paper.''

He glanced away. ''Once I knew you were an author and here on Maui signing books . . . it wasn't difficult.''

''I guess not. So what did you do? Show up at one of those signings, stand at the back of the crowd where you were hidden, and watch me? Then follow me to Kihei, to see where I lived?'' Just the thought of it gave me a squeamish feeling.

I knew I'd hit it right on the mark when he didn't answer.

''Oh, and let's not forget the missing film,'' I said angrily. ''You did take it, didn't you? Just how did that fit in?''

''Kate, I swear to you, I did not take that film.''

I pushed past him. ''God! How can you live with yourself? All those protestations of innocence, all that pretending you were interested because I looked like your beloved princess—''

''Wait a minute.'' His face darkened with anger. ''That was not pretense. It was all true. And if I deliberately set out to have dinner with you and get to know you the other night, I only did so because by then we'd had that conversation on the *Kaulana*, and I liked you. I was worried about you, and I didn't know what to do about Philippe Lanier. All I knew was that I didn't want to be responsible for bringing any sort of pain into your life.''

I laughed harshly. "Oh, well, you've certainly not done *that*, have you?"

"Kate, I was going to tell you. And this—last night. I never meant it to happen, at least not this quickly. I thought I'd tell you the whole story, get everything out in the open first. In fact, that's why I had the letter right there, where it was handy. I didn't try to hide it from you. It's just that things got out of hand between us—"

"You know what? Stuff it! I don't want to hear about that. The only thing I want to know is what you're going to do about Philippe. I assume you'll be collecting that check any day now."

"I, uh . . . I honestly don't know."

"You don't *know*? After all that hard work, you'd turn down cash on delivery?"

His jaw clenched, and he answered just as angrily, "I only meant that if you *want* this creep Gerard back in your life, I'll pass the word along to Philippe. Hell, Kate, I'll handle it any damn way you want me to!"

"Well, good. I think you should take the damned check, then. After all, you should at least get some sort of payment for sleeping with me."

He grabbed my shoulders. "Don't even think that. That's not the way it was. I *care* about you, dammit! Believe that, at least."

"Well, of course I will, now that you've given me so much reason to trust you. Why wouldn't I?"

His mouth tightened. "Don't do that. Don't put that kind of wall between us. Try to see that I was looking after you, trying to protect you. That's all it was."

"Damn you!" I said furiously. "*Gerard* is *here*!"

He dropped his hands. A confused look crossed his face. "Here? Gerard Lanier? He's here?"

"He arrived last night, and you damned well know it!"

"Kate, I swear—"

"You saw him at the pool. Don't pretend you didn't."

"That's not true! If I'd seen him, I'd have—"

"What?"

He shook his head. "I don't know. I'm not sure."

"That does it. I'm out of here."

"Where are you going?" he demanded as I headed for the door. "You're not leaving Pua'lani?"

"Oh, hell, no," I tossed back sarcastically. "Why would I do that? No, I'll just stay right here where you and Philippe and Gerard can play your little games and pounce upon me unawares."

Taking three long strides he reached me, blocking my path to the door. "Listen, Kate, if you want to leave, I won't try to stop you. But think about it—let me help you, now that I know what happened between you and that jerk. Let me figure out what's going on."

I pushed him away and yanked open the door. "Get out of my way before I break your jaw."

I half ran to the guest room, thinking to pack. But when I opened the small, mirrored closet, I found my suitcase was gone.

I stood there, confused, and almost went back to the main house, to accuse Dan Kala of having put it somewhere to keep me from running.

But that didn't make sense. He didn't know any of this would happen.

Nahi'ena'ena. She had tried to keep me at Pua'lani before, by taking my car keys. This was one of her tricks—again.

I glared at the portrait. "Damn you! You can't keep me a prisoner here. I'll leave without my clothes if you don't bring that suitcase back right now!"

The little princess remained mute—and I felt like a

fool. Had I imagined her too? Was *everything* that had happened to me here in Maui a product of my imagination? A lie?

No—one thing had been undeniably real: Philippe Lanier had hired Dan Kala to find me. And Gerard had shown up here, out of the blue, and tried to whisk me away to France.

One thing I knew about Gerard Lanier—he was not a prince on a shining white charger, arriving in the nick of time to carry the princess—no pun intended—off to his castle. No, he'd been up to something. And there was one person—only one—who might, if I were lucky, tell me what it was all about.

Margo.

I picked up the small white phone by the bed, then hesitated. Gerard had told me that the house was closed, and that Margo was staying with her family. I didn't have that number, but, then, something told me that even about that, Gerard had lied.

Once again I punched the redial. As the number rang I braced myself for the worst: Maybe she wouldn't talk to me at all, beyond the first hello. Maybe I'd severed the last tie in our relationship by my silence.

A female voice answered. "Hello. Lanier residence."

Thank God. "I'd like to speak to Margo, please."

I could hear breathing on the line, but no words. "Hello?" I said. "Can you hear me? I'm calling for Margo."

The woman at the other end seemed to falter. "I . . . uh . . . Margo . . ."

"That's right. Margo Lanier. Is she there?"

The voice gathered strength. "This is Margo's aunt, Lucinda Reed. Who's calling, please?"

Lucinda was Margo's "maiden aunt," I remembered, though I'd never met her. Margo had always lovingly referred to her as that, adding, "She's wonderful, but I think she trusts people far too much. A bit like you, Kate."

"This is Kate McKenna," I said, gripping the receiver. "I'm a friend of Margo's. Is she there? May I speak with her, please?"

The voice wavered. "I . . . I'm so very sorry, Ms. McKenna. You must not have heard . . ."

Dear God, then, it's true, I thought, *about the divorce. And Margo has moved out, just as Gerard said.*

"My dear, Margo died," the woman continued, her voice trembling. "I'm so sorry. She died two weeks ago."

The room began to tilt. I eased myself onto the bed, feeling weak. "Died . . . ? But that can't be. It just can't be . . ."

Margo was *young. My* age. She couldn't be gone, not like that. Not so suddenly. A sharp pang of grief struck me.

"She died in childbirth," Lucinda Reed said, her tone sympathetic. "I'm really very sorry you weren't told. I made most of the phone calls myself, and there were so many, I know I must have missed a few. Between that and all the other arrangements . . . well, it took me until today just to come here and put away her things. The whole family has taken this quite hard."

"I understand," I said numbly. "It's . . . it's just such a shock."

"Of course it is, dear. If you were her friend . . . well, it was dreadfully unexpected, for all of us. There was a fall, you see, down the stairs, and unfortunately, she went into labor prematurely. The doctors did everything they could to save her, but there was so much bleeding . . .''

The meaning of her words filtered through. ''Labor?'' I said tensely, interrupting. ''Did you say labor? Margo was pregnant?''

''Yes, of course, seven months. You didn't know?''

''No. She never told me.'' I gripped the receiver. ''You said she fell down the stairs? But how? How could that possibly happen?''

There was a moment of silence. ''I . . . I suppose it's all right to tell you, dear . . . after all, it's public knowledge by now. In all the local papers, don't you know. It was Gerard, you see.''

Every nerve in my body froze. ''Gerard?''

''If only we had known what he was like. But Margo didn't talk about their troubles, she kept everything to herself. Now, of course, all the servants are talking, so it hardly matters, does it, trying to keep things quiet?'' She sighed. ''They were having an argument, you see, and Gerard . . . Gerard pushed her. One of the maids saw it all and went to the police the next day. I only wish I had been here. Gerard . . .'' She lowered her voice to a confidential tone. ''It wasn't his baby, you see. And not that it's for me to judge, but he never seemed, to me, to be a good husband, and Margo finally turned to someone else . . .'' Her voice broke. ''Well, the maid said he did it deliberately, that he wanted them both to . . . you know.''

''But what happened?'' I asked, horrified. ''Why didn't they arrest Gerard?''

''Oh, they tried, dear, straightaway, but he ran off, you see, right after it happened. They did catch him, though, thank God—just two days ago, in London. They're holding him there for . . . extradition, is that the right word?''

I shook my head, bewildered. ''But, Ms. Reed, Gerard can't be in jail in London. He was here, in Maui—just last night.''

"In Maui? But that's quite impossible, dear. I've just spoken with the Seattle district attorney, and he assured me that Gerard is safely under lock and key in England. Dear, he's been there for the past two days.''

A sense of unreality shook me. None of this made sense. I had seen Gerard with my own two eyes.

Hadn't I?

Or had I conjured him up, out of some strange, sick need? What the hell was going on?

Margo's aunt was speaking. "Dear, you did say your name was Kate? Kate McKenna? My mind is a bit fuzzy these days. I'm sorry.''

"Yes," I answered. "I'm Kate McKenna.''

"Well, it's coming back to me now. Philippe, Gerard's father, has been trying to find you ever since this happened. He wanted to warn you, dear.''

"Warn me?''

"About Gerard. After he ran off, that is. Gerard had spoken of you often over the years, it seems—you are the writer, aren't you?''

"Yes. Yes, I am.''

"Well, Gerard, it seems, had clippings of your reviews all over his study wall. We didn't know any of this, of course, until after . . . Well, at any rate, that's why Philippe thought he might try to find you. It's all coming out now, dear, about Gerard, you see. I'm afraid this wasn't the first time he'd harmed someone. There was a young woman years ago, in France . . . a car accident . . .'' She paused. "It's a long and rather sordid story. I'm sure you don't want to hear that now.''

"No. No . . . not right now.'' The only thing I could take in, at that moment, was that Philippe had been trying to find me, to warn me. That must have been why he'd hired Dan Kala.

"The problem, as I see it, dear, is that they're such an ingrown family, the Laniers. So protective of their reputations." Her voice rose, becoming thick with anger and tears. "If Philippe hadn't covered that old incident up, even to paying off the officials in France, this might never have happened to Margo."

My own eyes filled. "I'm so sorry, Ms. Reed. I don't know what else to say. I really don't. Is there anything I can do?"

"I don't think so, dear . . . Well, actually, now that you ask, I'm sure the entire family would appreciate your prayers for the baby."

"*Baby?*" I nearly dropped the phone. "But I thought—I mean, I assumed—are you saying Margo's baby didn't die?"

"My dear, she made it through, but just barely. I'm afraid the doctors hold out little hope for her survival. She's two months premature, and there were complications, I'm afraid, from the accident."

Oh, dear God. "I . . . yes, of course I'll pray for the baby," I said.

As for Gerard—I would have killed him with my bare hands, if he'd been here at this moment. My hatred for him was overwhelming. If I'd known any of this last night when he was here—

But he wasn't here. Gerard was in London, in jail.

There was one other thing to ask. "The funeral? You've already had it, of course?"

"Yes, dear. Last week." Lucinda Reed blew her nose. "There was some delay because of the autopsy. Again, I'm so sorry you weren't notified. I'm not as young as I used to be, I suppose. It's all been so terribly difficult."

I barely heard her apology. *Last week*, I thought. *The funeral was last week.* Something began to knock at my heart. It was like that, exactly—a knocking at my heart.

Clarity, at last.

"Ms. Reed, what day, exactly, was the funeral?"

"We had it on the twenty-fifth, dear. The morning of the twenty-fifth. Barely a week ago."

The morning of the twenty-fifth. The morning after I'd met Dan Kala on the *Kaulana* and gone to dinner with him at the Hyatt.

The morning after I'd found that message on my computer: *Ask him who he really is . . .*

And the morning I'd had my first vision of the woman with long dark hair . . . the woman who had turned into Margo.

The knocking at my heart became a pounding: *You see it, don't you? You see.*

Yes, I answered, *I see.*

Margo had been calling me for weeks, leaving messages. Something must have been wrong, even then. Finally—unable to reach me for help till it was far too late—she had paid me a personal visit. And then another.

The visions had been real.

"He tried to kill my baby," Margo had said only yesterday. *"Help me,"* she had pleaded. *"Don't let him . . ."*

"Dear, is everything all right?"

I realized Lucinda Reed was speaking, and thanked her, offering my regrets once more. Gently, I set the receiver down as all the memories rushed back—the good ones, for once, not the bad—memories of my friendship with Margo, before Gerard. Saturday mornings, walking arm in arm along Telegraph Hill, stopping in at the bakery, buying croissants and espresso, sitting at the little green table outside. Watching the world go by, and poking secret fun, together, at the aging hippies in their tie-dyed T-shirts, their long beards and sandals . . . we, who were oh-so-smart and trendy in those days, so far above anyone the slightest bit different from us.

Margo . . . holding me tight when my grandmother McKenna died, rocking me till the tears stopped, then force-feeding me pizza and beer. Margo being there beside me at the funeral. Lending me her strength, when by myself I had none.

Margo sitting beside me in movie theaters, the two of us laughing or weeping together. Sharing popcorn together.

Beaches, I remembered now. A three-hanky movie about friends who stood by each other—in life and in death. "Let's always be like that," Margo had cried, hugging me outside the theater afterward as we shared the last bits of Kleenex in our pockets.

"Yes, let's," I had answered tearfully, hugging her back.

And it had been like that. The two of us together—always together.

Till Gerard.

I wanted so much to kill him in that instant, it made me ill.

Gerard had pushed Margo down the stairs, Lucinda Reed had said. He had murdered Margo—and possibly their child.

Gerard, who just last night had been here, telling me he still loved me, wanting to start over, saying Margo didn't care . . .

Except that he hadn't been. Here.

Or was Lucinda Reed wrong? Did Gerard escape? Maybe she just hadn't heard about it yet.

How long I sat like that, thinking and then not thinking, feeling numb, I didn't know. I felt dizzy, disoriented when I tried to stand up. A stiff breeze had come up, and I was cold. I wanted to shut the door.

Looking out onto the lanai, however, I felt a strong urge to be outside. To feel the sun on my face and look up into the sky.

But the sun had slipped behind a cloud. Though it must only be midday, the sky had grown dark. There was a storm on the way. A bad one this time.

As I stood on the lanai, a sound of drumming, and of light, airy, flutelike music reached my ears. It seemed to float up from the black-sand beach at the bottom of the cliff. I'd never been down there, as it hadn't looked hospitable from above. Mostly rocks and surf, with only a tiny patch of the gritty, lava sand.

But the music roused my curiosity. Who could be there in that remote little spot?

Without conscious direction, my feet took me to a narrow trail that crossed the front of the cottage next door and led to a path down the side of the cliff, to the beach.

"I wouldn't try that path," Dan had said the first day I'd been here. "It's not in good shape. The storms have washed much of it away, and it's quite steep."

The beginning of the path, however, seemed good. Smooth—and only a gentle slope. *I'll take it*, I thought, *till it runs out*. Drifting along with the waves of music, and now laughter, I passed the cottage. It was closed up, empty, the artist-in-residence still away on business, no doubt. I continued downward on the path, noting as I paused once and turned back that I could no longer see either the cottage or the main house.

The sky grew ever more dark. It became difficult to see. Stark white blossoms on either side of the path, however, stood out boldly, as if lit from within. I fancied they had been planted there to light my way . . . that someone had known I would come, and had set them there to guide my feet along this rocky, narrow trail.

As I came upon a curve in the path, the beach became visible again. Surprised, I saw there were fires there now, and the sweet, oh-so-tempting scent of roasting pork drifted up to remind me that I hadn't eaten all day. I could see figures on the beach, and the music and laughter grew louder. *There's a party. Someone is having a luau. They must have come down by the other trail, the one between here and Keanae.*

The beach seemed much larger from this angle, than from above. It stretched from one jutting point to another, and the sand, from this perspective, looked whiter, softer. Nearly everyone sat cross-legged, though some were half out of sight, with their backs against large rocks. Five or six men tended the pit where a pig, presumably, roasted in coals. They were dressed in the old Hawaiian way, with only their bottom half covered, by a cloth that was not much more than a G-string. Their figures were tall, sinewy, sexy, their chest and flank muscles gleaming in the reddish glow of torches that had been placed into the sand at regular intervals. As I watched, Hawaiian dancers, all women in skirts fashioned of large *ti* leaves, moved into a circle. They began their erotic, rhythmic swaying, the torchlight dancing over their dark, silky bodies as they moved to the haunting pulse of drums and flutes.

I hesitated, reluctant to descend any farther and intrude upon what must be a private party. *A very private party, indeed,* I realized, as I saw that beneath their flowered leis, the women's breasts were bare. They made no effort to hide this fact, and as they danced, the leis moved, exposing large, taut nipples, which glistened darkly and appeared, at least to my eyes, to taunt and tease. Men in the audience laughed softly in response, and women too—an easy, knowing laughter, one filled with a promise of things to come. I saw then that the breasts of the women in the audience were bare as well, and that each wore only a short, sarong-like wrap from the waist down. As the pulse of the music grew stronger, the dance more and more erotic, men pulled their women toward them to touch their breasts playfully, sensuously, and then to stroke between their legs. The women spread their legs in a delicious-seeming abandonment, giggling and sighing. Several couples began openly to make love on the beach, apparently oblivious to anyone else around. The sounds of ecstasy and lust, so often hushed out of embarrassment or inhibition—at least in the society I came from—floated softly, and sometimes wildly, in the air.

My legs grew weak as my own senses became caught up in the scene. I sank to the ground, though it was impossible to drag my eyes away. I felt like a voyeur, yet oddly, with no shame. Moisture trickled between my legs, and the heavy scent of sex rose to my nostrils. Involuntarily, I looked down, and was stunned to see that I was wearing not the shorts and tee I'd left the house in, but a long white garment that hung loosely to my ankles and was high at the neck. On my chest swung a silver cross—the body of Christ, crucified, affixed to it in the Roman Catholic way.

My hands flew up to the cross in astonishment, and my eyes fastened on those hands, normally white and soft. They were brown, now, and strong, with square, blunt nails. The palms were full of calluses.

"Melika!" someone called. "Melika! Won't you come down to celebrate with us?"

Reeling with shock and confusion, I was unable to understand, at first, that this person—this woman on the beach below—was calling out to me.

Squinting through the half-dark, I searched out her face. *Who are you?* I wanted to cry.

And then, trembling: *Who in the name of God am I?*

The woman held out a hand. "Come, Melika. You will miss the ceremony. Hurry!"

I thought to run back up the trail—to scream for help, as I was overcome then, by fear. But my legs would not work, nor did any sound leave my mouth.

The woman started up the path toward me. "What's wrong? Aren't you feeling well?"

As she drew close I saw that she was dressed like the others, her breasts bare, a brief piece of white cloth wrapped around her slender hips. Her hair hung in loose waves around her shoulders and was heavily salted with gray.

"Nahi'ena'ena will be so disappointed if you are not there for her wedding," she said. "My poor baby sister . . . why are you so shy? Won't you come down?"

I tried to tell her I was not who she thought I was. But as I looked into her quiet eyes, I knew suddenly that, however incredible it might seem, I was this woman's sister . . . Melika.

The moment I acknowledged that, something in me moved. A shift took place, and I somehow became that person—that woman with the strong brown hands. I knew her memories, everything that had ever happened to her in the past. I knew she was barely eighteen and had grown up in a family in which she was loved. I knew she had attended Nahi'ena'ena, along with her older sister, and that because of this, had come to know Kauikeaouli—Nahi'ena'ena's brother, Kamehameha III. I knew she—I—had come to love him, just as Nahi'ena'ena did.

She had come to love Kauikeaouli—who this day

was to marry not her, but his sister, Nahi'ena'ena, in a secret ceremony in the old, traditional way. This was why I, Melika, hid.

"I cannot go down there," I was astonished to hear myself, in the body of Melika, say. "I cannot bear to see them marry."

"Here, let me wipe away those tears, Melika. Stay here if you like." My sister dabbed at my wet cheeks with the back of one tender hand, then ran her fingers through my short hair, smoothing it. "It will be easier, however, if you do take part. Easier to forget."

"I will never forget," I said stubbornly, shaking my head. "Never." I felt as if my heart might break.

Below us, the music stopped. A hush fell.

"See, it is beginning," my sister whispered. "Shall I stay here with you?"

I didn't answer, and after a moment she sat on the rocky trail by my side and watched as the procession began. Nahi'ena'ena and Kauikeaouli walked together, hand in hand, to the center of a circle formed by torches. Ringing the circle, too, were the *ali'i*, of whom I was not a part. As trusted servants, my sister and I were invited to attend Nahi'ena'ena—to help her make ready, and to stay near her side. We were not, however, one of *them*. Nor could we marry into them.

That was changing, of course. But not quickly enough for me—or, more to the point, for me and Kauikeaouli. Even if Nahi'ena'ena did not hold first place in his heart, there would never be a time for us.

"I know what you are thinking," my sister whispered beside me. "But you can still have him, Melika. If that is your intent, you will find him in another life."

I wrapped my fingers around my cross. "I no longer believe in other lives, sister. My new beliefs tell me there is only this one."

"Melika, you have let them capture you—those priests of Rome—as surely as any conqueror who ever stepped foot on this land."

"I love my new church," I answered stubbornly. "In another year I will be more than a healing sister. I will take my vows."

"Perhaps in this life you will make vows to the Church, sister. But I promise you that in another, you will be with the man you love."

I watched the white ceremonial cloth being placed over the shoulders of Nahiʻenaʻena and Kauikeaouli ... who, only a month ago, had been in my bed.

"You are far too romantic for a woman your age, Leali," I said.

"And you are far too tart for a woman of yours."

Nahiʻenaʻena lay on a massive bed in her room in the palace, writhing in pain. Biting the back of her wrist to keep from crying out, she muttered words to allay her fear. Mingled with words of old were prayers the missionaries had taught her. "*Our father, who art in Heaven, hallowed be thy name ...*"

Kauikeaouli—brother, husband, and for the moment a king without power, as he could not take this pain from her—sat beside his sister on the bed, his strong dark hands tenderly rubbing her swollen abdomen.

"Better to pray to our gods," he said, though not harshly. "Our father who art in heaven does not seem to hear."

Nahiʻenaʻena arched her back as the labor pain blossomed, infusing every muscle, every bone, with agony. Kauikeaouli grabbed her hands, squeezing them hard. "Hold onto me, Nahiʻenaʻena. Hold on." His forehead creased with worry.

She fell back against the pillows as the contraction subsided. Shaking her head, she said, "I don't like you very much right now, my brother. Damn you for doing this to me!''

He stared at her, appalled. ''You can't mean that.''

''I do!'' She pulled her hands away and wiped the sweat from her brow. Short black tendrils clung to her forehead, and he reached to push them back, as when they were children.

''No—don't touch me! Go away!''

''But, Nahi'ena'ena—''

She refused to look at him. ''Get me Melika. It's time.''

He stood, a helpless expression crossing his face. As he walked toward the door, her eyes followed him with love. ''Forgive me, Kauikeaouli,'' she said softly. ''I don't know what's wrong with me.''

He turned back, hope rising. ''Please, Nahi'ena'ena. Let me stay—''

But then another pain seized her, a pain more fierce than all the rest.

''No! Get me my midwife—and then get out! You men know nothing.''

He left, looking miserably unhappy.

Nahi'ena'ena took the pain into herself, trying to breathe deeply as Melika had taught her to do. ''If you don't fight it, it will be easier,'' her midwife and friend had said.

So she tried not to fight it. Just as she had tried for so many years not to fight the feelings she had for her brother, had tried to convince herself that he was right, and the missionaries wrong—that they should follow the old ways, letting their love grow, and be natural, and good.

She had ended up with a foot in two worlds, a stranger to both, and that pain was far worse than the one that gripped her now.

As the contraction subsided, Nahi'ena'ena acknowl-

edged to herself that she wasn't really angry with
Kauikeaouli. But men did not understand. They rutted
about here and there—did he think she did not know
about his little affair with Melika and the others?—
giving no thought to the consequences of their acts.

So now here she lay, going through all this pain for
a child that might not even be his, but that of her other
husband. Why did Kauikeaouli care?

The door opened, and Nahi'ena'ena looked up, expecting Melika. But Komohu stood there—Komohu,
dreaded *kahuna ana'ana*—dressed not in the old
ways, but in the current-day shirt, jacket, and trousers
of those who had come to "save" Hawaiians from
themselves.

Komohu—who had the expedient ability to change
who and what he was, according to his needs.

"What are you doing here?" Nahi'ena'ena raged.
"It's my midwife I need, not you!"

He drew close to the bed, a formidable presence,
not only because of his height, but because his *mana*
carried untold dangers. One must protect one's spit,
even, from Komohu, for he would take bits of spit,
hair, and blood, and use them in his magic, to seize
one's soul.

"I've come to bless your labor," he said silkily, his
cold eyes meeting hers.

"I don't need you to bless my labor. I want Melika.
Where is she? What have you done with her, Komohu?" Again, the princess began to arch, the terrible
pain nearly taking over her mind this time.

"I have done nothing but ask her to wait."

"*Melika!*" Nahi'ena'ena cried out. She tore at the
silk sheets, then drew blood as she bit again on the
back of her hand. Tears filled her eyes. "Oh, Melika,
where are you?"

"I told her to wait in the gardens, Nahi'ena'ena.

You might as well be still. Your precious Melika cannot hear you.''

Komohu drew from his pocket a yellow vial, fashioned from a miniature gourd. There were markings on it, and feathers attached to it. He set it on the table beside Nahi'ena'ena's bed and began to mutter words over it, in the old way.

"This will help you,'' he said then, lifting it to Nahi'ena'ena's lips as she settled back once more, drained.

She shook her head and pushed at the vial. ''I don't trust you, Komohu. Take that away.''

His mouth tightened in a frown of displeasure. ''Remember, Nahi'ena'ena, when you were young and we met in the woods? You trusted me then.''

"How well I remember,'' she said bitterly. ''I came to you then because I trusted you to satisfy my need for pain. I no longer have a need for pain, Komohu. There is far too much in my life as it is.''

"I provided the chants, Nahi'ena'ena. The prayers. You provided the pain, from your own mind. If you had wanted happiness, my spells could have given you that.''

"What are you really doing here, Komohu?'' she said in a voice just above a whisper, as she was growing weak. ''What do you want?''

"Only to persuade you to do the right thing.''

"Oh? And what is that? Tell me quickly, evil one. There's not much time left now.'' Taking deep breaths again, she began to arch with a new contraction.

"Nahi'ena'ena . . . this child must not live.''

Momentarily shocked, the princess forgot the pangs of labor. ''Not live! You madman! What are you saying?''

"I am saying that a child born of yourself and Kauikeaouli can only bring more distress to our country.''

She half rose on her pillow. "Distress? What are you talking about? Have you lost your senses after all?"

"Not I. Kauikeaouli. He refuses to make peace with the new order. You and he have fought together for the old ways from the time you were born, and if this child lives, Kauikeaouli will raise it to carry on that fight."

Komohu's voice turned persuasive. "Hawaii does not need this, Nahi'ena'ena. We must make peace with the new order. You must see to it."

"Get out of here!" she cried, afraid now for her child. "Get out of my room this instant!"

He ignored her, holding the yellow vial out to her again. "Take this. It will assure the child is born dead."

Nahi'ena'ena recoiled from the vial as if it were a poisonous snake. In the next moment her eyes narrowed, and the princess who had inherited her ancestor Kihawahine's powerful *mana* appeared, bringing a different presence to her body and into the room. No longer was she frightened.

"Get out of my sight, Komohu," she said in a low, deadly voice unlike her own. "Never come to this palace again."

Komohu drew himself up to his full height. His eyes bored through her—dark, cold, and lethal. "I had hoped you might see the wisdom in my suggestion. However . . . there are other ways." His hands moved over her abdomen.

"Melika!" she screamed, in a voice designed to make itself heard from one corner of the palace grounds to another. "I need you! Now!"

The door flew open. Melika stood there in her long, white "nun's" habit, the cross of Jesus at her breast. The cross took on light. It began to blaze.

"Get out of here, Komohu," Melika said. Her voice was soft, not raised. Gentle, not angry. Yet there was power in it that well matched Komohu's.

The *kahuna* sent Nahi'ena'ena a furious glance and strode away, slamming the door so hard it rocked the walls.

Nahi'ena'ena grabbed her abdomen and curled into a fetal position. "Help me," she whispered. "Help me, Melika. You are the only one who can."

I knelt next to Nahi'ena'ena's bed and took her hand. Nahi'ena'ena opened her eyes, and her gaze fastened on the cross I wore. "You're the only one I can trust now, Melika. The only one who does not believe in Komohu's power, and therefore cannot fall under his spell."

Leaning close, I said softly, "I heard what Komohu said to you. You must not even *think* of doing such a terrible thing, Nahi'ena'ena! To do so would be a sin, a crime against God. You know this. Your missionaries have taught you well."

Nahi'ena'ena shook her head. "I've thought that at times. But look at us, Melika—Kauikeaouli and me. Half our people are against us. And what of our poor baby, of which they would all make a pawn? The missionaries, and those who would align themselves with them for political gain, have left us with nothing but grief."

"That isn't true, and you know it, Nahi'ena'ena. You speak now out of your fear of Komohu. But you yourself have told me often that the missionaries brought good, as well. It wasn't so long ago that the leaders of our islands waged bitter war on each other, slaughtering everyone in their path. Remember the stories, Nahi'ena'ena? How here in Maui, the streams ran red with blood, right to the sea? Now, with the new

Christian ways, our leaders no longer do such dreadful things—nor must you. You *must not* think of killing your child.''

"Oh, my friend, of course I am not thinking of it! Truly, I am not. But I am so afraid for my baby. Komohu will never let him live. He'll be watching us every moment of the day, looking for a way to do my baby harm. He's an evil one, Melika. An evil *kahuna*. If he does not actually murder my child, he will find a way to capture his spirit and enslave it. I *know* this. I feel it in my heart.''

"Shhh . . . hush.'' Seeing that a new pain was coming, I gripped Nahi'ena'ena's hand. With the other hand I stroked her abdomen, massaging it in tiny circular motions. Together we breathed, in the way taught to us by the old midwives, who had been taught by the ancestors. The pain came and went. Nahi'ena'ena, drained more than ever, now, closed her eyes.

Tenderly, I rubbed perspiration from her forehead. "There is another way,'' I said softly. "It would call for a great sacrifice on your part, however.''

She met my worried gaze. "What is it?''

I leaned closer, to speak in a low voice. "Nahi'ena'ena, I fear you are right. Given even the smallest of opportunities, Komohu would do his best to harm your child. However, what if we tell everyone your baby died? Komohu would be the first to believe it. He would think he had persuaded you to drink from the vial.'' I motioned to where he had left it by the bedside. "We can take your baby somewhere to hide—''

Nahi'ena'ena's eyes widened. "Tell everyone he . . . died?''

I hushed her, a finger to her lips. Pressing gently on her shoulders, I settled her back against the pillows.

"Remember the story, Nahiʻenaʻena, of Kekuiapoiwa—the niece of King Alapai—and her child? Remember how the question of his paternity was such a disgrace to the old king that Kekuiapoiwa was forced to run to Halawa and hide while giving birth to the child? She and her husband then pretended to have the child 'kidnapped,' and spirited him away. When Kekuiapoiwa returned to the court in Kailua, she swore that her child had been stillborn."

"Yes." Nahiʻenaʻena's lips curved into a weak smile. "Of course I remember. The child was called Paiea. He lived hidden away in the Valley of Waipio for years, being educated and cosseted in the ways of the *aliʻi*. Later, when he was grown and all the troubles had been forgotten, Kekuiapoiwa and her husband took him back . . ."

"And he was given the name Kamehameha," I said softly. "Later to become King Kamehameha the Great. Your own ancestor, Nahiʻenaʻena."

She shook her head despairingly. "Are you saying I would never be able to see my child? Not till he was grown?"

"It would be a great sacrifice for you, I know. But think, Nahiʻenaʻena. Would you rather raise him in fear that Komohu might harm him one day? He would have no freedom. He would have to be watched every moment, unable to be with his peers . . ."

In Nahiʻenaʻena's dark eyes, I could see the struggle taking place. "You are right . . . he would be just as much a prisoner of my fear as Kauikeaouli and I were of our mother's religion. And he would never be truly safe." She closed her eyes briefly. "I . . . I will have to think, Melika."

"There is no time to think, Nahiʻenaʻena. Your child is about to be born. And there are so many babies dying now of the diseases the foreigners brought. Let me find one of those poor souls and bring his body here. We can say he is yours. I promise you, no one will be the wiser.''

''But where would you take my child?''

''I know a perfect place. It is secluded, and so beautiful, so peaceful and quiet. There are good people who would take care of him until he is old enough to join you and be safe.''

A frown formed between her brows. ''But, Kauikeaouli? My brother? He would believe his child is dead?''

''Nahi'ena'ena, forgive me, but neither of you can be sure the child is his.''

''*I* know it is,'' Nahi'ena'ena said vehemently. ''I know it in my heart.''

I stroked her cheek, gently, to calm her. ''Your heart must do what is right now for your child.''

Nahi'ena'ena grasped my hand. ''Melika, I cannot stand how much things are changing! Even you . . .'' She looked at my cross again, biting her lips, then glanced away.

''I have not changed,'' I said softly. ''I am still your friend.''

She met my eyes, then, and I saw that she knew about Kauikeaouli and me. She knew I had been in his bed only days before her marriage to him, that day on the beach below the cliffs. And though she had since forgiven me—she did not know whether to trust me.

''You and Kauikeaouli belong together, Nahi'ena'ena,'' I said. ''It will be all right. You will see.''

''Love conquers all?'' she said bitterly. ''Not for me.''

''It can,'' I insisted. ''If you let it.''

The princess released my hand and turned away.

"Pour me a glass of wine, Melika . . . and let me be for a bit."

I did as instructed, pouring from a gold-encrusted decanter into a matching goblet. A breeze came through the open window, bringing with it the scent of plumeria, which Nahi'ena'ena so loved.

She drank deeply of the wine. The pain of her life, her labor—and soon her death, I saw in a moment's flash of vision—began to dissolve. I shivered, afraid for her. My eyes filled with tears.

"Kihawahine . . ." Nahi'ena'ena whispered. "Great ancestral spirit, guide me."

Her eyes closed. The long dark lashes glistened, and tears trickled down her cheeks. "Melika?"

"Yes, Nahi'ena'ena. I am here. I will always be here." I took her hand again.

"Protect my baby. Do what you must, but see that he lives. In return, I promise to watch over your family. In life or in death, if I am needed, I will come."

The child was born swiftly after that. I handed him to Nahi'ena'ena, who held him close, her tear-filled eyes memorizing every inch of his perfect face, his tiny hands and feet.

"He looks like Kauikeaouli," she whispered. "I was right, Melika, the child is his." Her mouth shook. "I cannot bear to give him up."

I stood with a reassuring hand on her shoulder. "The decision is yours, Nahi'ena'ena. I have already brought the other . . . child, however. We must hurry if we are to do this."

"Melika? My dearest friend? Where did you get this poor dead child?"

I shook my head. "Do not trouble yourself this way."

"But I must know. I must know who is buried in my baby's tomb."

"He was a beautiful boy . . . born dead, to a woman my sister Leali was midwife to."

Nahiʻenaʻena's voice cracked. "The poor woman. Does she know? What we are doing?"

"I told her only that I would see he was buried properly. She is too poor to do this herself."

Tears sprang to Nahiʻenaʻena's eyes. "In the old days, it did not take money to bury a child, Melika! Don't you see? The new political ways are evil, they do not honor the soul."

I touched my cross, pressing it close to my heart for strength. "I agree with you about that, my princess. It is why I have chosen this path."

A full moon lit the way as I stole through the gardens of the palace with my precious bundle. The silver cross so lovingly given to me by the sisters who had come to our shores, gleamed against my chest. I brought Nahiʻenaʻena's baby, carefully hidden in the basket I carried, to my chest, hoping to hide the cross and not attract attention.

I would have preferred that the night had been more dark. There were too many people about this night, all of them mourning, or pretending to mourn, the death of Nahiʻenaʻena's child. Word had spread quickly throughout the palace, amongst royalty and commoners alike. Komohu, *kahuna anaʻana*, was said to be gloating that he'd had his way. There would be no child, at least for a time, of these two upstart royals who—in his opinion—could only have held Hawaii back.

There would be no holding back Komohu's gains, either, in terms of the vast amounts of land and money that would now change hands as the politicians forged ahead—less fettered by royal command. The king would be in mourning, would he not? And after that, who knew? Men have a way of changing, of seeing things differently, once they've known loss.

I slipped outside the palace walls, and then along paths that were hidden from the road. Heading north to the harbor, I paused now and then to listen: *Was that a footstep behind me? Was someone following? Did someone know?* Each time, uncertain, I would move ahead.

The way was long and treacherous, the paths I chose not entirely cleared. Several times I stumbled as my legs grew increasingly tired. At last, overwhelmed by exhaustion, I stopped. The moon was high now, and much too bright. I would find a place to rest in the shadow of the mountain, I thought, beneath an outcropping of trees. There I would feed the tiny infant with the milk I had brought from another woman's breast, a woman I had helped to midwife months before.

Settling in, I fed Nahi'ena'ena's baby. I rocked him and sang to him, holding him close so that he would not feel the loss of his mother. Finally he slept, and I found myself so tired, suddenly, I could no longer keep my eyes open. Drifting off, I dreamt of Komohu finding out what I had done and chasing me, his tall, threatening figure nearly upon me. In my dream he was naked except for a covering of *ti* leaves over his groin. He held a spear in his left hand. His chest was bare and painted with symbols I did not know the meaning of, as they were from long before my time.

"*Give me the child!*" he demanded in a voice that echoed from hill to hill. "Give the child to me!"

I sat up with a start, rubbing my eyes. Nahi'ena'ena's baby was crying. I looked down at him, then up. My limbs turned to ice. Komohu stood before me, just as in the dream—except that now he raised the spear above his head and brought it down with all his might to pierce my heart.

Blood spilled onto my white robe. My fingers lost their strength, and from them slipped Nahi'ena'ena's child. The basket fell to the ground.

No! I screamed, though no sound left my throat. My vision grew dark, and my last thought was, *I have failed my friend. Dear God, forgive me. I have failed my friend.*

I knew, then, that this had not been a dream.

I, Kate McKenna, looked down to see Melika's blood on my chest—my chest, that was clothed in her white robe. Horrified, I saw her drop Nahi'ena'ena's baby, then slump to the ground. At the same time, it was I who did these things—I who bled, who tried to scream, who died. My life's energy left me, slipping away. I tried to hang on, but could not.

If you need me, I will come, I heard Nahi'ena'ena whisper. *I will come.* Her words filtered through from far away, from the other end of a tunnel steeped with the purest golden light. I wanted to go to her, to walk through that light to where she was, where I knew all was peace. My heart longed for that peace. I reached out my arms for Nahi'ena'ena—only to hear her baby cry.

With a loud crackle and roar the tunnel disappeared, and along with it the light. In Melika's place lay I, on the ground, in her blood. My own body began to form from hers, from the white mist that was the only thing left of Melika now. I looked at the hands, and they were mine. I felt my face, the familiar features taking shape. I saw that I wore the same shorts and T-shirt I had left Pua'lani in.

I thought, *I have somehow crossed back to my own*

time. But then I knew I had not. Before me stood Komohu, raising his spear to slay the child.

"*No!*" I screamed, just as Melika had. Rising, I threw myself in his path. My hands flew up to ward off the spear, and the force that filled me then was like none I had ever known—powerful *mana* coming from deep within. By some knowledge that came to me then, I raised my arms and caused the wind to pick up speed. It roared in from the south, from the islands of the Marquesas, and from every ancestor this island had ever known. It came from the north, from the east, and the west, creating a vortex that picked up the evil Komohu, despite his strength, and thrust him backward, slamming him against a tree.

Bending down, I grabbed up the child, holding the basket tight to my chest, and began to run. "*Help me, Nahi'ena'ena,*" I prayed, "*help us both.*"

It seemed I ran for hours before I found myself on a trail that was parallel to a road, leading north and south. Following the trail, I headed north as Melika had done. But then there were lights behind me, and ahead. They were on the road, not the trail, and they were moving toward me from both directions at amazing speeds. Growing closer, they became huge spotlights, blinding me. A roaring sound came from each, accompanied by a fierce clatter of metal. I jumped back into the shadows, frightened and confused. The lights, I saw, came from trucks—army trucks, their style rounded and bulky, like those from World War II. As they passed I saw there were other cars on the road, cars from the same era. I had been thrown into yet another time.

"God help me," I prayed despairingly. Then, looking down, I saw I still carried the child in my arms. *Help us both*, I added fiercely, sensing the vengeance of Komohu fast on my heels.

There was nothing to do but keep running. All about me, tension and fear filled the air. Was this, too, the work of Komohu? Had *he* thrown me into this time and place, for his own depraved purposes? And where, precisely, could I be?

My feet carried me to a cliff overlooking some sort of harbor. Amazingly, night turned into day. Even more astonishing, the harbor held no water. It was as if a giant scoop had removed every drop of sea, leaving behind only a basin of wet sand. Scattered here and there in the sand were the rusted bodies of discarded army trucks. Coral and sea grasses stood exposed. Several people stood or walked in this basin, presumably for a better view. It was an awesome sight, yet frightening—this revelation of what was always there, but hidden, beneath the sea.

I looked about at houses along the beach, and then farther on. Quonset hut warehouses, loading platforms, and amphibious World War II tractors lined the shore. People stood on the cliff beside me, now, observing the spectacle of a harbor gone dry. I turned and spoke to a man, asking him what had happened. He did not see or hear me.

A terrible, thundering sound issued then from above, and the ground beneath my feet began to shake. The cliff began to crumble, threatening to dump us all from its edge. Terrified, I found myself caught up in the pushing and shoving of bodies beside me, as everyone tried to escape the cliff. Those immediately surrounding me ran for a path to the basin below. I couldn't move, other than to go with the crowd.

When we reached the bottom of the cliff, the crowd dispersed. People ran in every direction. I turned to look back up. At the edge of the cliff—where I had been only moments before—Komohu stood. His legs were splayed in an angry stance, and in each hand he held six spears. Beside him stood a giant black hog, its breath spouting flames. The flames grew larger and larger, and the hog slowly turned its head till the flames caught on dry brush, then began to climb up the side of Haleakala. Reaching the top of the ancient volcano, they scrambled like a hungry lizard, over its rim. Haleakala erupted, shooting streams of fire and ash hundreds of feet into the air. Cinders turned the entire sky red, like a gigantic burst of fireworks, then fell, the hot ash scorching my eyes, my face, my hair. Thick, monstrous streams of lava, blazing from thousands of degrees of heat, began their slow but terrifying slide toward the sea.

Or what had been the sea.

Clutching Nahi'ena'ena's baby from his basket, I held him close to me, running across the empty basin of sand. From behind me came Komohu's vicious laughter. "Your *mana* is not so great now, is it, Nahi'ena'ena?"

I whirled about and heard her answer through me. "I will show you, Komohu! You will see how much more powerful than you I can be!"

I felt my right arm go out, making sweeping motions up and down the face of the cliff. The cliff began to crumble again, and I saw that the path I had taken down here, with the others, crumbled with it.

Komohu stood with his arms outthrust, the spears in each hand shooting bolts of lightning toward the sky. As I watched, his face and form changed. He laughed, and the sound was hideous, like that of a multitude of tormented, burning souls. My mouth went dry and I began to shake as Komohu's hair turned from black to blond, and the face looking down at me became Gerard's.

"You've aligned yourself with the wrong people,

Kate!'' he taunted. ''You're lost, now. You'll never make it home.''

As I watched, stunned, the features formed, then reformed, the hair that was blond became black, then blond again. The voice—

''Murderer!'' I screamed. ''What monstrous things have you done?''

''Margo was the monster!'' Gerard's angry voice rang out. He laughed, a revolting sound. ''She cheated on me! Isn't that rich?''

I started toward him, to kill him. It was all I could think of—I wanted to kill.

But the path to the top of the cliff was gone. I would have to put the basket down, and climb. I'd have to leave the baby behind.

Before me swam Margo's face, Margo's tear-filled eyes. ''Run, Kate! Run!''

I turned away from Gerard, running farther into the dry basin, stumbling over coral and losing a shoe. My foot left a bloody trail, but still I ran, faster and faster, not looking back but only down, to Nahi'ena'ena's child.

The wrap had fallen away from his head, and his tiny face was exposed. Then, as in my vision at Pua'lani, another face began to form over this one. There were two babies, now, coming together, one transparent over the other—

I stopped running, my mind going numb. In that instant, Margo and Nahi'ena'ena appeared just in front of me, floating as in a mist. They reached out. Tenderly, a hand of each touched the babies in my arms. Tears streamed down their cheeks.

''You've done well, Kate,'' I heard them say. ''You've done everything you could.'' Gently, they took their babies from me.

The terrible sound of Komohu's laughter thundered

from the cliffs. "Well, now, you have come straight
to me, I see. And now that I have the three of you
together—"

Whirling back, I screamed, "For God's sake, what
is it you want?"

"To end your line," Komohu said in a silky voice.
"But you know that, don't you? You know this cannot
go on. You women are more and more trouble all the
time. It never ends. If you had listened to the churches,
to your teachers, if only you had understood your
rightful place—"

From beside me, then, came a scoffing sound. Looking about, I saw Melika standing beside me. Beside
her stood Nahi'ena'ena and Margo. Then, as I
watched, another woman appeared—a woman I barely
remembered—my mother, Luce. My heart seemed to
turn over, fear becoming love, as the four women gathered in a vague, ethereal mist, their faces forming
about me, faces of light . . . transparent, without human form.

Melika stepped forward, then, taking on more essence as she came between Komohu and me.

"You think you've won, do you, Komohu? Dark
over light? I think not."

The evil *kahuna* began to laugh, but his expression
changed suddenly to one of fear as the other women
stepped forward, the four of them together forming a
barrier of light between him and me. The light shim-
mered, it grew brighter, then brighter yet, till all about
me were streams of that pure, golden light, and Komohu could no longer be seen.

"Go, now, Kate!" I heard the women's voices, like
a choir of so many angels. "Go quickly!"

I hesitated only a moment. Then I began to run,
while to my ears came the sound of Komohu's roar.

Glancing back, I saw the light, and the women, disappear. At the same time, Komohu lost his footing and began to fall. The giant black hog disappeared in a burst of angry red flame and became a fireball, speeding toward me.

Cries came from the observers on the cliff. People were pointing out to sea, or rather where the sea should be. A mountain of water—a huge, solid wall of water thirty feet high—was now rolling in through the harbor, aimed directly at us. Men, women, and small children began to run back toward the cliff. Screams arose from the mouths of small children. Mothers picked up their toddlers and carried them on their backs. *"Tsunami!"* came the cry from first one, then another. *"Tsunami!"*

Tidal wave.

There was no time by then, I knew, to run for cover. I watched helplessly as the monstrous wall of water reached the first rusted truck, then the next, lifting and tossing them into the air like so many miniature toys. Waves came from every direction, one grinding into another as they filled, then overran the harbor. The sound was terrible, like a thousand freight trains barreling in.

The last thing I saw before being struck by that terrible liquid avalanche was the face of Nahi'ena'ena. She stood above the murderous waves, reaching for me. I felt our hands touch. Then she was gone.

Epilogue

I cannot tell you that the foregoing truly occurred. Not in "reality"—for your reality, of course, will not be the same as mine. Did my ancestor, Melika, attempt to hide Nahi'ena'ena's child? Was another tiny corpse buried in the royal baby's place? And did the child of Nahi'ena'ena and Kamehameha III secretly live on, hidden away somewhere in Maui, or on some nearby isle?

And if so . . . who are his heirs now? Do they know they are directly descended from the royal line?

It is a question, I suppose, for the historians. I only know what I saw and heard. I know what I felt. And because I saw, heard, and felt these things in Maui, Hawaii, in this summer of my own time, I would like to bear witness to them. Therefore, I have written my account on these pages so that you may read and decide for yourself.

If I were to argue the point, however, my argument might sound something like this: If Nahi'ena'ena's baby did in fact die—then Komohu got what he wanted. Why, then, would he still be seeking revenge? Rather, it would seem that Melika (and I, with Nahi'ena'ena's help) did succeed in saving the child—

for the simple reason that Komohu's wrath has followed Melika, and our entire family line, down the years.

My grandfather tends to agree, and adds, "One might even surmise that the royal baby's heirs are among those fighting today to restore Hawaii's sovereignty, and return it to the old ways. Divine justice, wouldn't you say, Granddaughter?"

"Except that you and Grandmother have paid the price."

"We have all paid a price," my grandmother said quietly.

We were sitting on her verandah when we had this conversation, shortly after the incidents described above.

"I believe," my grandfather said, "that Komohu must have known about your connection to Gerard Lanier, and decided to use it once you appeared and began to connect with Nahi'ena'ena. As a *kahuna*, after all, he could see the past, present, and future. He knew precisely what would happen that fateful night when you went into the past and ran with Nahi'ena'ena's child. He also knew the only way he could stop you that night would be to kill you."

"Or lure me away beforehand, pretending to be Gerard," I said thoughtfully. "It was Komohu that night, I'm sure, at the pool."

"I agree. I've also no doubt it was Komohu," he added, "who—in the form of Gerard—murdered your friend, Margo. In his twisted mind, he tried to lure you away from Maui, so that you would no longer travel into Nahi'ena'ena's world. What he did not count on was that Margo Lanier would come to you here, after her death. He must have been outraged when she, Nahi'ena'ena, and you, connected beyond the veil."

"There's one thing I haven't figured out, though,"

I said. "Did I actually become Melika? As in taking over her body, I mean? Or *was* I Melika, in that age and time? Did I simply reconnect with myself in some odd way?"

"You must spend some time with your grandfather, now that all this is over," my grandmother said, smiling. "The two of you can study about space and time, and how everyone, and everything, exists all at once."

"In other words, it may not ultimately matter who was who, or what was what," Dan said from beside me, laughing softly. "Since we are all seemingly one, and anything can change, anyway, in less than a nanosecond."

It was all too much for my tired brain, and I settled at the moment for relaxing on the porch swing and gazing at the wonderful Maui sky.

There are a few things I do know for certain, however—or as certain as anything can be. The four women—Melika, Nahi'ena'ena, Margo, and my mother—all came together at the end for one purpose: to give me their love and protection. For that, I will always be grateful.

As for the rest, it was Nahi'ena'ena, I know, now, who, in some form, stole my film. She did it to make me go after Dan Kala, hoping that would bring me to Pua'lani. As indeed it did.

The reason I know this is that I found all my wonderful sunset photos, fully developed, on the table in the guest room when I woke up, the morning after that day on the cliffs.

So the princess was up to her old tricks, right from the first. But I don't believe she drew me in maliciously. She knew—because she, too, could see past, present, and future—that Komohu was already after me. She knew I'd need help. And she—and Margo—both hoped for mine.

As for the warning on my computer, about Dan? That almost certainly was Margo. She couldn't have gotten a clear fix on Dan from "over there." All she knew was that Philippe was looking for me, and Gerard was close on his heels. Dan, she must have thought mistakenly, was their willing tool.

After the *tsunami*, I had been found by Dan at the top of the cliff at Pua'lani—unconscious, but otherwise unharmed. I was "out" for thirty minutes before I awoke on the bed in the guest room with Dan, Sharon, and my grandmother watching anxiously over me. I was battered and bruised, my arms and legs scratched and bleeding. Until I told them what had happened, they assumed I had fallen on the path leading down to the beach, injured myself, and crawled back up.

My grandfather is worried, even now. "You must guard yourself well, Granddaughter. I wouldn't trust that Komohu is through with you yet."

He may be right. Shortly after the incident at the cliff, I had a phone call from Lucinda Reed. "I felt I should warn you, dear. Gerard somehow disappeared before the authorities could transport him from London. It was strange. The guards claim he was there one moment and gone the next. We think they must have been drinking—either that, or Gerard bribed them to let him go. At any rate, no one has seen him since."

I couldn't tell her that the person who was imprisoned in London might not have even been Gerard. I couldn't tell her, because there was no way I could know this for sure. But I haven't been able to stop wondering just where Gerard ended and Komohu began—and for how long all that had been going on.

"And how is little Kate?" I asked Lucinda Reed that day.

"Oh, my dear, she's been thriving, ever since she had that miraculous turnaround, the last time we talked."

Margo's baby had made a remarkable recovery at the exact time Nahi'ena'ena and Margo received the two babies into their arms, that day below the cliffs. I didn't know until much later that Margo had left a letter for her family, requesting that if anything happened to her, they would name her baby "Kate."

I know what you may be wondering. Was my grandmother right about Dan Kala and me? Did Nahi'ena'ena bring us together because we were starcrossed lovers in that previous life? If so, I have my theories about that, lately. While I do recall that Melika's sister, Leali (my great-grandmother several times removed, it turns out), promised Melika she would be with Kauikeaouli one day, I tend to think it's not that cut and dried. Rather, I wonder if it's only that a piece of who they were—some tiny essence of soul—found a way to cross time and space and plunk itself down in Dan and me.

We were married, shortly after that day on the cliffs. We were married in the gardens at my family's house, and Damien even got over being a surly teenager long enough to clean up the backyard. Sharon was my maid of honor, and our wedding was all I'd ever dreamed of . . . or, for that matter, written about. Like Carolyn in my book, which finally got finished, I'd married the "rich, handsome plantation owner."

Of course, Dan Kala isn't precisely "rich." He still does his consulting, and we both work hard to keep the cottages ready for guests. In fact, we hope you'll visit us here one day. Just take the Hana Road to Huelo Point . . . and cross your fingers it doesn't rain.

As for life in Paradise, I sit here today on the lanai

at Pua'lani, and my free hand instinctively goes to my swollen tummy, to protect the soul that lies there, waiting to be born. Komohu, I know, does not give up easily when he's obsessed. I must not let him get by me this time. And he is on his way . . . I know that now.

Only this morning, I stopped my writing to lie beneath Nahi'ena'ena's portrait and close my eyes, breathing deeply and surrounding myself, as Sharon has suggested, with a protective circle of light. I saw Margo, then, as she appeared the first time to me in Kihei, the time she became the woman with long dark hair. She was beckoning to me, and with such urgency I felt drawn in, though I resisted at first, wanting only to enjoy my pregnancy, my new life, for a time.

"You must protect yourself," she seemed to say, though I heard no words. "Protect your child."

After she told me that, I spent a lot of time in thought. What I decided was that "Gerard" would not show this time. Komohu can't possibly believe I'd fall for that again.

But *someone* will come. He'll arrive in some form, around the time my baby is born. A doctor, perhaps. Or a nurse.

And I will be ready. I'll be prepared.

As for Dan, he worries incessantly about me. "If that bastard tries to harm you, or our child, I swear to God I will kill him," he said the other day.

Well, as to that, I doubt Komohu *can* be murdered. If so, my band of angels would have finished him off on the cliffs. No, the evil *kahuna* has too many tricks. So I wait. I make ready. Meanwhile, I write a bit more every day in the new book I've begun, and every day—little by little—more light comes through. I write about Nahi'ena'ena and Kauikeaouli. I write about Nahi'ena'ena's child. I study, and there are days when I ask the question: Is there something else I should know?

By the time I reach those magic words, *The End*, I may well have the answers I seek.

Meanwhile, I will tell Dan about Lucinda's phone call regarding ''Gerard'' when he comes in from the taro fields tonight, and we will talk. I will do this now because I am learning what it is to trust, and I love this man with all my heart. He deserves to know what I plan.

There is nothing, however, he can say, that will stay me from my course. I have been studying with Sharon and with my grandfather. I have learned things. And I am calling them in, even now—Nahi'ena'ena, Margo, Melika, my mother . . .

We, too, will talk. We will plan. And when Komohu arrives, in whatever form, we will know precisely what to do.

Kate McKenna
Pua'lani, Maui, Hawaii

Author's Note

The story of Princess Nahiʻenaʻena and her brother, Kauikeaouli, King Kamehameha III, is largely true, according to Hawaiian history. The personal scenes between the brother and sister sprang from my imagination, as did my speculations regarding the fate of Nahiʻenaʻena's child. Details surrounding the location and time of the child's birth have been fictionalized.

After Nahiʻenaʻena's death in 1836, the grieving Kamehameha III built a mausoleum at the royal palace, on the sacred island, Mokuʻula, on Maui. There he placed the remains of his sister and her child, in coffins that were covered with scarlet silk and a variety of richly gilded ornaments. The coffins rested on a bedstead which stood in the middle of the room. The mausoleum was described by a visitor as a large, elegant chamber with beautiful china matting and a small organ, which Kamehameha III played for the enjoyment of his guests. Splendid dresses, formerly worn by the princess, were on display in a cupboard with glass doors. This elegant room opened onto a piazza, commanding an exquisite view of the harbor.

Kamehameha III was the last royal monarch of Hawaii to follow the tradition of brothers marrying sisters, and the custom passed into history with his death in 1854. Meanwhile, the royal court had moved to Honolulu, and in 1883 the remains of Nahi'ena'ena and her child were moved from the sacred island, Moku'ula, to a nearby cemetery in Waine'e.

Moku'ula, and its magnificent royal palace, eventually fell into decline. The island now lies submerged but largely intact beneath the town of Lahaina, Maui.

Joanna Carr awakens in a hospital after six months in a catatonic state, only to be told that her beloved husband, David, has been brutally murdered, and police are still searching for the killer. Grief-stricken and confused, she flees to the safety of the country home they once shared to try to piece together the crime—and her life. But Joanna knows that something is dreadfully wrong—and that the nightmare is just beginning...

MEG O'BRIEN

I'LL LOVE YOU TILL I DIE

A WOMAN'S DESPERATE SEARCH FOR THE TRUTH PLUNGES HER INTO A WEB OF DECEPTION, DESIRE, AND DANGEROUS OBSESSION.

It has been almost a year since Beth Lambert's body was recovered from a ravine on Whidbey, a tranquil island community near Seattle. Now Naomi Wing, full-blooded Wintu Indian, who turned her back on the old ways to become a high-powered attorney, has returned to her ancestral home, haunted by the tragic death of a girl she had come to love as a daughter—and caught up in a love affair that may have played a role in Beth's death.

What Naomi finds will pit her against Susan, Beth's dangerously unstable mother, and force her to confront the Native American heritage she has denied for so long. On the mysterious, forested shores of Whidbey, she will pursue secrets only the dead can reveal—secrets that lead her to the shocking truth about Beth...and into the dark shadows of her own past.

A DEEP AND DREAMLESS SLEEP

by Meg O'Brien